I'm a
Registered Nurse
Not a Whore

I'm a Registered Nurse Not a Whore

stories by
ANNE PERDUE

INSOMNIAC PRESS

Library and Archives Canada Cataloguing in Publication

Perdue, Anne
I'm a registered nurse not a whore / Anne Perdue.
ISBN 978-1-897415-30-6

I. Title.
PS8631.E7325I17 2010   C813'.6   C2010-904613-7

The publisher gratefully acknowledges the support of the Canada
Council, the Ontario Arts Council, and the Department of Canadian
Heritage through the Book Publishing Industry Development Program.

Printed and bound in Canada

Insomniac Press
520 Princess Avenue, London, Ontario, Canada, N6B 2B8
www.insomniacpress.com

 Canada Council   Conseil des Arts   Canadä
for the Arts   du Canada

for my mom,
always

and Julie,
I am so lucky

TABLE OF CONTENTS

I'M A REGISTERED NURSE
NOT A WHORE

"A HAIR DRYER'LL fix it," said Stu — stepping forward to inspect the situation after Eugene told the guy from Premier Appliances that he had to pay for the damages to the floor. The delivery guy snorted like a donkey, wiped his nose on his sleeve and demanded a signature. Eventually Eugene gave in just to get the dumbfuck out of his face. He yelled at Tim to measure the height of the fridge and took off. Twenty minutes later he reappears — his wife's hair dryer in his hand.

"Put the setting on high," says Stu.

Sure as Eugene wants everyone to think the sun shines out of his ass, the heat reverses the compression and the soft pine floorboards spring back until the dents are hardly noticeable.

"Looks good, eh boss!" blurts Stu.

"What the hell would you know?" Eugene sneers.

"Fridge is sixty-four inches," says Tim.

"Can't be. Measure it again," Eugene orders.

"Oh boys," Mrs. Wilkinson calls out, peering into the kitchen. "I'm so sorry to trouble you. The appliances are delightful but I didn't really want them in the dining room if at all possible." A Polish chap was going to be re-lining the fireplace next week and he'd need access to the east wall.

"No problem don't worry that's what I'm here for," says Eugene, asking himself why the hell HO's always think it's better to do several projects all at once.

Thirteen steps down to the basement — Eugene, Tim and Stu lug the kitchen table, the dishwasher, four chairs and several boxes of kitchenware. Back in the dining room they renegotiate the rest of the furniture with the fridge and the range until there's room enough and more for the fireplace guy. Mrs. Wilkinson is concerned that some of the assembly bits and bobs might go missing so she stands by, watching. Eugene strains his back pretending he isn't about to blow a gasket and begins boasting about how much Katia loves her new Crossfire convertible.

Then Mrs. Wilkinson leaves.

An hour later she returns carrying a case of cold beer. Damn, thinks Eugene. If there's one thing he has a rule about, well actually two, it's that shirts stay on at all times and there's no beer drinking on site. Ever.

Ten minutes later Stu, helping himself to his third beer, starts telling Mrs. Wilkinson how much he loves her oil paintings of ships and harpooners. He asks her if she's ever read *Moby-Dick* because she would probably enjoy it and she screams, "I love *Moby-Dick*!" Although it's in that precise give-every-syllable-a-chance diction that holds dainty traces of an English accent so it's hardly a scream.

Eugene, completely pissed that Stu has the audacity to chat up his client, is mortified when Stu uncaps beer number four and coaxes Mrs. Wilkinson into having one too (serves it to her in the bottle!) and makes his way through the maze in the dining room to plant his dusty rear end on one of her chairs. Thank God they're wooden not upholstered, thinks Eugene, as Stu blabbers on about the wild and salty seas and how greed makes men's souls grow stupid and small.

Eugene tells Tim to go on home. He takes his time cleaning up, listening from the kitchen, whistling now and again. As he winds an extension cord around his arm he hears Jean Wilkinson ask Stu what he likes most about *Moby-Dick*.

"It's a lot about how we, I mean mostly us guys, live our lives. We need to work. But the way we work is competitive and chaotic, like the madness of the whale hunt, and so we continually live in fear that we're gonna be eliminated. We go crazy — "

Eugene's face appears in the doorway.

"Chasing and getting things we don't need and probably aren't meant to have."

"Stu!" Eugene puts on his most charming smile. "Time to call it a day. Enough of taking up Mrs. Wilkinson's time."

"Oh Eugene, don't worry," Mrs. Wilkinson insists. "Stu and I haven't finished our book club meeting yet. Run along. I'll send Stu off in a few minutes."

Eugene looks at his steel-toed boots. He's been way too patient with Stu and his beer buzz bullshit. That's *his* client telling him to run along like *he's* the hired hand. Shoving his tired arms into the sleeves of his coat he hears Mrs. Wilkinson ask, "Now, should I call you Ishmael?"

"Yes!" shouts Stu, "Call me Ishmael."

There's a wild burst of laughter. And a clapping sound. Mrs. Wilkinson and Stu high-fiving?

"You two behave yourselves," Eugene warns as he closes the door, noisily — wondering why he's letting himself be upstaged by a fat fuck who lives in a rooming house and can barely afford toothpaste let alone a skanky girlfriend. Please, he says to the sky, please let Katia be home. He feels a desperate need to see her. She can yell at him because he hasn't hooked up the barbeque yet (like there's been time). It assures him that their life together is real. That the antique lights in their hallway and the softened water in their taps and the elegant wine cooler in their kitchen are not fabrications of his imagination. (Despite the latter having been acquired through the redemption of 75,000 American Express points.)

Next morning it's confirmed: the fridge is two inches higher than it's supposed to be and the fucking room isn't squared off properly. Stu returns from another smoke break, stands around coughing on everything, then walks to the foot of the stairs and shouts to Mrs. Wilkinson that he'd be happy to take her empties back to the Beer Store. She calls out that that's a wonderful idea, as long as he agrees to keep the refund.

In the afternoon Eugene backs his truck into a pole at the pickup bay smashing the back end to the tune of two grand all because he has to get away from the noisy drone of the compressor and the incessant *ka-pung ka-pung ka-pung* of the nail gun. And Stu. Stinky Stu. All the guy has to do is bloody well show up at seven-thirty, trudge in with his mud pan and trowels. He's too clumsy for carpentry or plumbing or electrical and he expects to get paid just for standing around. Guy comes from another era. Never thinks about plugging in a Shop-Vac or doing a little clean up.

At five-thirty Eugene says to call it a day but be back at nine (tomorrow's Saturday). Tells Tim to go on over to the bar. He'll meet him there in twenty to review *the plan.*

It's early April and warm enough that someone's propped open the door. Following on Tim's heels, Stu heads inside, wound up and confident with twenty bucks he convinced Eugene to advance him. A few regulars are gathered at the bar — early evening ones who come here after work and stay for an hour or two or sometimes six if the mood of the place is enticing enough for them to forget about anything that might be waiting for them at home. A cat. A girlfriend. Leftovers in the fridge.

Stu's not a regular here; he's an occasional. Stu doesn't have enough cash flow to be a regular, so he makes it in here now and again when a profusion of factors collide to provide an unambiguous pull or push through the doorway. He tries not to come in here alone. Being so close to home it would be too easy and to survive this life you need some kind of definition for your haunts and your habits. He's learned the hard way that leaving everything wide open with possibilities can lead to terrible fun and tragedy.

Pint in hand, Stu stands at the bar and looks through the doorway. It rained dark and hard in the afternoon and the amber sunlight, sinking low, glares warm off the shiny wet sidewalks. A bus barrels down the street, lurching on its hydraulic haunches. He turns to Claudia — a sour, lethally honest public defender pushing fifty with a reptilian stare, who's perched on her usual stool.

"The tongue," he explains, "is the strongest muscle in the body."

"Really. Then be strong for me. Hold yours," she begs. "Hold it!"

Roly-poly Stu snaps still. The only way he can hold his tongue is to freeze. Everything. Legs, arms, belly, head, eyes. But it's torture. "Geez," he cries out. His body slumps, his head lolls to the side and his fists swing downward. "I can't do it!"

Claudia raises an eyebrow. "You're too easy. Learn to control yourself or I'll have to give you a tongue lashing."

Jake, from a couple of stools over, says something about not wanting to miss *that*. He raises his glass. The bartender catches the gesture and another round is ordered.

Stu clears his throat, rolls his big marbly eyes. Tells Claudia about this guy he knows who went to see a psychiatrist.

"He starts explaining about his life. *I got a good job … great wife … two healthy kids … but I'm unhappy. What's wrong with me?* And the psychiatrist says, *I think you're stupid.* So Arnold says, *Well thanks a lot. I want another opinion.* The psychiatrist says: *Okay then. You're depressed because you're fat and ugly!*"

Claudia barely swallows her beer before the slightly familiar punchline makes her abdominal muscles tighten, causing what would have been an unfortunate spray of cream ale from her mouth and nostrils. Leaning back she flings her blondish hair. "Stu baby," she coughs, "you're killing me."

Jake, his eyes on the television screen, pipes up how amazing it is, all those people lining up to see a dead Pope. Not really, suggests Stu, everyone loves a dead person. Claudia remarks it's history in the making. Jake says John Paul II travelled more than any other Pope so it's only fair, like the saying goes, an eye for an eye, that others are now coming to him. Claudia says that doesn't sound very Christian. Someone no one knows mentions that with all that garbage everyone is leaving in St. Peter's Square, the Pope's gotta be happy he's not around to see it. Jake says when the Pope came to Downsview a few years back and those half million Christian youth plugged up the sewers, flooding an Idomo store, he got a real steal on a wall unit.

After four days on the job, Stu's shoulders and neck are tight. And that bloody tooth. But man it feels good to be here, undemanding and soft, as if time itself, kidnapped for a little while, is being held ransom until it's necessary to induce an action. Such as taking a piss. Squaring up. Parting. But Christ, the tooth is gonna kill him. Goddamn trench mouth. A dentist, if he could get in to see one, would just pull the damn thing out and leave a hole.

"Hey, check this out!" says Claudia loudly, waving a hand toward the TV that's running an update about Charles and Camilla's delayed nuptials. She begins to describe a dream she had. She was Camilla Parker Bowles. In anticipation of marrying Charles she was being very quiet and proper, sitting in a dark bedroom with wallpaper everywhere. "Even on the floor. People kept running by telling me how lucky I was. Then I looked in a mirror and I looked like Princess Diana, but I had a huge mole in the middle of my forehead." Claudia looks at Stu, then touches her forehead.

"What else?" asks Stu.

"It was growing bigger and bigger, expanding by the second, like a bubbly burnt pancake. I was scared to touch it … then I woke up."

Stu raises a hand to signify he's got this one. "Your subconscious," he says, clearing the mucous in his throat. He explains that the mole represents the subconscious. Lady Diana knew she should never have married Charles. The dream is a reminder to pay attention to what is going on deep down inside.

Claudia lowers her voice, "You're scaring me, Stu."

"Nahh," Stu puts his beer down on the bar, lifts his baseball cap and runs a scaly hand through his chalky hair. "Women are naturally more connected to deeper patterns and energies," he says, sounding serious. "That's why I always say, if the world were run by women, it would be a better place."

"Whoa, don't know about that," Claudia says quickly. "With our tendencies toward consensus and inclusion and our proclivity to share feelings, eventually we'd screw things up just as much — maybe more."

With a nod to the bartender, Claudia reaches around her stool, grabs her bag and puts a twenty on the sticky counter. She smells something slightly oily and dank, traces of the outhouse. Odours and all, she loves Stu. He's smart and he knows a lot of things. Like where to find old bricks or where to get a pack of cigarettes for five bucks, and what he doesn't know he makes up. Pulls it right out of his cap.

"You're a rare bird, Stu. As rare as a virgin in a whorehouse."

"Hey, that's exactly what I was once upon a time."

"Next time, darling! Next time I want to hear all about that," she says, as she jumps off her stool, gives Stu's arm a squeeze and heads to the door. As she walks away, Eugene marches in.

"Hey boss," Stu calls out. Eugene ignores him. Punches Tim's shoulder as he swings his legs around a stool. Tim, his elbows on the counter, leans his lanky frame into Eugene. "Our Pillsbury Doughboy's dancing tonight."

Eugene grunts. "Stu, don't have too much fun," he hollers. "You can't afford it."

"Yes boss," says Stu, bowing. Fuck his tooth hurts.

"I mean it fish meal," Eugene barks like a drill sergeant.

Stu watches Eugene tell Tim how to shim up the bottom cupboards and how to cover the extra four inches above the fridge and is reminded that Eugene never seems to learn that what he needs to fear most is not that he's not perfect, but that in an effort to appear perfect he repeats the same mistakes. If Jesus Christ were a contractor he'd conduct himself like Eugene, except he wouldn't keep forgetting job after job that everything in a kitchen has to be precise to an eighth of an inch and you need at least three coats of mud on your joints if you want to do it right.

Stu touches his back pocket where his wallet holds Vanessa's picture. His very own Lady Godiva. He knows

there are two things you need in life. Someone or something to love. And something to do. You need both. Or
you need hope that you're gonna have both. And right
now he has it going on. In the mornings he aches so
much he can't sit up so he rolls off the mattress (at six-
thirty like all good drywallers) and tries not to land with
too much of a thud on the cold floor. He stays there momentarily making sure he hasn't disturbed his sweetheart
who lets out a tiny sleepy moan and shifts her naked
body just slightly toward his side of the bed. He gets a
little hard and his heart beats louder. It is happiness. Stu
knows he'll never get the knack of respectable living but
he knows what it is to be in love. It has a sound: *thuu-
ump ... mmmmmm.*

He wobbles over and leans on the bar next to
Eugene.

Eugene's telling Tim he's gonna head out to the
Depot to get some edging tiles. "If we use them to frame
the stove area, it'll look like it was made to be that way."

"Sweet," says Tim.

Eugene orders another pint. What a frustrating week.
Katia started up again about their summer holidays and
he didn't know how to tell her about his truck. And fuck,
how was he to know one side of a room could be five
inches shorter than the other? Whoever built it in the first
place was a fucking idiot.

"You guys need to relax a little," Stu offers. "Did I
tell you what the drill sergeant said to the squad about
what would happen tomorrow if it rains?"

Eugene glares at Stu's round belly, barely covered by
a thin T-shirt with a faded Tweety Bird across the front.
There isn't a part of him not peppered in dry floury com-

pound dust. Eugene can't believe this dusty blubbering dink works for him. He ignores Stu's punchline, something about amphibious landings and duck waddles. "Stinky, how many beers you had?" he shouts.

"What is this? The inquisition?"

"I don't want you piss-headed tomorrow, showing up like a junkyard dog in heat. Give me back the twenty bucks I gave you and get on home."

Eugene's mouth is tighter than a spring-loaded clamp.

"You heard me."

"You don't need to do this."

Oh yes I do, thinks Eugene. "Listen you rat weasel, if I don't see your ass at nine tomorrow morning you're toast. You understand?"

Stu wonders if he means he'll never hire him again, or that he won't pay him for the work he's already done.

"Come on," Eugene warns. Christ, I got to get to the Depot, *now*. Some Friday night this is. "Give me the fucking money I gave you and get outta here."

Stu reaches in his pocket, takes out a ten and puts it on the counter. He'll keep the other. That's fair. An honest peace offering. Raising his hands to his head like a man surrendering at gunpoint, he starts backing up, slowly. After knocking into a stool and almost falling over a magazine rack, he exits through the doorway never taking his eyes off Eugene who stares back expressionless, his eyes burning cold and hard, like stainless steel screws.

Eugene stretches. It's Saturday, the bonus day, the add-on. Picking up the Shop-Vac filters he bought last night, he inspects the free sample of hand cream wrapped in cellophane that's nestled inside the box and reminds himself that nothing is free. (Katia loves to explain this stuff to him.) Someone in front of a computer somewhere determines the cost of things. Rationalizes the payoff of partnerships. In this case, Black & Decker and Neutrogena.

He props the filters against the Shop-Vac, thoughtfully, and stands back to admire the upper cabinetry and the way the microwave fits seamlessly between the glass doors. No one would ever guess it's a discontinued model sandwiched between economy-priced cupboards whose styling has been copied from some hotshot Italian designer. Eugene congratulates himself and is convinced that he was right to mark up the microwave for a hundred more than MSRP, because they used to sell for triple what they go for now and it cost 215,000 Amex points. His aching shoulders tell him he deserves more credit than he gets.

"Eugene! Are you planning the rest of your life?" Mrs. Wilkinson — dimmed and distorted behind the foggy blur of a polyethylene sheet taped to the doorway as a dust barrier — is putting on her coat. Eugene blinks hard. How long has she been there?

"Just thinking through the day before my guys come," he says, cheerfully, while a little voice tells him *now*. Now is the time to ask about the money he needs for the extra work required because he didn't measure every single possible length, width and depth. And he didn't tell her days ago when he should have that it's more expensive to vent through the ceiling. And he didn't add on the extra fifteen percent admin fee Katia keeps bugging him about, because he worries it'll price him right out of the ballpark even though he always under-quotes and ends up working way too hard for way too little.

"I'm heading out for a couple of errands. Can I get you anything?"

"Don't worry about me, I'm absolutely fine." Eugene nods at the kitchen windows. "It's a beautiful day out there." His voice is sure and smooth and he turns to offer a life-is-great wave but Jean Wilkinson's disappeared down the hallway. Every click of her heels knocks his confidence. His armpits are wet. Christ — yet one more job where he barely makes as much money as Tim. Barely as much as Stu once he factors in depreciation on his tools and the two grand to fix the crinkled back end of his truck. If the job goes on much longer he might as well start paying for the privilege of working for Jean Wilkinson.

But damn it. She's got pull with the Committee of Adjustments and said she could recommend him to a lot of real estate agents who work this area and that's just the connection he needs to keep his business humming with the kind of jobs he likes — jobs that don't require a zillion permits and an inspector breathing down your back. Jobs that are right in your own neighbourhood. You can hop on home if you need to take a crap and don't want to run out to some scuzzy donut shop to do it because your client's sitting on the couch, leisurely reading a magazine, just an arm's length away from the bathroom door. Eugene had a big one this morning before he left home and it's got him feeling light with confidence that he and

Tim will get a lot done today while Stu gets the vent boxed in and the ceiling finished. Today there will be no distractions. And no beer — even if it is Saturday.

"Hey Gene," says Tim, stepping in through the back door. "What's the plan?"

These words are heaven to Eugene. Ask him whether to use a cross-brace or a parallel-hinge, he'll know. Nails *and* glue boys. Double reinforcements all around. That's the kind of guy he is. A gentleman contractor. A class act.

Tim grins at the sanding kit. "Someone's been watching the shopping channel." He tells Eugene to be careful. Starts out simple, then the wife goes crazy in the middle of the night and your basement's crammed with balls and benches and a Bowflex with more attachments than the joists on a dance floor.

"Ha!" says Eugene. "Katia doesn't go all crazy for cheap things."

Tim smiles, thinks better you than me. He's glad he's not marrying into money like Eugene did. Nikki may be bossy sometimes but she doesn't try to wear the pants. Tim watches Eugene take the attachments out of the box and he's overwhelmed with pity. The guy works so hard for twenty-eight bucks an hour, then tries to make extra money by trading in his wife's American Express points for building materials and small appliances. Makes it seem like it's all cool and you should envy him the silver spoon in his mouth but it's more like a horseshoe up his ass and eventually, as with anything up the ass, it fucks you. Eugene still wears a good veneer, walks around with the resilience of a younger person, but these are his prime earning years! Ten more and he'll be half-deaf and younger guys will be outbidding him on these small-time reno jobs he pretends to love because he's too scared to take on bigger projects with real money.

Not me, thinks Tim. I'm gonna buy time through the magic of compounding. Everyone knows you have to start early. It's the only way to go. You need investments that generate dividends or capital gains. As the value of your investments increases you generate income on income. Asset allocation is essential. Time is everything.

Tim looks around. "Should I set up the tile cutter?"

"I need you to take measurements for the board Stu's gonna need. Remember, we're going to centre it up." Eugene stands in front of the microwave and gives a military-like gesture with his arms to illustrate symmetry. Tim nods, leisurely drags a ladder into position.

There's a flustering of muffled noises. Someone shakes the door. The glass rattles as it swings open. Stu holds on for dear life but unable to stay standing on two feet, he falls to one knee, then his side, landing hard with a whistle fart.

He rolls onto his belly, retches lightly and swallows. "I hear the sergeant singing. Please ... don't read me the riot act."

Every second that passes is an insult to Eugene.

"Well, if it isn't Mopy Dick himself. Stand up, whale boy," he commands, before he kicks the orange casing of a measuring tape across the floor. It bounces like a curling rock off Stu's hand.

"Let me explain," says Stu. "I've had a long night and ... my tooth ... it's killing me. I just need some painkillers. And a coffee."

But Eugene doesn't want an explanation. It's always the same. Stu can stay sober for months, then no matter how hand-to-mouth his existence, the guy still finds a way to do himself in. But not this time. Not in Jean Wilkinson's house. "Get out of here," says Eugene.

Tim, standing on the ladder, watches with wonderment. Stu's lack of self-respect doesn't compute in his books. The guy's got at least some kind of a life. A place to live. Some kind of a girlfriend. What's wrong with him?

"Please," says Stu. "Can you give me what you owe me?"

For a moment it was so quiet you could almost hear the tulips in the backyard poking up through the ground.

"You don't understand. You work for *me*." Eugene points his index finger at his chest. "You're supposed to help me make money so I can pay *you*. Get it? Now get your stinky tweety bird ass outta here."

Stu turns and crawls toward the door. Grabbing the frame he pulls himself up and looks back at his boss who's peering silently into the black tiles of the backsplash. Stu steps outside, pulls the door shut, wobbles along the garden path careening wider than usual.

"Ssufferin' ssuccotash," sputters Tim as he steps down from the ladder.

Eugene shrugs. "Same old shit," he says, pretending he's not ready to pick up his drill and hurl it through the window or pound his fists into the stainless steel appliances. It's one thing to have Stu around when you have Tim, but without Tim he's going to look like one half of a sorry pair. The gentleman contractor and his smelly lowbrow sidekick. Can't downplay appearances, even in this business. Tim's been good for him. He never spits or pisses against a backyard tree or smokes cigarettes without his hands. Or even with his hands.

"Let's get this goddamn vent finished," Eugene says, feeling jumpy and panicky. He doesn't need this headache. He has to protect his reputation and he's got to make some money.

To understand the pain Stu's in, take the severe hangover kind that makes your head tight and your stomach feel like it's going to blow chunks with terminal velocity, and add, mix and stir to that the kind an abscessed tooth creates when it pulses and robs you of rational thought and sleep and never goes away and then hurts so bloody bad it feels like someone keeps jabbing at your jaw with a syringe full of ice cream, twisting and injecting it real good until you start to get a little paranoid that you're being tortured because you did something really bad that you can't remember. And when you think it can't get any worse, it's as if someone's taken a sledgehammer to your jaw and the whole side is so ruined it's a wonder your face still has room for your eyes. Stu's gone over the crack in his molar so many times his tongue's lost feeling and his mouth has the acid taste of bile and blood.

He wanders through the laneways, then sits next to a garbage shed and dozes until the sun is directly overhead and the pungent smell of fish rotting and soiled baby diapers wakes him. Stu closes his mouth, tries to swallow, but dryness has shut off his throat. He decides to head over to the convenience store where Tony sells a coffee and a cigarette for a buck fifty. Hopefully he can do a deal because seventy cents is all he's got.

Forgive me please, Stu mutters, uncertain who he's talking to. It would have been okay if he didn't have the tooth problem, and if he hadn't run into Jack behind the beer store who was sitting on a few cans of Max Ice and was happy to see him, and if the antibiotic someone gave him a few days ago hadn't got lodged in his esophagus where it spent twenty-four hours burning a hole in the soft tissue and messing with his sinuses and his balance before dislodging itself. Stu has control over himself, in spurts and starts, but at the end of the day — or sometimes in the middle — he looks at himself and all he can see is a five and a half foot, fifty-nine-year old windbag, coughing up blood and compound dust.

Inside the store the air is stale except for the hopeful smell of fresh newspapers and plastic bread wrap. Tony nods at Stu as he and Charlie continue their card game across the counter. After a few words, a buddy this and a buddy that, Stu's got a coffee and cigarette, which he's allowed to smoke in the store. Tony gives him a couple of milk crates to sit on. He and Charlie take turns dealing fast and machine-like, neither showing any reaction until one of them grunts. Eventually the cards are stacked, Tony unlocks the till and slides a twenty to Charlie who leaves.

As he exits, a woman wearing a brown wool coat and a clear plastic shower cap over her thin nicotine-coloured hair, shuffles in. Slow and steady, like an old Austin Mini hitched to a conveyor and being drawn through a car wash, she heads toward the back of the store, rounds the corner, returns up the other aisle. In contrast to her feet, her eyes dart about as if picking up clues. As she passes Stu, he nods. She frowns, takes a licorice pipe from a plastic container and puts it in her pocket. Digging through another pocket she finds a dime and places it on top of the plastic lid that shields the lottery tickets. Tony, reading a magazine spread open on the register, mutters *tanks*.

A moment of silence.

Then a voice, with zero tolerance for monkey business, snaps through the dim air. Piercing out high and mighty, it sets the record straight: "I'm a registered nurse not a whore."

Tony, startled, agrees. "Yes, ma'am," he says, obediently, as the woman heads out the door and into the sunlight. Tony goes back to his magazine and Stu sips the last of his coffee.

Bang. It hits him. The infection is too healthy so it keeps expanding. That causes pressure, which causes pain. The pressure needs to be released. Bodies aren't a whole lot different from houses. They're made of matter and they crack and tear and sometimes things grow in them that shouldn't.

"Thanks buddy, you're a registered nurse," he says to Tony as he leaves the store.

The coffee and cigarette have drained Stu's head of some tension and his stomach is slightly more stable. His tongue, raw and swollen, slides back and forth over the worn edges of his front teeth and along the metal wires that hold his incisors in place.

He thinks about Vanessa, and as he does everything fits together like a jigsaw puzzle and he recognizes that he can't help messing it up sometimes just so he can put it back together again, and the possibility that one of these times he won't be able to is what drives him to act recklessly. But right now he knows what he has to do.

Back at Mrs. Wilkinson's, Eugene and Tim are both up on ladders trying to do what Stu knows he can do better. Stu shuffles to the corner. Picks up Eugene's drill and a case of bits. The heft of the power tool, firm in his grip, comforts him. The room is unnaturally quiet. Eugene feels Stu's presence as an effrontery that renders him speechless; Tim wonders what Stu's up to and what Eugene's going to do about it.

Stu heads outside. Helps himself to a garden chair. The sun feels warm and he shifts around until its fullness is on his back. He feels something in his chest open up. It breathes softly and although he knows his hearing's not what it used to be, there's no mistaking the rosy rhythm and the soothing sound of the syllables. *Va-nes-sa. Va-nes-sa.* His hands are vibrating slightly but inside he feels calm. For a moment he imagines he's dead. When you're dead people admire you for a short while. Funny old Stu. But that's not the point. Actually there is no point. There's only Vanessa and things to do. And knowing that, he takes out the second smallest bit, puts it in the chuck and tightens it. With light pressure on the trigger he checks that the axis is straight and the drill's set to forward. He touches the tip of the bit. Torque's good. Resting the drill on his legs he looks up, pulls out a pack of matches from his shirt, lights one, picks up the drill and slides the bit into the flame until the heat of the match begins to burn his fingers. He flicks out the flame and puts the burnt stick in his sweatshirt pocket because Mrs. Wilkinson's backyard is too perfect for a used match. Elbows firm on his knees, drill steady in his hands, he opens his mouth. Positioning the bit on the back molar he holds firm and presses the trigger while gradually applying force. With as little fanfare as Mrs. Wilkinson's tulips exploding from the earth, Stu pokes through the enamel, drills a hole into the abscess, and being careful not to puncture the inside of his cheek he bores through the tooth, pushing out the infected pulp. Then gently pressing the toggle into reverse, he pulls it back out. The vibration tickles his lips and his arms are shaking. He sits with his mouth open for a few seconds. The pressure, that goddamn incessant pressure is replaced by a hot sting that tastes like copper and makes his mouth water. His tongue, all-knowing, slowly tests the terrain. There's a sharp edge and the tooth is a little loose but it's still intact. Leaning over, he discreetly spits out a piece of grit and lets out a big *ahhhhhhhh*. He brushes off the bit and in a moment of pride and relief, kisses it. He feels, all things relative, a frantic joy. Like a dog who needs to run and bound and catch and chase and dig and twirl. He can fall on his knees and get up again because he has love for life. Big cosmic love. The moon spins around the earth and he's going to howl at it tonight while the sun and the stars keep it all in balance.

"Back to work," Eugene orders Tim, as Stu walks into the kitchen and puts the drill and the bits back on the counter.

"You got too much mud on the tape there," Stu says, as a white bit of something flies out his mouth. Coughing, he rubs his nose with his sleeve. "Let me get up there and fix it for you."

"My fucking ass you will," says Eugene. "Your arms

start to ache, you gonna use my circular saw?" Eugene stares so hard Stu looks away, sees his favourite trowel sitting in a bucket of water.

Something through the window catches Eugene's eye. It's Vanessa, loitering in the laneway. Vanessa, shifting her weight back and forth.

Stu follows his boss's gaze.

Eugene turns back, studies Stu's wide-set eyes with their fish-like intensity. His thick lips, smooth and pink, ooze an undeniable sensuality from among the dry silvery bristles that cover his face.

"Get the hell outta here," Eugene growls as he steps off the ladder and rattles it. "Don't you dare show your face around here again unless I give you permission."

Stu backs up. Heads toward the door.

"I mean it dentist boy. And don't forget to collect your crack whore hygienist on the way out."

"Registered nurse," Stu says softly as he closes the door behind him.

"What?" yells Eugene.

He and Tim watch as Stu makes his way toward the laneway, and waddles up to kiss Vanessa's neck.

She is sexy — in a skinny, well-worn way thinks Eugene. Taller than Stu and half his weight, her head's always tilted, demurely, like she's a little lost — but underneath it's pure sass, she knows what she's doing. She and Stu are both pigeon-toed and it gives them a childlike quality that's innocent and brattish. As they turn down the laneway Vanessa punches Stu in the arm.

Tim loses interest and looks at Eugene who appears to be mesmerized. Tim flicks a bit of compound off his hand and heads up the ladder to move some more mud around.

Eugene can't figure it out. She's sleazy for sure, but Stu? She could do a lot better than that. Her skin is so marbly white, her hair so blond and fine like a handful of sunlight. He hates to admit it, so he rarely does and only to himself, but lately when he's making love to Katia, he imagines he's with Vanessa.

Vanessa and Stu's home is a good-sized room with a good-sized window. Located in the back corner on the second floor down a creaky, barf-stained hallway that smells of urine and yesterday's cigarettes, it's a place to rub their brains together and then their bodies. And dream and snore and wheeze. Stu feels strangely that their brand of love could go on forever. It's the world he isn't sure about — the house they live in, the streets they walk, the people they need to rely on in order to have some money. It's life's first rule — the business of needing money for food, shelter, shoes, and a luxury for Vanessa, like lingerie or a winter coat. That rule always makes him feel like he should brace himself for a swift kick to the back of his head.

When Stu and Vanessa arrive home Stu tells her not to worry. Eugene's got lots of work for him. In his soul he feels like he is sinking. His mind tells him he can't afford to feel that way.

Over the summer and into the fall Eugene throws a bone to Stu every couple of months. Makes him feel good to know the guy's still alive and it also satisfies a practical consideration. Like what if, at some point, he's absolutely stuck? These days all the top drywallers are busy building those mega subdivisions. Eugene knows he can't compete with the big-time developers so there's always Stu. You can't call him, he doesn't have a phone, but if you swing by and throw a rock at his window he'll look out and ask what you need. And he amuses Hal who's working for Eugene now that Tim's moved on.

Vanessa lands a job three days a week as a New Career Candidate at a discount clothing store run by a not-for-profit. Stu feels guilty he doesn't make enough for them to survive on and worries about her being out in the world without him — she could slip into old ways — but Vanessa says she likes meeting people and putting all the clothes on the racks.

Occasionally Stu gets up early, having told Vanessa the night before that Eugene needs him over at a job site. He walks the streets and laneways, hoping to find himself in the right place at the right time and sometimes he does. One day he scored a few hours work unloading and spreading gravel; another time he made a few bucks guarding the back door of a catering business while the owner went off in search of lost keys.

On these morning searches he often thinks of another morning, back when he and Eugene were working on Mrs. Wilkinson's kitchen. It was early enough that the streetlights were still on and as he made his way along the sidewalk, Walter Castle appeared out of the dawn, riding down the street on his electric scooter, the stem of a thorny red rose in his mouth. With his large pointy nose stretching out between piercing eyes and stringy white hair tucked behind big thin ears, he motored right up to Stu like a man used to giving orders with no time to waste hanging around discussing the price of gas or the amazing benefits of pomegranate juice. Coming to a sudden stop, he took the rose out of this mouth and with a clear-eyed stare announced, "I love that woman and I'm gonna marry her." Stu whistled through his fingers then clapped his hands as the groom propped the stem back in his mouth and took off. The moment so full of unaffected happiness that everything in it appeared invulnerable to failure.

One afternoon in early November, Stu — restless — is hanging around outside the No Frills. He's hoping for work and this is as good a place as any to do that. Mrs. Wilkinson, walking down the street, is headed to the hardware store when she spots him. She stops for a moment and mentally searches through her house, room by room, for something that might require a man for hire. Stu, looking up, spots her coming toward him.

"Can I call you Ishmael?" she calls out. He opens his arms wide and bows to her. She asks how he is and he says *fine fine,* and asks about her kitchen and tells her how much he liked working on her house. Mrs. Wilkinson asks Stu if he wouldn't mind helping her out with something. A lot of light bulbs in her house have burnt out. "I'm getting too old to even look at a ladder. What I'd like is if you could just replace all of them for me."

"Like a maintenance checkup. Change them all before they have a chance to burn out?"

"Yes! I feel silly asking but it would make me feel better if I didn't have to worry about them," she explains.

There are a lot of light bulbs in Mrs. Wilkinson's house: bulbs and tubes, floods and spots, all different wattages of incandescent, halogen and fluorescent, so Stu spreads the job across four Saturdays. The last one he replaces is a trilight she uses in a floor lamp in the living room next to her reading chair. Stu came across a line of bulbs for specific tasks and found one designed just for reading. It casts a soft rose glow that minimizes reflection and is easy on the eyes.

"Stu, it's brilliant. Absolutely brilliant!" she cries out. There's a little confusion about the money. Stu's sure she's overpaying him but eventually he accepts her remuneration with a gracious bow and a discussion about what Mrs. Wilkinson is reading, which leads her to ask, "Would you like to read them?"

Stu looks at the books. His head rolls and his eyes open wide. "I'd love to hear what you think," Mrs. Wilkinson adds with a nod of encouragement.

Stu steps back, zips his sweatshirt, looks at the books with their sewn pages, serrated sections, hard covers and fancy dust jackets. The top one has stylish lettering rendered in foil. "I can't. I'm honoured but I don't read hardcovers."

"Stu," she pleads, "I'd like you to have them." He hums and haws, swings his head to one side, then the other, then agrees.

"Wonderful. I'm so happy to share my books with you."

"You know," he says, "I used to buy books like this. Back in the 80s it was us drywallers who showed up on site in sports cars wearing fur coats. It's harder now. Everyone's a drywaller."

Mrs. Wilkinson asks Stu to wait a minute. He stays as still as he can, looking down the hallway and into the living room at various lights, remembering each one with particular detail, a dusty socket or the tightness of the thread contacts. Each one a unique variation on a theme, all of them ready to be lit through the magic of electricity. Electrons passing from atom to atom, moving by the grace of conductors. Mrs. Wilkinson reappears, a fur coat draped over her arm. "It was my husband's. I'd like you to have it."

"Mrs. Wilkinson, I can't." Stu shifts his weight from foot to foot. "You know my girlfriend, Vanessa, it's *her* dream to have a fur coat." Stu puts the books on the antique hutch, pulls out his wallet and opens it. "Here's a picture of her."

"Beautiful, she's very beautiful. I tell you what. Would you promise me that once you get Vanessa a fur coat, you'll come back for this one?" Stu agrees, picks up the books, and asks her if she knows how many dry-wallers it takes to change a light bulb.

"Hmm, I think you've stumped me. How many?"

"Just one," he says, "but you also need someone kind enough to ask." As he heads down the walkway Mrs. Wilkinson turns on the porch light.

The winter was a mild one. Cold enough that no one tried to play tennis on the court in the schoolyard that Stu and Vanessa's window overlooks, but not so cold that people who live in the ravine a couple of blocks away were losing any toes to frostbite. The end of the year passed. Vanessa was promoted to Cashier and offered a full-time position but Stu urged her to stay part-time. He wanted her to feel she could rely on him to provide. He wasn't doing a very good job of it but he was doing a good job of convincing her that things were going to pick up for him in the spring.

On one of Vanessa's work days, Stu, returning from the laundromat, was trudging up the street with his arms full of clothes. He would put them on the radiator and in a couple of hours shuffle them. By late afternoon they'd be dry and he would fold and pile them into tidy rectangles, like well-read books, and put them away before Vanessa came home.

"Stinky," a voice yells.

Eugene, his head hanging out of his truck, veers right onto the sidewalk and grins at Stu like he's caught him robbing a bank. "I need you to come with me. Cleaning out a garage over on Sumach."

"I'm busy," says Stu.

"Have to pick up something. I'll be back in ten. Be ready." Stu watches Eugene drive away. His head, through the back window, is motionless and perfectly shaped like a crash test dummy's.

At home, Stu arranges the clothes on the radiator, then heads outside to wait for Eugene.

After sorting and coughing their way through old carburetors and tires, paint cans, garden tools, exercise equipment, abandoned sports gear, broken electronics, seasonal decorations and stir sticks from bars all over the world, they take off for the dump. Racing down the street and flying over a speed hump, they sail right past a group of young boys on the sidewalk kicking a pigeon. Its feathers are bent out of shape as it flits and flaps to free itself. Stu tries to get Eugene to stop but Eugene tells him to mind his own.

At the dump they drop the goods into the appropriate containers and Eugene heads off to sign the paperwork. Stu leans against the truck and admires the sunset glowing golden over the cityscape. Thousands of hungry birds are lined up against the sky, chirping from the hydro wires. Despite being January it smells like late fall — worms and burning leaves. He's winded and sweating badly. But he's working! Tonight, Vanessa will insist he take a shower. He will and then he'll put on a clean T-shirt and sweats. He looks around. His eyes focus on a green forest of Christmas trees, stacked on their sides, piled three or four stories high. He and Vanessa hadn't had a tree this year — always needing to save money they don't have. Holy shit! He'll surprise her. Next week's Chinese New Year, they'll celebrate that. Why not? There was a string of lights he'd seen somewhere. Where was it? Oh yeah! In the bin behind the Bargain Shop. They'll decorate it with lights and popcorn on a string and have a Chinese New Year Christmas.

Nope. No matter how hard Stu pleads, Eugene refuses. He isn't a goddamn scavenger. No way is he going to put someone's used tree in the back of his truck. "The needles will all fall off. And by the way Stinky, Santa's already come and gone." He pays him thirty bucks for four hours of his time (it isn't drywalling) and takes off.

Halfway up River Street the pain in Stu's chest is severe. His breathing's loud. His arms tingle. He stands the balsam fir in front of him. It's dropped a trail of needles but what's holding on is healthy. He raises a hand to check the upper branches. A sharp pain shoots out like a bullet. Minutes later, a taxicab pulls up and the driver yells at him. When Stu doesn't respond the cabbie calls 911, gives the details and heads off to his fare. That's how the paramedics find Stu, arms stretched out, his round weight prone on top of the tree, its prickly branches having cushioned his final fall.

Vanessa is too distraught to leave the house. Dan from the room below uses his cell to call Eleanor, who works with Vanessa, then leaves with the police to identify the body. Eleanor comes right over and uses Stu's phone list — written on a piece of cardboard which was once the inside of the bright orange back cover of Gail Sheehy's #1 Bestseller, *Passages* — to call Stu's sister. When she places the call Vanessa screams so loud Eleanor worries the girl won't make it through the night. She tells Vanessa she'll be right back — returns twenty minutes later with a muffin and some chicken soup, which Vanessa refuses. Her eyes are so puffy she crashes off the walls as she wanders down the hall to the toilet. Eleanor decides to keep an eye on her since no one else is.

Over the next few days Eleanor makes arrangements at a home that the coroner says is the best deal in town. Initially she'd tried to secure a little church just a few blocks away but it wasn't available because it's being used for advanced polling for the federal election. And anyway, it would have cost more and it wasn't really clear how expenses were going to be covered. Eleanor tells Mr. Beattie, the funeral director, to keep things simple. Polly, Stu's sister back in Halifax, said she was coming but then her daughter Keri got the bug. She sends beautiful flowers.

Inside the funeral parlour there's no mistaking the artificial air of death. Eleanor sits Vanessa down on a wooden foldable chair set against the wall in a tiny room with plastic flowers in china vases glued to heavily lacquered tables. Sitting next to Vanessa, she holds her hand, asks her how she met Stu, but Vanessa, unable to speak, shakes her head. After a while Eleanor goes to the common room to get some coffee and a plate of butter cookies. Vanessa refuses to eat. Eleanor quietly goes to Mr. Beattie's office to confirm final arrangements, then sits a bit longer with Vanessa before reminding her that unfortunately she can't stay the full two hours. She has to be at the academy by eight for her son's graduation. Really, she should have changed the night of the memorial, but at the time she thought Polly would be here. She hadn't anticipated she would feel so responsible for Vanessa.

Mrs. Wilkinson is in Florida. Eleanor's message is waiting for her on the tiny cassette tape of her old-style answering machine. Dan and Jennie and Blade from the rooming house were coming but they hadn't been around when Eleanor and Vanessa left and now they're walking way out Dundas West instead of East wondering why there's no funeral home between Tim Hortons and the Honda dealership.

Eugene decides to stop by the bar before heading over. He tells Tim and Hal to meet him there and they'll go together. At the last minute Hal calls. He can't make it. Wife's working late, gotta stay with the kid. But Tim shows up and he and Eugene raise their glasses, "to Stu."

Jake is there talking to some bald guy. Claudia's on her usual perch.

"What's the occasion, boys?" asks Jake.

Eugene tells them the news.

Claudia gasps. "I had no idea." She asks when? Eugene provides as many details as he feels appropriate.

"That guy always made me laugh," says Jake. "Had quite a mouth on him."

"I don't remember him," says the bald guy.

"You would if you'd met him. He was always talkin' up a storm about funny stuff," says Jake. "What was his last name anyway? Stu what?"

I don't know, thinks Tim.

"Smart," says Eugene.

"Stu Smart, eh," Jake says. "Funny guy. Stu Smart. Reminds me of one of them tongue twisters I used to know. How's it go? If Stu chews shoes ... should Stu choose ... the shoes he chews?"

The bald guy tries to repeat it. "If Stu shoes chews..."

"Give it up guys," Claudia says with a look of disapproval.

Eugene tells Tim that Stu's passing has created a bit of a situation. Would he be available to help him with some drywalling on the weekend? Tim says maybe and tells Eugene to call him Saturday. They decide to have another round.

Eugene talks about the jobs he's been working on. Mostly small neighbourhood projects. Kitchens. Bathrooms. Real estate agents say these are the best rooms to renovate, you get your money back, but those granite countertops are a bitch to install.

"Where are we going anyway?" asks Tim.

Eugene pulls out his agenda from his shoulder bag. "Out Dundas somewhere." He puts a newspaper clipping on the bar. "Got the address here."

Tim picks up the announcement. "Born 'forty-eight. What's that make him?"

"Fifty-nine?"

"A year shy of sixty," says Tim. "Wonder if he was eligible for CPP death benefits."

Eugene asks him what he thinks is going to happen to housing prices. This leads to a discussion about capital gains and investments. "All comes down to where do you put your money?" says Tim. "It's an old question and a good one. Keeps me in business."

Eugene tells Tim about a new set of Callaway irons he just ordered (125,000 points). And about this property in Creemore that Katia keeps talking about. Ten acres with a little river running through it. "Second property, of course," says Eugene. "I couldn't live out there full-time."

Fuck, he thinks, Vanessa's going to be there. "Let's have another one," he says to Tim.

"It's getting close to closing time. I'm so sorry for your loss. This must be a very difficult time for you. I've seen this before," Mr. Beattie continues. "Sometimes people just can't make it."

He sits beside Vanessa, aware of her influence over him. And how skinny she is. Wonders if it's grief, poverty, drugs or all three. He realizes he has no idea what her voice sounds like. He lets a few minutes pass.

"I'll call you a cab," he says gently, standing up.

"No." Her voice is high and thin, not what he'd expected.

"Don't worry," he says. "It's on me. Please."

When the cab arrives, Mr. Beattie escorts Vanessa through the heavy oak doors. He reaches around to open the door of the cab. Vanessa looks up at the sky. She realizes she has no idea where Stu is. The basement maybe. Could she touch him? Is that a bad idea? She wants to ask but can't find the words. The cabbie leans over and looks to Mr. Beattie who gives him the hand signal for one minute.

Mr. Beatty touches Vanessa's shoulder, then holds her arm and guides her as she twists herself into the darkness of the cab. The light of a streetlamp catches her hair. In a moment absent of logic he strokes the top of her head, then leans into the vehicle, takes her hands and folds her thin fingers around two tens and his business card.

Back at the bar, Claudia gets off her stool and quietly waves goodbye.

"See ya later," says Jake.

Eugene looks at Tim. "Here's to Stu, a gentle soul," he says, holding up his half full glass. And he means it. And for a second he misses the guy but then tells himself to stop. No use crying in your beer. We all die. Some day I'll die too. That's life.

THE ESCAPISTS

EVERY YEAR, Doug and Sharlene beat a retreat from the dreary complications of January — dry skin, diminished daylight, streets that disappear after snowfalls — and board a packed charter fight to Puerto Vallarta or Puerto Plata or Santa something or other. They book their vacation the first day of November, in honour of The Day of the Dead, hoping their packaged week will fulfill a travel brochure promise of memories that last forever. And when the big day finally arrives and they find themselves descending the steps of the noisy jumbo and squinting across the scorched tarmac at the quivering green-brown horizon, inhaling hot air mixed with the leaden odour of aviation fuel, they see themselves as they appear in their finest daydreams. Full of their best feelings. The brazen seductive sun wraps around them and melts away their apprehensions and insecurities. They nod agreeably at an agent who wants nothing more than to direct them to their carrier's air-conditioned coach. *Don't worry,* they tell less experienced travellers who sweat and panic when the short, greasy-haired representatives yell at them all to move along. *They're not going to slit your throat.*

Hola amigo, they call out to demonstrate the best way to deal with these Third World workers, many of whom lack both subservient humbleness and good customer service skills.

Seated in the transfer operator's luxury vehicle, they uncap their first *cerveza* and urge their vacationing *compañeros* to join them. As they help themselves to a second and then a third — *gracias* — with nary a concern about needing to pee (you sweat it off down here) they welcome back an old feeling: they, Doug and Sharlene from Canada, are built for fun and adventure.

Don't worry be happy, they joke with others.

What happens here stays here.

We're all just outlaws looking for a little fun.

Is it time for a drink yet? Oh wait, we've got drinks in our hands!

As a couple they discuss their options. Maybe they'll make new friends. Acquire a piece of art. Liquidate everything and buy a little property down here.

Doug always gives Shar the window seat. He holds her hand as the bus speeds along the dirty roads, past ramshackle buildings housing businesses called Servicar and Super Shalom. Seems no matter what seaside paradise they land in there's always some old lady at a card table ready to braid hair into cornrows, emaciated dogs running around with their rib cages showing, and some leather-tanned skinny guy with a python around his neck. Shar can't remember where they were when they swam with dolphins. Where it was that Doug was bitten by a jellyfish. If San Juan is in Costa Rica or the Dominican. But Doug knows. If she were to ask him he would answer *Treasure Reef. Juan Griego. Puerto Rico, baby.*

And to the last one he would add a slinky salsa sidestep while singing *she looks like a flower but she stings like a bee … like every girl in history. She bangs, she bangs. I'm wasted by the way she moves, she moves …*

But Shar doesn't ask because she doesn't care. Names are just details that men obsess with so they can throw them at each other and feel like they're gaining territory or scoring points. And my husband, she thinks — look at him, will you? He doesn't need anyone to egg him on. As for her, as long as the sun shines she's pleased as tequila punch because some places in the world are just inherently better at producing happiness. It grows in the plants and flows in the underground rivers and darts about on the backs of the tiny rubbery geckos.

Doug leans into Shar and as they peer out through the tinted glass they know they've arrived. They're doing what people do to reward themselves. It's the stuff of dreams. It's the stuff of screen savers, for Christ's sake. And the pleasure of leaving their lives behind is accompanied by a sense of stepping into themselves more fully. Their feelings heightened with a traveller's alertness. They are, during these breaks, what they are most proud of being: adventurers, explorers, sun gypsies. Doug wears his bandanas and his Hawaiian shirts, Shar her halter tops and sometimes that oversized T-shirt with the life-sized naked woman airbrushed into position, front and back.

Yet their desires to have no worries can be more intense than their sense of being somewhere. Sometimes they experience uncomfortable embarrassments that make them feel defeated or damaged. Like the time they landed in a crowded airport (Doug knows where) and a beefy guy reached in, yanked a gigantic duffle bag off the carousel and swung it across his back, obliviously side-swiping Shar and knocking her to her knees. The cold grimy floor felt harder than a sheet of black ice and she couldn't stop weeping. Or the time Doug joined a friendly beach volleyball game but couldn't connect on any bumps or spikes. Fists clenched, he stomped away complaining that the Brits were cheating and then stepped on a bee, which left him mute with pain and humiliation.

But after these inconsequential episodes, and always by the following morning, they wake full of love for each other, and for wherever they've landed, and set out to put their towels on a couple of loungers before heading to the breakfast buffet. Mornings are spent quietly with magazines and discussing other guests — where they're from, their jobs, their tattoos. The rest of the day gets worked out in due course, beginning with the first pina colada and ending with the chatting up and toasting of others in the bar. By midnight they fall in bed and lie on their backs, listening to the sound of the waves approaching the shoreline and the wind undulating the sheers, and drift toward dreamland anticipating doing exactly the very same thing tomorrow. Which amounts to not much really. But it seems like everything.

"We used to be peacekeepers," Doug laments, inhaling his Benson & Hedges and casting an eye out from the balcony into the warm, windy, early-evening darkness that's particular to the Caribbean. "I gotta get a beer," he says, dropping his cigarette into the sludge in the bottom of the green champagne bottle he's holding. "You guys wanna free beer?"

As her husband heads for the mini-bar, Shar takes over.

"I love my son but he's an idiot. He's in Military College near Kingston. Wants to go to Afghanistan. If he does I'll kill him." She squints across at her neighbouring vacationers, a pretty blonde and her husband Jonathan, but isn't clear-headed enough to read their faces. Nodding towards the bright, cavernous privacy of her room, she adds, "*He* doesn't get it. Matt's my son, not his."

Just then the country music playing in the background explodes, bursting out of Doug and Sharlene's junior jacuzzi suite with the brazen cockiness of a rooster strutting across a barnyard. Shar closes her eyes and lets her body sway as the deep baritone floods the balcony, overflows, spills across the illuminated turquoise waters of the swimming pool, and sails into the darkness behind the swim-up bar where the bartender is all alone restocking the tiny fridge with juice mixers. Showing no need to excuse itself, it barrels across the manicured gardens and invites itself into the ocean-view jacuzzi suites at the far end of the property.

"You know this guy?" Doug asks, stepping back out, extending a can of beer across the concrete balcony divider. "Josh Turner. He's got a voice to kill."

"No, don't know I do," says Jonathan. "You? Claire."

Claire frowns and shakes her head no.

Remember, Shar tells herself. Her name's Claire — like Cher.

"You guys ever make it out to BC? If you do, you

gotta come up to this festival we go to. We're really like rock and roll all the way. Saw the Stones five times. But now we're turning country." Doug sings along: "*If I gave you my hand would you take me and make me the happiest man in the world?*"

Shar smiles vacantly and wraps her white robe tighter across her throat.

"This festival, it's country and folk. Goes for three days. Everyone comes in trailers or with tents. We met Josh Turner's brother. You guys would love it."

"I want to win the lottery," Shar says, clapping her hands wistfully. Her eyes flit around the balcony looking for a lucky spot to land on, finally choosing her husband's torso that's showing through the front of his white robe. She grins as if Doug's chest hairs had just told her a deep, dark secret.

"Better get dressed for dinner," Doug suggests. "Where's my wife?" he asks Claire. He looks at Shar. "Oh! There she is. Go get dressed for dinner, hon. Supposed to be there by eight, I think," he says, giving her bum a cheeky slap.

Shar holds her arms above her head and circles around, as if so intoxicated with life she's no longer part of it, and twirls into their room.

Doug watches her fade away. "I love it when she gets dressed up for dinner." He steps toward the room. "Put on a dress, will you," he yells, then looks back to his new friends. "Sorry. I've been talking away. You guys probably think I'm nuts. You wanna join us for dinner?"

"We can't. It's assigned seating."

"Oh. It's like that, is it?" Doug turns away from his neighbours and gazes into the night sky. His hips begin to swivel as he sings along with Josh, "*Would you accompany me to the edge of the sea, help me tie up the ends of a dream? I gotta know ... would you go with me?*" Doug stops dancing. "You guys can bonk me on the head for this, but seems to me the Afghanies just need better education and more job opportunities. If they had more security and prosperity they wouldn't go side with the Taliban." He looks at Jonathan and Claire who are smiling at him, a little too politely for his liking. "Whaddya think?" he asks them. "Whaddya think about the Taliban?"

"A definition is by no means clear," offers Claire.

"Graeme Smith in the *Globe* wrote a very informative series," says Jonathan.

"That's right, it was superb," says Claire.

"Sorry I missed that," Doug responds. "Listen, you guys been here two weeks, right? What's good to do here?"

"Read and relax," Jonathan says informatively.

"What else?"

"Claire and I go jogging along the beach every morning."

"We're training for a half-marathon in May," adds Claire.

Doug keeps waiting for more. "That's impressive," he comments. "So what else? Where's the party?"

"Cancun. Two hours north of here."

By the time Doug and Shar head off for the restaurant they're both well enough tanked that food no longer seems necessary. And the layout of the resort is bothering Doug.

Walking along the softly lit stone pathways, a mild feeling of despair climbs into his jet-lagged body. Where the fuck exactly do people have fun here? Everything so spread out and there's no energy to the place. No main bar where you can just hang out, chat, watch the game while the wife takes a boo through the gift shops. All the bars next to the restaurant (and the tequila tastery that's really only a makeshift kiosk) close at dinnertime, leaving just one tiny outdoor bar where they play Enya music.

Inside the enormous, busy, glass-walled restaurant their hostess, Lucia, checks her list to confirm their names. "Follow me, please," she says. As she leads them to their table, Doug spots two familiar faces in the back corner of the room.

"Look who it is," Doug shouts with astonishment, as he rushes past Lucia.

"Fancy meeting you here!" Doug lands a chummy pat on Jonathan's back.

Jonathan and Claire stare at each other, incredulous.

"This table here's empty." Doug looks to Lucia. "Look, nobody's sitting here, right? Why don't we sit here?"

"I will check. I think for tonight it may be fine," Lucia says, turning on her heels and heading back to her station.

"This is fun," cries Shar.

Doug hands his wife the wineglasses from the table and begins rocking the heavy metal frame back and forth, nudging it sideways across the plush carpet until it's almost touching Jonathan and Claire's table.

Shar puts the glasses down and she and Doug move their chairs over and settle into their seats.

"Good evening. My name is Aurelio," a tall man says, as he snaps open Shar's serviette and drapes it across her lap. "I understand you are sitting here tonight."

"Apparently we've made friends," says Claire.

"I see. I'm very happy," Aurelio says laughing. He hands Doug and Shar their menus. "Would you like to order drinks?"

"*Si si,*" says Doug, rearranging his weight in his chair before leaning across the table. "Now what's that you guys are drinking?"

"Lagoons. Vodka martinis with curaçao," says Claire. "It's our favourite drink here."

"They're blue," explains Jonathan.

"We'll have that too, don't you think Shar?" And so their drinks are ordered, which helps Doug feel a bit better because this place is hoity-toity. "You guys don't mind if we sit here, do you?"

"It's okay," Jonathan says.

Doug can't stop sweating. He surveys the room. White tablecloths and big glittery chandeliers. Not what he'd expected. Where are the scruffy terracotta tiles and the ceiling fans whirling off-kilter? And the folksy decorations that Shar likes to buy? Artisan stuff. Mariachi bands and donkeys made of straw. Wood carvings of worn out looking women carrying water jugs. Some of the male guests are wearing ties. What the hell's that about?

Doug sits up straight, puts his elbows on the table and tells himself to suck it up and try to fit in. Probably better than a buffet every night anyway since he's not exactly one for self-control.

"I work as a bookkeeper," says Shar. "What do you two do?"

Claire and Jonathan look at each other. "I'm a lawyer," Claire says. "Jon's in advertising."

Doug looks at Shar. Wishes they were sitting side-by-side rather than across from each other because he'd like to be able to rest his hand on her thigh. From the back his wife's a real knockout. It's only from the front you see the creases and the worry lines and the mouth with those front teeth that reach out a bit too far. But he doesn't give a damn. He leans back, inhales the sweet scent of her perfume for which he, Doug Petersen, is the intended, honourary recipient, and that alone convinces him that rightness commands his life.

Doug listens as Shar asks Jonathan about the world of advertising and as he does he hears a voice in the back of his head assure him that yes, he does love Shar as much as (but not more than) his first wife. He and Vivian had never come to a place as expensive as this one. In fact, he never realized the depth of his love for Vivian until she had withered away, her eyes the only part of her body that became larger, shinier, more intense as she shrank from chemo and radiation, all of which lead him to the logical confusion that if only Shar would die, he could really feel all the many levels of compassion, tenderness and pride that make up his love for her.

In a voice austere and triumphant he announces, "Family's very important to us. You guys got that? People in the trades are decent. I don't mind. If someone needs something, I'm there. I don't care who they are."

"Doug's a plumber," says Shar.

"Good job. Sanitary and storm. Maple Ridge water

works. Twenty-one pumping stations. I do inspections, oversee flushings, repairs. I work independent," Doug shares with a shrug. "No one breathing down my back."

"He's gonna get a good pension. Thank God because I do bookkeeping." Lowering her voice to almost a whisper, Shar adds: "Just a couple of small clients here and there, so I ain't got a pension or security. I'm fifty. We met when I was six. He was eight. He asked me out in Grade Eleven — *so I'm going to this dance, do you want to come? No way*, I told him. He was an asshole."

"Oh that's a nice thing to share," says Doug.

"It's true, you were an asshole, but you're not anymore."

Shar and Doug, their faces bloated from humidity, tilt their heads at each other, then turn to their dinner companions. Jonathan and Claire are smiling deeply into each other's eyes. "What do you feel like eating?" Claire asks quietly, as they glance down at the menus in front of them.

Doug looks at his menu but he can't focus. The trouble is going to be the evenings. It's always okay during the day but what do you do here at night? And this restaurant. It's too stuffy and he can hardly make out the fancy words on the menu. It's too fucking hot. And unexciting. His mind is full of thoughts. It has a mind of its own. It launches itself three thousand kilometres away. Back to reality, where he's a supervisor. He thinks about the various opportunities his job provides him. Constant blockages — tree roots, grease, disposable diapers that need to be cleared out, usually just sewer snaking and camera shit, literally — that take him right up to the property lines of some bored and lonely women. *We got everything working for you,* he always says reassuringly with a polite nod, soft leather briefcase in hand, as he steps across the threshold having sent the boys off to the next site.

He doesn't play around that much anymore though. Not as much as he could, believe you me ...

Shar's mesmerized. She's drawn to the creamy perfection of Claire's well-toned shoulders, completely bare and unblemished above the neckline of her slinky black dress. They're so marvellous she wants to lick them but the suddenness of that would be vulgar so she undresses Claire slowly and delicately. Pressing the nakedness of the silky young body against her own she can hardly believe how good it feels. Her hands can't stop touching all that softness. Claire's nothing like Doug. Everything about her body is warm and light and receptive. Shar climbs right on top of her and kisses her mouth. She's betraying her husband but only with a woman and it feels oh so good. She kisses Claire's neck, then her dainty breasts. As the perky nipples respond to her tongue she lets her hands roam down to the narrowness of Claire's waist and the sensuous curves of her hips. Her hands slide right underneath Claire's buttocks, and as she slinks down planting more kisses she feels Claire's long legs wrap around her back. But that's enough. Beyond that it's all too yucky and complicated really. Much as Doug wishes she were into it — it's never been her thing.

Doug clears his throat. "Sounds like, ah, you guys got good jobs."

"We think so," says Jonathan.

"Demanding," Claire adds. "Sometimes we hardly even see each other through the week."

"That must be hard," Shar suggests sympathetically.

"May I take your order please?"

"Oreo, you're back!" Shar shrieks, wiggling in her chair. Aurelio bows.

Claire and Jonathan clearly know their way around the menu, ordering *tostonillas*, *ceviche* and the *papillot* — all in some convoluted combination that seems to please them both no end. Jonathan hands back their menus, concluding with "*Gracias, Aurelio*," rolling his r's so naturally and effortlessly Shar can't help it, she has to tell him. He sounds like Antonio Banderas and did he ever see him in Madonna's *Truth or Dare?*

"No," says Jonathan.

Shar looks at Aurelio, holds up her menu and points at something. "*Par favor*, I'll have this." Aurelio compliments her on her choice but suggests she might like to have something else to accompany it, so Shar orders a soup too.

"Steak," Doug says. "You got steak?" Just about a full minute later, after Aurelio has explained about the menu cycle which revolves through an eight-day schedule and there is filet mignon topped with sautéed mushrooms, tomatoes and cilantro but that's not tonight or tomorrow night or the night after, Doug discerns that the answer is no. No sirloin, no porterhouse, no rib-eye, no T-bone, no strip, no flank. Frustrated, he gives a quick wrist-toss of his menu and inadvertently stabs the starched white shirt that contains Aurelio's belly. "Just get me the closest thing you got to a steak then."

"We have a delicious pork filet stuffed with *fufu* and onions, very good, would that be to your satisfaction?"

What the fuck is *fufu*? Irritation and disappointment

cripple Doug's vocabulary. He gives Aurelio an annoyed but affirmative nod while wondering who the smart ass is who decided to bring high falutin gasasstronomy to this piss-poor country? The stress of restraining his anguish leaves him thirsty. Claire and Jonathan are having two more of those blue things — but Doug's ready to move on and he decides his wife is too.

"We'd like a bottle. What's your best white?" he asks. Aurelio immediately bows and then hustles over to a rotund guy behind the bar who whisks to their table and introduces himself as Norberto, their sommelier for the evening. Norberto scans the table. Jonathan points politely toward Doug. A brief discussion unfolds regarding the merits of a dry French Pinot Blanc versus a slightly sweeter German Riesling. Norberto keeps shoving the wine list in front of Doug's eyes. "Please, see here sir," he pleads, but Doug insists he doesn't need to look. What's the guy think — that he's gonna study it? Isn't that why some places have a someallyeh or whatever you call it — so you don't need to figure it all out on your own?

"We could have them both," suggests Shar.

"We'll have the French one," Doug instructs. "And get me one of those double Xs too, please."

"I prefer reds," he says, as Norberto hurries back to the bar, "but in these countries you risk your life drinking the piss-rot they pass off as red vino. It'll clean out both your ends." Doug eases back in his chair, looks around, hunches his shoulders, opens up his arms wide and explains, "It's not their fault. It's all imported and other countries only send their bottom of the barrel shit here. Pardon my French."

"I can't tell the diff," says Shar. "I like it all!"

Drinks arrive. Then the food, which everyone agrees is not bad. Shar shares that she's watching her salt these days and asks Claire if they have kids (not yet) while Doug asks Jonathan where they usually travel (no particular place). Shar says how much she loved being pregnant and that she's fifty and she met Doug when she was six and that every mother should get life insurance because you never know — *my son was only nine when my first husband died unexpectedly and I had nothing to fall back on* — while Doug suggests to Jonathan that they might like Cuba — *food's lousy but great beaches and cigars and culturally quite interesting being that they're all critical and against the bourgeoisie but they don't say no to our tourismo dollars, you follow me?* The conversations duel diagonally across the table, growing louder, exhausting everyone. Shar wants to know how Claire met Jonathan but Claire doesn't offer much except that it was at a wedding, while Doug keeps pressing Jonathan, *whaddya think about Castro?* Eventually everyone gives up and lets Doug talk about being in Thailand. "It's Moslems there, right, where we were. And they don't drink. I kept thinking what are we doing here but it was on the tour. They're extremists — the big J's there, you know. When we were there three monks were dilapidated."

"The big J?" Claire says.

"Could we not talk about that?" Shar says turning to Doug.

Doug notices Shar's face is getting bonier and it makes him feel a sad kind of love for her.

"Jihad," Jonathan says softly. "De*cap*itated."

"That's right, extremists, mostly in the south," Doug

says. "Anyway it was fun but getting a drink was a real chore. It's why we like these cluesives."

"These what?" Claire asks.

"All-inclusives," says Jonathan.

Suddenly Shar remembers a TV ad, for a financial or insurance company or something, called Clarica. She leans forward, touches Jonathan's arm affectionately. "You're a Claire-i-ca advisor, aren't you?" she teases.

Jonathan nods ever so slightly.

Come on advertising guy, Shar thinks, it was funny. "Do you know that TV ad?" she asks. "It always makes me laugh so hard. An old one with the skier from Quebec, who was it?"

"Jean-Luc Brassard, gold, 'ninety-four, moguls," Doug says.

"Right," says Shar, "in a commercial about ..."

"PertPlus."

"That's right. Where he says, he says, get ready," Shar warns, "I use it because it gives me the cunt-roll I need." Doug hollers and Shar laughs so hard she starts to cry, but Claire and Jonathan barely smile.

Shar's eyes narrow and she lets out a tiny grimace to let Doug know what she's feeling. She's had just about enough of trying to share life stories with these people. She could continue on, explain the part about how when she was twenty she'd married Jamie, who was Doug's best friend, and the when and what-for of how she'd eventually ended up marrying Doug, but why? This perfect pair aren't exactly talking much about their triumphs and tragedies, their life secrets.

Doug replenishes Shar's glass, then his own, then stares into the shallow blue pool still remaining in

Jonathan and Claire's martini glasses. He understands. He feels it too, that there's something deceitful about this couple. Jonathan announces he works in advertising but then he explains he's a comptroller. What's that got to do with advertising? These two are the kind that figure he and Shar would never pick up the subtleties of their lingering glances, or the sarcasm of their body language, that implies that *their* devotion is more profound than what they consider to be the buffoonery of love, called Doug and Shar, that they got cornered into eating dinner with.

Doug reaches for his wine. Takes a gulp. "Not bad for free wine," he says.

Claire addresses Doug. "It's not free."

Doug looks at his glass suspiciously.

"Drinks are included, but not wine. Anything beyond the house you are required to pay for," explains Claire.

"Says who?"

"That's why there's prices on the list," Claire continues.

"That's why the sommelier kept trying to get you to read it," adds Jonathan, calmly.

"That's bullshit. It doesn't say that anywhere. They don't tell you that." Doug looks around as if searching for someone famous, while wondering — if you can drink all the top shelf vodka, gin, scotch and tequila you want here, what fucking sense does it make that you have to pay for a stinkin' bottle of wine?

Aurelio appears, wants to check how things are going so far. Jonathan takes it upon himself to mention that there's been some confusion about the wine and the price list. Aurelio excuses himself and returns a minute later with Norberto who shows Doug the list of wines and the prices next to each. "I am so sorry sir, but you asked about our best white."

"Listen, no one said anything about paying for nothing so don't take me for a fool."

Norberto apologizes and points to the number next to the wine and softly reads it aloud. "One thousand six hundred thirty-two. Pesos."

Doug is unable to focus. He looks at his plate, stabs his pork with his fork and takes a bite, then another. When Norberto leaves, Doug drops his cutlery, letting it clatter on the glass tabletop. What kind of fucking conspiracy place is this? Before he can count to ten Norberto comes back with some guy named Alex who tells Doug he'd like to offer him a discount on a special romantic candlelight dinner on the beach. Normally a hundred-fifty dollars, includes a free bottle of champagne but he can have for only one hundred American dollars. What night would he like to schedule it?

Doug lets out a deep growl. His hand flies up and swats the muggy air.

"Get outta here," he shouts, so steamed up he can't even swallow. "Get the hell outta my face will yah?"

"Hey, cowboy," Jonathan says. "Cool it, will you?"

Norberto and Alex silently back away.

"At least now you know," Claire says, her face lighting up.

"What happened to the happiest man in the world?" Jonathan asks. "Where'd he go?"

Doug's face is redder than the rare steak he'd wanted but couldn't order.

Sweat drips down the side of his forehead. He bursts

from his chair, grabs the bottle of wine and storms from the table. It's hard to move in a straight line and he realizes he's shit-piss drunk but criminal thoughts and adrenaline keep him upright.

Jonathan, Claire and Shar watch as Doug heads to the bar holding the three-quarters empty bottle out from his side as if it were a squirmy, disobedient child. A discussion with Alex begins politely but very quickly Doug's loud enough that a good number of people are watching.

"Sometimes he gets heated up," Shar explains. Her husband's movements are jerky as he paces to the bar, turns back to the table, heads back to the bar.

"Let's go," says Claire.

"Excuse us, please," says Jonathan. "I think we'll be leaving you."

"It was great to meet you. Have a safe trip home," Shar says as she watches them point their knives and forks to ten o'clock, loosely fold their white napkins to the left of their plates, and quietly tuck their chairs in. At the hostess lectern Claire says something to Lucia while Jonathan slips some bills in Aurelio's palm and shakes his hand as if congratulating him.

Just beyond them, Doug is having more words with the bartender. He stomps over to the tropical plants beside the bar. He pounds the bottle of wine into the soil between the colourful dahlias. Just as he swings around to head back to his table he catches a glimpse of Jonathan's backside exiting through the glass door. With a sudden jolt of relief and freedom he charges back to the dahlias, grabs the bottle, and lets out a major "heeeeee-haaaaaaaaw," as he pours the last sips of the sweet white nectar into the earth. He has nothing fucking

left to lose and what's a vacation if not an opportunity
to let it all hang out? What the fuck does any of it matter? Everyone pretending to be so ultra civil. No one for
even a second understanding his frustration and the need
to rail a little because he never learned to read good or
use the computer right. He tosses the bottle back into the
plant box.

As Shar sits watching her husband duck and dart under
the arms of Alex and then successfully dodge Norberto's
clumsy tackle before jumping onto a bar stool from where
he yells at the top of his lungs, "Hello, Mexico. It's great
to be here," — she smiles. He's wound up tighter than the
strings of an Ozark banjo. She hasn't seen him perform
such splendid maneuvres since he wore number 22 for the
high school football team. And as he slips and falls on top
of the ice sculpture — a mermaid emerging from a rock
— that is melting anyway on top of the shiny mahogany
bar, she wonders if somehow everything is her fault. She'd
married Doug because it was what he wanted and she
thought it would make her life easier and it had but that
didn't make it right. As the sculpture breaks into several
pieces and Doug falls to the safety of the floor she tells
herself that what was right is what she'd done some thirty
years ago when she first turned him down. But what to do
about it now? If anything.

As the top of Doug's head rises from behind the bar
she tells herself she will need to tell him gently, kindly,
knowing it's the dividing up of things that can cause hor-
rific rows. She'll let him know he can have the dog painting they bought somewhere. And the TV. Even their

whole Stones collection. She'll pose no threat even while he proceeds to be a raging hurt asshole.

Doug begins his stumbling journey back toward his table, a leery Alex shadowing his every move.

More than his chubby knees, receding hair, stubborn paunch, eyes swimming in the pink of broken capillaries, what Shar sees is a wounded man. His face is furious and frightened and he needs her. I'll never leave him, she thinks, he's my margin of safety.

Shar stands, steadies herself, then climbs atop her chair. "Hello everyone," she calls out. "I'd like your attention. Let's hear it for a man who needs no introduction. Give it up, please, for Mr. Doug Petersen ... from Maple Ridge, Canada!"

The room registers her suggestion with momentary stillness.

Then a red-faced, heavy man sitting at a table in the middle of the room, eyes fixed on Doug, pushes his chair back and starts clapping. "Encore! Encore!" he shouts.

As Shar slides down from her chair, Doug stops, turns to the man and takes a full bow. Then heading to Shar he stares into his wife's beautiful eyes. His own wild eyes beg for her pardon as he yells, "Tomorrow night, buddy. Same time, same place."

INHERITANCE

It WAS ONE of those warm and clear summer Sundays. The kind that makes people say, *don't bring anything just come as you are,* and you actually believe them. So very perfect, really, that you develop an undeniable urge to punch the air to see if you can poke a hole through it. You tell yourself you want to live in a day like this for the rest of your life and never again have to schedule a furnace checkup or lose an umbrella or book a holiday. And then you wonder how your life became so precarious that the weather counts among the petals you pluck from the daisy to discover your fate. It's sunny. It's sunny not. She loves me. She loves me not. I love me. I love me not.

Laura had finally put her foot down and demanded that Leo seek professional help. Although his outbursts of anger never really hurt anyone, his temper echoed off the walls of every room and Laura was tired of feeling haunted by a looming beast. After putting up a fuss and suggesting that maybe Laura was the one who needed help, Leo had obliged. Now — he's all for it. He has the sense that his therapist sees into his soul, at least the parts he chooses to reveal, and although he has a penchant for brilliant mimicries that can sidetrack their discussions and exasperate her, their weekly sessions have given him a new lease on life. She validates that he is in fact a smart, funny, useful man. A decent father, husband, human being. She's taught him how to breathe and count, to help dissipate his anger. Recently, they have been working on being mindful of small moments of happiness. When he's in a custom-tailored suit on the precipice of closing a deal, and his witty remarks about that new HBO show have sent everyone buckling over in howls of laughter — it all makes sense to him. He grins with confidence knowing his Botox injections are hiding the cracks and crevices around his eyes.

Today, however, is not one of those days.

"Shut it," he yells at the family dog. Shaker — leashed to an upside down golf club stabbed into the lawn — stops barking, twirls and hops on his hind legs in a gesture of adoration toward the master of the house whose frustration is heating up as hot as his neighbour's barbeque. But at least they're busy barbequing now instead of pounding those pan drums. All afternoon while Leo struggled with the rinky-dink miniature levels you suspend on a string, the entire Jones family had been out in their backyard, sitting on lawn chairs, practicing "Love Me Tender." Leo figured that if Ronald Jones were better educated or knew how to read music he'd go over and help him with the harmonies, but what's the use? Better to refrain!

He rubs his hand along a field joist, then turns to his two oldest daughters who are sitting at the edge of the deck frame looking bored and hard done by. "Leeann. Luisa. One of you grab the plane from my workbench and bring it here. Now. Please." He hears a tsk and the rustle of legs moving. Crouching to alleviate the pain in his lower back, he imagines what's ahead: his mother-in-law settled into a folding chair wearing one of her wash-and-wear summer dresses, complaining about how she's being hounded by telemarketers, the spotted skin on her arm jiggling like rice pudding as she raises her glass to let someone, anyone, know it's empty; his sister-in-law babbling on about her brilliant little team of hockey wannabes as if anybody's interested; and Laura, plopped in her Muskoka chair wistfully waving a glass of white Burgundy, happily and blindly convinced there's not a care in the world to be had — my husband who works fifty hours a week will fetch my mother a top-up *and* cook the steaks *and* entertain the troops. Leo stands back up. *I* need a vacation.

"A vacation, that's what I need," Leo repeats the thought aloud for anyone who might be within earshot. "From everyone and everything. Shaker, note the emphasis on *every*!" he yells. The dog, silenced momentarily, wags his tail.

Leo squints toward the back of his property where his two youngest are chasing each other in a circle. He grabs a couple of screws, fastens a corner bracket, reminds himself that he'd always wanted a family since he'd been an only child and his parents hated each other. But the thought isn't enticing enough to divert his attention from the real problem, which is he never signed up to be the single preferred supplier of an endless profusion of clothes and iPods and tampons. How many times does he have to plead? His wife's either too busy or too clue-less to realize that batteries need to be recharged and a man needs his weekends to relax, uninterrupted please, to play his guitars and just be himself. Laura used to find him amusing. *You're so funny* she would laugh, as he yelled *Lau-raaa* while performing a perfect Dick Van Dyke pratfall over a milk crate full of records. Now, she just looks away; her allegiance has moved to her chil-dren. Four. All girls. Enough of a brood for sure, but still, Leo can't believe that Laura had her tubes tied last winter without consulting him. Ever since, she's become soft and doughy in the hips and breasts. And she has a new annoying habit of leaving her mouth open, as if nothing-ness holds a fascination for her.

It's my own fault, thinks Leo. I've spoiled my kids. And I've spoiled my wife.

No wonder she clings to him, even now, twenty-three years after they met in the record-lending section of a downtown library. He'd been so full of purpose back then, hunting through the bluegrass section; she was idly browsing for something that might move her. Well … she found it all right! He taught her about guitar picking styles and the beauty of lyrics and how chord progres-sions are handed down and modified with each genera-tion. Everything is traceable. And what had she taught him? She who had spent two years of high school in the pristine hills of Switzerland and learned to sail at the family's summer cottage in Muskoka. She managed to get him out on skis and tried to teach him how to make a perfect downhill turn. Leo, with his brown wool hat and leather gloves, had felt threatened by the fluorescent colours and sleek synthetic materials of the born and bred skiers. He quit after one outing. Looking back he understood. He'd been a sea urchin caught in an undertow of privilege and luxury.

"Thank you," he says, as Luisa hands him the plane. "Do you girls want to see what I'm doing?" Leeann and Luisa both shake their heads no and look away. Fine. Have it your way he thinks, but the sting of their disinterest gives rise to one of his least favourite thoughts: one day soon his beautiful daughters will look at him and see an old man with a thickening neck who never graduated from university. He dreads the day his kids overtake his own level of education, knowing it will fill him with a bitter self-pity that'll haunt him for the rest of his life. Well, what can he do about it? Things weren't handed to *him* on a silver platter. He'd gone to a tough school, Eastern Collegiate, and he'd dazzled everyone at special auditorium events playing "Classical Gas" on a twelve-string with open tunings. And a number of girls had followed him around asking him to play James Taylor songs.

He grips the handle and the knob, bears down and begins planing the joist. Shavings curl up and fall away. He runs his hand along the seam where the joists abut and caresses the silky surface. "Perfect," he exclaims, overcome with an intense desire to go to the garage and snatch a cigarette from his secret stash. But there are too many eyes on him. And he doesn't have any left.

"Perfect, perfect," the little ones chant. Leo looks at his two youngest and asks himself, why do all kids today need braces? Apparently your kids are guaranteed social problems if they don't have straight teeth. First it was Leeann. Then Luisa. Now the little ones both need tracks, surprise surprise, because of malocclusions. All that fine Italian muscle and style he needs to flog to pay for it gives Leo a sinking feeling. These days, every time a customer drives another two hundred thousand dollar racing machine off the premises, and he heads into the boss's office for a glass of Dom, he has a dreadful feeling he's just witnessed his last sale. Amazing how some things get harder to do the better you become at doing them. Selling cars is like that. But not playing guitar. That's what he was going to tell his therapist last week, but she went and made reference to a husband — even though she doesn't wear a ring — and he'd been thrown off his game.

Leo tosses his plane into the wheelbarrow where it clanks against the metal sides. He picks up his drill and a hurricane anchor. Drives a screw into the beam.

He can still feel the electric pang of jealousy that had shot through his spine, causing him to ramble on about his eavestrough, Laura, the garage, the dog, Leeann's boyfriend, and how his mother-in-law and sister-in-law are coming over and Laura expects the deck to be finished because it was finished weeks ago but he had to pull it apart because it didn't slope properly. It's the rebuilding that is particularly difficult. It's taken nights of setting the boards at different angles and pouring water on them to see how well it rolls away from the house. I'm more of a thinker than a doer. And I'm a perfectionist and my wife doesn't understand. *Just average it, pick a number, how important can it be?* That was her input. It's always the same: you learn how to build a deck the hard way and once you're done you're an expert. But once you're done what does it matter because you'll never want to do it again. Ever.

The whole thing got him so worked up, before he knew it, Rachel was telling him their time was up and he never got to tell her the one thing he really wanted to say in the first place, which was that he recently made a huge discovery. He was on the Internet, tracing his genealogy, and he'd almost had a heart attack at what he'd unearthed. He, Leo Rosoff, was a three-times removed, blood relative, of Lenny, fucking, guitar-genius-Breau.

The whirl from the drill slows its tempo. Fucking fuck fuck.

He pulls the battery out of the drill, orders Leeann to put it in the charger. "It's next to where the paint cans are," he yells. "Luisa, get me my ratchet screwdriver. Now. Please."

He hears his two youngest screeching like banshees. He closes his eyes, wipes the sweat off his forehead. If he'd known about the Lenny Breau connection thirty years ago he would have taken music more seriously and God knows where he'd be. Instead, he's here.

The doorbell sounds. Fuck. Shaker barks madly. Leo opens his eyes, steals a look through the sliding back doors. The inside of his house appears dark but there's no mistaking who's coming through. His mother-in-law stands straight but shuffles duck-like with a cane — her weighty waddle a constant reminder that you pay a price for living, especially if you've spent most of your evenings anaesthetizing yourself with drink in order to enjoy an hour or two of euphoria followed by several hours of sleeplessness and self-loathing. She may have money but she's weak, Leo reminds himself. And there's his sister-in-law, trailing behind her. He digs through his tool belt, pulls out his watch. He knew it. They're two minutes early. He stuffs the watch back in amongst the brackets and braces and hangers and fasteners, rage building up in him like rainwater in a backed up storm sewer.

He grabs the screwdriver from Luisa. "Thank you. Luisa." And counts the joists. One two three four five six. Six to go.

"It was so tasty. So different," says a familiar voice. "My bowels are working overtime." No denying it, his mother-in-law's been overindulging.

He reaches in his tool belt for another screw, fits the bit into the cross-hatch, marvels at the magnetic pull between the two metal surfaces, male and female, and screws another anchor into a joist. Five more.

"I can hear my grand-dog," Alice calls out.

"Can I say hi to Grandma and Aunt Jodie?"

"Does it look like we're done here?" Leo shouts over Shaker's barking.

"Here comes the out-of-town guest," Alice sings out.

"We're coming through," Laura announces.

Leo continues twisting the screwdriver. Righty tighty his hands are aching, and his thin white T-shirt and faded Bermuda shorts are wet with sweat. Leeann looks up expressionless at the sliding doors. Luisa, next to her, untangles the string on a yo-yo, waves and makes a hey sound, then retracts the gesture. The two little ones continue to chase each other, crying out, "We're coming through. We're coming through." Shaker barks and yanks on his lead to get to the visitors.

"Leo?"

Leo keeps tightening a screw but the pressure of five sets of eyes on him is too much. "What?" he yells as if everyone were three houses away.

"We're here!" Laura warbles.

We're here! Leo repeats to himself. You're my wife. You live here. You're always here.

The screen door slides open slowly. Behind the soft hollowness Laura and Jodie appear on either side of their mother. Jesus Christ. If they try to walk across the joists I'm gonna kill them, Leo thinks. He turns to his two oldest who are staring at the two tiny beige plasters on each of his white spindly legs. "Leeann and Luisa, go check the deck boards. Make sure they're piled with the crowned edge upward." He reaches for an anchor. "Now. Please."

He hears Jodie hop down between the joists. "Okay Mom, looks like we're not playing with a full deck, but it's really just getting you out the door that's a problem," she says.

A discussion ensues about the possibility of using a stepladder or some milk crates, or maybe some boards to create a plank. Alice is worried she'll fall over.

Leo pretends to ignore them. He hears his mother-in-law laughing and gasping for air while her daughters tease her about putting Lyn's mini-trampoline below her, so she can just jump out the doorway.

"I've got an idea. I'll crouch here, like this. Laura, you stand behind Mom, put an arm underneath each of hers, like this. Then Mom, you step on my back, but not on my spine. A foot on each side. Then I'll count one, two, three, and lower you down like an elevator. Once I've got you as close to the ground as I can, you grab a hand on each of these joists, and step off my back."

Fucking fuck fuck. Why the hell couldn't they just stay inside until he's done? It's like he's fucking not even here.

"I should exercise more," Alice notes, as they complete a mock practice run.

"Okay, I'm ready for you Mom."

After much coaching and encouragement, Alice steps onto Jodie's back and steadied by Laura, is slowly lowered. With a squeal that's part delight, part fright, she leans over, grabs the joists, and stumbles off her daughter's back on to the ground.

"One small step for me. One giant step for my daughters," Alice calls out. Laura claps, Jodie whistles, Shaker barks excitedly, and the little ones change their chant to, "One small step. One small step."

Alice announces that she thinks she has a sliver.

"How bad is it? Should we get you back inside, Mom?" Jodie asks.

Fuck. "Lau-raaa," Leo screams. "Do you or do you not want a deck?"

Laura, Alice and Jodie all turn to him. "It's okay, Leo," Laura says.

"Now let's not bother him, he's working hard," Alice says. "Come on girls."

Each holding an arm, Laura and Jodie escort their mother to the end of the framed-in maze and help her step over the end rim and onto the grass.

Leo glares at Leeann. "You're not even checking them. Crowned edge upward. Please."

Luisa makes her way to her grandmother and gives her a hug. "Sweetheart, you're taller than me!" observes

Alice. Luisa shrugs, looks at her feet, lets the yo-yo roll off her palm, then turns her hand over and suspends it in the sleeping position before gently tapping it. The yo-yo coils back up.

"Well now," says Alice. "Look at you, little missy! When did you learn all this?" She wants to exhibit a grandmother's bursting love but the still-fresh humiliation of being lowered into the backyard like a cast stone bird bath, has injured her pride. Her tone is patronizing. Luisa says she waxes the string.

Jodie wanders over to the whirling dervishes who have stamped a well-worn spoor in the grass and are now chanting, "Guess what. Guess what."

Running into the middle of the circle, she calls out, "What? What?"

"We're taking swimming lessons," they scream in unison.

"You've become fishes!" Jodie yells as the fishes swim away and over to their grandmother, nearly toppling Alice before darting away from her too. They jump onto the joists and march to the back door with the symmetry of synchronized swimmers. Arms linked for balance, bums swaying with full haughtiness, they sashay away from their father who yells at full volume, "Lisa, Lyn, off the joists."

Jodie brushes the grass with her foot and looks at her mother who's smiling vacantly into the evening. Laura has given her a chair to sit in and headed back into the house to find some tweezers.

Two more to go. "Shaker, shut it," Leo cries.

"Can the dog be let loose?" Jodie asks as she kneels down to pet him. "Backyard's fenced in."

"As long as you run after him when he digs his way out."

"Just asking."

"Just saying."

From the corner of his eye, Leo watches Jodie wander over to Alice. No wifey. No kiddies. Easy for her to pretend to be superior. What is it they chant? We're here, we're queer, we're … who cares? he thinks, as he stretches his tongue out as far as it will go and licks the salty sweat off his weekend bristle.

One of the back legs of the chair Alice is sitting in is wobbly and the whole thing slants awkwardly to one side. Seated still as a garden statue and clutching her purse on her lap, Alice leans to the other side to compensate. Jodie lies down on the prickly grass beside her, hears the next-door neighbour whistling, the lid of a barbeque slamming shut.

"Mom is your sliver hurting?"

"Look. I managed with these old nails to poke it out."

"It feels okay?"

Alice nods yes.

"That was quite a reception wasn't it? Leo's in a good mood." Jodie rolls over to face her mother, hoping Alice will express frustration or disappointment or better yet some kind of festering animosity.

"Oh, they play this game all the time."

"Hockey's a game. This is more like a puck in the face."

Her mother looks at her and raises her index finger. Seemingly needing to point at something, she leans forward and taps Jodie's nose. "We don't do ourselves any good to be so harsh."

Irritated, Jodie rolls back on the grass. Although it's still early in the summer the cicadas are singing, their high voices circle the yard providing a single note of accompaniment to Shaker's incessant barking. She thinks about the ugly grab bars she installed last week in her bathroom, just for her mother's annual visit. "What do you think?" she had asked, as she put the final bead of silicone around the flanges.

"Leo told Laura I should have a toilet seat raiser too," Alice had said.

"What would Leo know about it?" Jodie had shot back.

Alice pointed a finger at a crack in the tile where Jodie had drilled a screw a little too tightly. "I love that guy," she'd said, before patting her heart and exiting the bathroom, limping more than usual.

The sweet and salty smells wallowing over from the Jones's barbeque are making Leo hungry. He touches his stomach with his left hand. Back and forth across the tiny cavern of his bellybutton he strokes the calluses on his fingertips that he keeps thick by soaking in rubbing alcohol twice a week. He looks over at Leeann and Luisa who are staring into space and bores one last screw before rising from between the joists to stretch his neck. Last one! He wipes his forehead with his T-shirt.

"Leeann, Luisa, stay there. Lisa, Lyn," he shouts, "come out here. Now. Please."

Leo unbuckles his tool belt and throws it in the air toward the barbeque. It crashes through a patch of asparagus ferns beside the wheelbarrow, creating a hole in the feathery softness. "Lau-raaa," he shouts, long and military-like.

Laura appears behind the screen door. Her weary eyes suggest she's getting ready to answer the needs of a demanding toddler.

"I've asked your two youngest to get out here and they're not listening. Could you be so kind as to round up their little behinds?"

"Leo!" Laura blurts, "stop it."

"Mom-meee," a voice wails from the house, as Leeann makes her way over to her grandmother to give her a hug.

"Coming," Laura calls out. Leo watches his wife slip back into the house. He admires her patience but he can't stand her inability to orchestrate others. She's never deliberate or loud enough. Her voice so light you can't ever criticize her performance. In fact, she doesn't perform. She has no ambitions that way. Her joy comes from watching others. Her children. And occasionally him.

"Okay," he cheers, once all his girls are gathered outside. "You know what's next. Place the boards into position. Don't line up all the shorter ones so they land on the same joists. Stagger the full length ones with the ones that need to be married up. Leeann! Which side do you put facing up?"

Leeann stares at her father as if he is defective. "Why don't you just tell me and I'll do it," she says.

He pounds his head with his fist. "When I ask a question I expect an answer. It's very simple. Put the boards with the crown edge up, but make sure there's no ugly knots or holes showing."

Leo announces that Leeann is to supervise then calls out, "Finally, I can go have a shower."

The girls soldier on. Leeann studiously inspects the lumber, and Luisa, Lisa and Lyn lay them into position until Lisa and Lyn begin swinging boards at each other, like gladiators in training.

"You two are total spazzes," Leeann moans. "Get lost." Lisa and Lyn chase each other to the back of the yard. A window on the second floor slides open and a threatening voice yells, "It better be done when I come back down." Leeann looks up and scoffs. Exasperated, she goes inside as the little ones chant, "It better be done. It better be done."

"Maybe I better help," Jodie suggests, as she stands up.

Alice waves a hand as if to say I'm stuck here so don't worry about me.

"Hey Luisa, let's get this done."

Luisa's unhappy about it but moves a few more boards around before also abandoning the project and heading inside. Leeann appears behind the screen. "Mom says you need these," she says, holding up a pair of tweezers.

"Oh that crisis has been solved," says Jodie, "but thanks." Leeann disappears. Jodie keeps at it until the deck — with unattached boards that shift slightly from side to side and need to be trimmed on one end but slope ever so perfectly from the ledger board — is assembled. "Hey," she announces to no one in particular, "we're all decked out."

From the back of the yard, Lisa and Lyn begin circling and chanting: "We're all decked out. We're all

decked out." Then they turn and throw themselves at
each other, chest butting in a full body high-five. Again
and again they pound their thin little fronts together until
a clank, so tiny it might have been imagined, is followed
by a silence, then a piercing wail rising higher and higher
in painful protest. Fat drops of blood drip from Lyn's
nostril. Lisa gives the back door a look of fright. Jodie
runs over to Lyn who spits most of a tiny front tooth into
her hand. At the sight of the sharp broken pearl she
screams louder. Jodie puts an arm around her and shep-
herds her toward the house.

"You'll be okay, sweetheart," says Alice, as they pass
by.

Lisa scurries over to Shaker, lies down and pats him.
"I didn't do it. I didn't do it," she insists.

Alice opens her purse and pulls out a mickey encased
in soft, sturdy rawhide. Its Royal Canadian Yacht Club
insignia breathes another era, one of dignity and legiti-
macy. She takes a quick gulp, realizes the bottle's empty.
"Alice, you silly old goat," she says as she buries the bottle back in her bag, then looks at Shaker who barks at
her.

"Lisa honey, do you think you could get your old
grandmother a drink?"

Lisa squints, shakes her head no.

"Well, hell's bells. I'll get my own then." Alice stands
up. Lisa watches her grandmother take a few jerky steps,
then runs and grabs her arm and together they make
their way to the deck. The boards clap as Lisa jumps on
them. She offers her grandmother both her hands. Gripping the tiny fingers, Alice manages to hoist herself onto
the deck. "Isn't this nice," Alice repeats over and over as

she shuffles forward. The roar of a plane overhead excites Shaker and he jumps in circles barking.

"Shut it," Leo's voice calls out from the bathroom window.

Alice looks up with a smile while she takes a step forward. She can't help herself. He's a kook but she loves her son-in-law so. He has a particular brand of enthusiasm that makes him excited about odd things, like the time he told her that houseflies hum right smack dab in the middle octave, the key of F, and the time he explained that his birth date, January 1, is exactly between the birth dates of two famous Capricorns: Jesus and Elvis. Alice is grateful that he accepts her with her slow ways and all. Years ago he'd told her she was welcome in his house anytime and she's never forgotten that. Alice knows Leo considers her family — he feels comfortable enough to yell in front of her. As you get older, family becomes more important and then it's the only thing you have. You wake up one day and realize you no longer have a driver's licence, your passport's expired, and you have absolutely no good reason to renew it. Then it hits you. You'll never again be able to tell yourself that the future holds better possibilities than the present. You are a dusty old bag of loose flesh on brittle bones and someday others will rummage through everything in your life — sharing, laughing, maybe crying, while throwing away dresses, underwear, shoes. Her foot, in its flat-heeled sandal, lands on a board that shifts ever so slightly but enough to send her over on her side — *oh God, here I go* — with a slow, single whump as Lisa darts out of the way.

"Oh dear," Alice chuckles to let all who may have borne witness know there's no reason to be concerned.

"I think I've fallen over."

"Can you stand up, Grandma?" Lisa asks softly. Alice rolls onto her knees. Startled and embarrassed from the shock of a sudden landing, she playfully taps Lisa's foot, then looks behind her and clownishly barks at Shaker. He barks back and as she and her granddaughter laugh, a noisy burst of gas shoots out Alice's rear. Lisa screams and dashes inside. Alice crawls forward and makes her way through the doorway calling out, "Grandma hurt her ankle!"

Inside the house, Leo has emerged fresh from his shower wearing butterscotch linen pants and a silk shirt the colour of oatmeal. Casual yet sophisticated with a European flair. Wrinkled with weary leisure they drape off his frame with an elegance that suggests a relaxed manner until you look into his eyes, which smoulder inward.

"Well well," he calls out, looking down from the second floor landing. Lyn is lying on the couch. Luisa's put a folded napkin on her head as a makeshift nurse's cap and lightly pressing a spoon into Lyn's mouth, is sharing her prognosis that the patient may require amputation.

"What have we here?" Leo asks eagerly.

Laura, fishing in her purse for her keys, says, "I have to take Lyn to the clinic. She's knocked part of her tooth out. I'm worried she's damaged the root."

"What happened?"

"She fell."

Leo suggests *he* should take her to the clinic. "No," Laura insists. "I'm going to take her. I've left the steaks on the counter. Leeann and Jodie are in the kitchen looking after the vegetables." Alice, climbing one stair at a time, announces her ankle is a little sore and perhaps they should call an ambulance big enough for the whole lot of them. She smiles, says she's only teasing. She'll be fine in an hour or so. She just needs to put her lower appendages up and have a little drink of something. Consensus is reached: Alice will be okay; Laura will take Lyn to the clinic.

As Laura calls out that she won't be too long, hopefully, Leo feels content with only the slightest tug of angst. Really what's the point of switching things up? Rachel has horribly fat calves that don't match the rest of her figure.

"Hello?"

He looks around. His mother-in-law is clinging to the banister for dear life.

He opens his arms wide. "Hey-hey," he says, like she's been waiting all her life for this. He reaches down, pulls Alice up to his chest. "If you keep carrying on like such a wild and crazy gal we're going to have to Taser you." Alice sinks into his arms, breathing in the lemony fresh masculine bulk. There's nothing like a man right after he's showered and patted himself with cologne. She loves her daughters, but God...her son-in-law!

"I'm so happy to be here." Alice looks up at Leo. "You do look good. Laura says you're seeing a counsellor. I hope it eases the pressure." She gives his hand a reassuring squeeze.

"It helps," he admits, amazed at how light the world feels right at this moment. The deck's more or less finished. Lyn will be okay. Fortunately it happened before the braces and he can probably do a deal with the orthodontist. He and Laura have a great house, two cars, four healthy, beautiful daughters. And Alice rewrote her will to specify that he would inherit the family's prized collection of vinyl. First pressings and rare recordings. There's even a signed copy of Eddie Condon's original *Bixieland* release. Leo had checked the going price for some of the records on eBay and was absolutely floored at what they could fetch, not that he would ever auction them off like some unsentimental pimp. He's already started to build special shelves for them in the upstairs hallway. He anticipates hours organizing his collection by decade and by artist. He can literally hardly wait! He rubs his mother-in-law's back and tells her to go sit with Luisa who's flaked on the couch staring at the TV. He'll get her a drink.

As Leo serves up two gin and tonics, Alice tells him she's proud of him.

He checks on Leeann and Jodie who are sitting at the kitchen table looking at something in a magazine. "Potatoes on?"

"Yeah yeah," says Leeann, without looking up.

Leo whistles "What a Wonderful World" — not an easy tune to pull off — and walks through his dining room. Laura polished the table this afternoon and put together an impressive arrangement of wild flowers. Reminds him of a Tom Thomson painting he saw last summer at the McMichael Gallery — an unusual one for Thomson. He steps outside and walks across the deck, pours a bit of water from the watering can and watches it trickle away from the house. Perfect! He takes a deep breath, mindful that he's having a moment of happiness, and finishes off his G&T. Temperature's dropped a bit and the air conditioner's off. He doesn't like to keep the house cooler than twenty-five degrees. The Jones's is working overtime though. He looks at his backyard, admires the flower beds around the periphery. Shaker, over by the barbeque, is quietly chewing at his paws. Leo decides to tease him and shouts out his name. After all, he isn't above a little fun. Luisa or Lisa might even be watching their dad through the living room window. Scratching his armpits and lurching like an ape, he leaps at the dog, thinking maybe sometimes he is a little rough. He needs to be a little softer and more tolerant. Shaker stares at him, expectantly. There's something in his mouth.

Leo freezes.

"Fucking fucking little bastard."

Leo charges. Picks up the little terrier by the neck.

"*Fuck.*"

A jumble of miniature gears, fasteners and washers lies on the grass, smeared with the mushy remains of a muffin Leo stuffed in his tool belt this morning. The leather strap is slimy with saliva, the mechanism totally destroyed.

He yanks the dog's collar off, throws it hard against the fence, opens the lid of the barbeque, shoves the animal inside, lets the lid slam shut. Muffled barks echo from under the lid, followed by whining noises accompanied by deep sniffs.

Leo looks down at the cracked crystal and the large roman numerals on the face, mangled forever. The only surviving possession of his Armenian grandfather. Destroyed.

He grabs his tool belt, throws it on the edge of the deck, picks up the crown and the dial plate, holds it close to his eyes and lets out a wail of anguish. He hears Shaker whimper.

He walks the length of his backyard, clamps his fingers, knocks his knuckles together and counts one, two, three, four, five, six ... His father worked as a roofer and never wore the watch. Somehow he always knew the time without needing to check. Got up at the same time every day of his life. Never called Leo by his name, just shouted "you." "You get up now." Leo looks at the ruined face. He was going to give it to Leeann when she graduates from high school next year. She's always admired the weight of it and the large elegant numbers. There's a noise, gentle steps on the deck. There's a loud empty clank, the barbeque starter.

"*No. No.*" His heart explodes.

He lunges toward her.

"*Lift the lid,*" he screams. Leeann returns his plea with a confused look.

He opens the lid and *oh my God please God* he grabs the dog by his head and his rear. Leeann starts walking backwards toward the house, her hand over her mouth. Leo quickly releases his hold on the dog, letting it rest on the cushiony grass. It lies still. He charges to the side of the house, grabs the garden hose and runs back tripping over a patio stone.

"Here boy. Here boy." The dog's eyes are open. Leo sprays the branded animal with the cold water and its tiny body heaves upward, wet and mangy. Is it air in the lungs or the pressure of the water? The eyes look at Leo with exhaustion and devotion. Leo drops the hose, falls to his knees on the wet grass and puts a hand on the singed and drenched coat. He leans in, whispers, "I love you." A sulfurous stench makes him cough and his nose runs as he kisses the dog's tiny, motionless head. He sits back. Looks at his house. Five motionless faces look down at him from the living room window.

Nothing moves. Seconds tick by.

In a desperate panic he picks up the hose and sprays it full blast at their faces. Behind the wall of rushing water they appear untouched, like marbled stonework glistening beneath a hardened polish.

CA-NA-DA
(One little two little three Canadians)

SALLY SNOW HAD had it with men but as for people en masse, she still liked them enough to desire their presence in her life. With Lyle set to fly the coop one of these days she was starting to consider how dull it was going to be living alone with the Discovery Channel. She decided it was time to do something and it hit her one day, unexpectedly, like a ton of books. She would join Mensa. Just for a lark! Why not? These days everybody is hooked on Sudokus and she can finish off a Suicide level faster than anyone she knows. And although she doesn't know a lot of people — so you have to consider how big both the fish and the pond are — she knows enough people to recognize that she is a member of that increasingly endangered species: people-who-actually-know-things. "What you are," her old friend Adele says, "is a factoid." Lyle is smart too, when he wants to be, so Sally offered him $1000 to take the home test with her. It would be fun and it might help Lyle realize he isn't living up to his potential. Deal was they would get up early Saturday to complete it. If he passed, Sally would give him another $2000. It was a bribe he couldn't refuse. He wanted the money to buy a gun.

Sally woke Saturday with excitement. She felt as if the numbered balls that bounce inside the hollow Plexiglas containers on the late night lottery draws were inside her, vaulting off the elastic cavities of her stomach. After the home test she would take the supervised test. Sally knows IQ measurements are biased and don't take into account emotional or creative intelligence, but no one's stupid enough to completely discount them. We all want to know where we sit on the bell curve. Although you better be prepared Sally, she warned herself, in that funny way she has of talking as if she exists as a separate person. It's easy to forget a name, or whether you paid last month's Visa bill, but it's really hard to forget a specific number — 108 (average), or 116 (above average), or 136 (genius) — that attaches itself to you. If you're Mensa material you're above 131.

These busy thoughts rummaged through Sally's brain as she lay in bed, listening for the crashing thump of the morning paper being hurled against the door. Larry from three houses down hollered at his poodles to stay on the sidewalk. Lord love a duck, must be close to eight. Sally, you've slept past your usual time.

She recalled words and ideas from the book she'd been reading last night — a surprisingly lucid text about genes, chromosomes, dominant and recessive traits — and thought about her first husband. According to Adele, who had run into him at a gas station north of the city, he had been diagnosed with Crohn's disease. As Sally stretched her legs, she imagined Wayne rising from the toilet, turning around to reach for the handle and seeing blood on his feces. For a second she felt the sudden panic that accompanies the discovery of losing a credit card. Does she still love him? Is it too late? People do marry, divorce, and marry each other again, although usually to no better resolution.

She remembered Wayne's dirty, calloused fingers and his scaly eyelids that were always swollen. How he over-ate fast and mindlessly like an unrestrained swine. How other than pizza, he never knew what he wanted to eat for dinner. How even though it had been the 70s and Sally was expected to make dinner and not need her husband's input, she yearned for something more. Someone who might actually come home one day with that fondue set she openly coveted. And help her use the goddamn thing. No, she doesn't love Wayne. Not one bit really. What she feels — she imagines — is compassion. Compassion for Wayne. For everyone with Crohn's disease. For the whole damn human race.

She flipped back the comforter, sat up and hopped onto the broadloom. Raising her arms, she stretched up toward the ceiling. Sally Snow is not so tiny you feel sorry for her — the crown of her head reaches almost four-feet-seven (four inches shorter than Mother Teresa) — but she is tiny enough that you might wonder what went wrong. Did a pituitary gland impairment cause a growth hormone deficiency? Was she denied emotional comfort and caloric nourishment in her formative years? Assumptions have always pervaded Sally's life with an air of misfortune, which explains why others rarely consider it cruel when she's denied easy access to mortal love, or can't reach the upper shelves at the grocery store.

She tiptoed across the hall. Listened outside Lyle's room before heading to the washroom. Listened again before heading downstairs. Oh, how he can sleep, long and still. He doesn't snore but he does occasionally moan and shout out sounds. Lord only knows what that's about. Sally knows better than to traipse in on him unannounced. Doesn't matter whether she's enquiring about his dead-end job or his dull-headed girlfriend or if he has underwear she can add to the white load, he can be terribly nasty. She accepts that like many young men he's convinced he needs to hide his life from his mother.

It had rained hard during the night and sunlight, radiating off the wet patio stones, brightly illuminated the kitchen. "An auspicious morning," Sally said aloud, looking at the dewy vapours rising from the yellow blossoms of the forsythia. The wisteria and azaleas were exhibiting new foliage. Sally, that high-bloom fertilizer with low nitrogen has really paid off.

She made her usual coffee blend: two-thirds Dark French, one-third Colombian decaf, and sat at the kitchen table holding the hot mug. Minutes later she was up to the front door to retrieve the paper. She would relax with it for half an hour before waking Lyle — he'll need a good hour before they can begin the test. On the way back to the kitchen she removed two envelopes from the safe in the dining-room hutch. One contained the tests; the other a stack of fifty twenty-dollar bills. From a drawer she took out her instamatic camera. She'll use the self-timer to take a picture of her and Lyle completing the test. Later she'll paste it in her scrapbook with their scores.

Sally is hell-bent on making sure Lyle doesn't waste his days waiting for life to script his next move. He's just completed a general bachelor's degree and Sally knows it's time for him to move on. There is no way on this earth she's going to let him live out his twenties working at that shooting range with those restless rednecks who can't put together a sentence. "Ly'l 'ome?" That's what his work colleagues grunt when they call. "Ly'l 'ome?" When exactly did we stop using words? Or decide that a sentence no longer needs to contain a complete thought, usually with at least one independent clause? If Lyle doesn't find a better job soon he's going to start to lose his verbs, or his hearing, and end up an unambitious aging security guard like Wayne.

After making her way through the front sections of the paper, Sally looked out at her backyard. The dew was disappearing and the long moody shadows had pulled back to form more agreeable patterns. Sally doesn't want to exhaust her brain but good grief, it's hard not to get worked up. Hundreds of bodies being dumped and burned in Haiti. Millions of chickens and turkeys being slaughtered in BC. If SARS and foot-and-mouth disease aren't enough, now we have the avian flu. And closer to home, police have confirmed what everyone already knew: the remains they found in a ravine belong to the little Asian girl who was abducted months ago. Sally closed the paper thinking perhaps it would be better if the whole human race were culled and left to burn on a hillside somewhere. The big nest is foul and we are beyond turning things around. If global warming doesn't destroy us some pandemic will. Who knows what's left. Seventy-five? One hundred years? The only hope we have demands something we're not capable of — cooperation, on a global level. That'll never happen, so we're doomed, but in the meantime international law is the emerging discipline and Sally knows that that's where Lyle's future is. But before knuckling down to law school he needs to expand his horizons. Europe, Asia, Australia. What a year he'll have! Sending home emails from Internet cafés which Sally will take to Mensa meetings to share with her friends.

If only she had sought out real adventure in her twenties when it's easy to leave your life behind for a little while. She could still hear her old self, young and stubborn, suggesting with know-it-all authority: "I'll go next year when I have more money." "Can't, I just started a new job." "I shouldn't, I've met someone, a man named Trevor."

Trevor lived for hockey. It was 1967 and the Leafs were making a convincing run at the Cup. Trevor loved how Keon consistently shut down Béliveau. "And fucking Punch Imlach," he would say. "Guy scatters three-thousand one-dollar bills on the dressing room floor during game six. Good way to remind the players what's on the line."

"Literally and figuratively," Sally would add, aware that Trevor probably didn't know what that meant.

There was nothing like it and there never would be again. It was the last season before the league expanded from the original six to twice that number. Trevor laughed, Sally did too, at how those old geezers beat the Canadiens four games to two! She scrapped plans with Adele to travel to Europe because she and Trevor, riding high on Stanley Cup euphoria, decided to spend two weeks at Expo 67 in Montreal — a once in a lifetime opportunity. They had their passports stamped at over fifty pavilions, spent a lot of time smoking and had sex every night in a dark, heavy room in an Auberge des Voyageurs with an exposed brick wall, thick red carpet and a rough, meringue-like stucco ceiling that was the colour of beach sand and looked like mountain tops.

Trevor would orgasm, then pull out slowly and ask, "Did you come?"

"Yes," she would whisper, rubbing Trevor on his back while keeping her eyes on the ceiling. While Trevor snored and his seminal fluid turned cold between her legs, Sally would lie awake imagining she was an Expo 67 hostess — fluent in three languages. She would slide — never bounce — into her white plastic chair at the information booth. Elegant and gracious, her long arm would unfold like a wing to reveal a white glove waving with kindness, inviting visitors to join her. Leaning forward in her fitted blue uniform and pillbox hat, Sally would elicit respect and admiration.

The toilet upstairs flushed. Sally jumped up, put a piece of multi-grain in the toaster, shook some Mini-Wheats into Lyle's favourite green Bakelite bowl and placed the milk and sugar serving set beside it. She poured herself an orange juice, turned the radio on low to her favourite classical station and ate her toast covered with the thinnest layer of honey. Scuffing and dragging noises filtered down from upstairs. Waiting for the familiar shuffle of Lyle's approach she wiped the table for errant crumbs, lined up the test booklets and put a sharpened pencil and an eraser on top of each.

"Hi honey," Sally said breezily as Lyle ambled into

the kitchen, his body hidden inside a huge T-shirt hung loose over red nylon running pants.

"Huuuhh."

"Did you sleep well?"

Lyle slumped in his usual chair and stared at the cereal in front of him. Then the test booklets. He had shaved and a faint smell of musk and nutmeg emanated from his rosy cheeks.

"The home test honey. I thought it would be good to start at ten-thirty." Lyle looked blankly at her, then back at the Mini-Wheats.

Sally took this opportunity to let Lyle know what was on her mind. If that couple hadn't tried to make money the easy way by renting out rooms to foreign students, their daughter would still be alive. We're all tired because our soil is infertile. Our meat and dairy products are carcinogenic because factory farm animals are full of synthetic hormones and slaughtered before their time. She'd be okay. So would he. But the next generation? Not so good. "As gloomy as all that sounds one has to look at the bright side of things." Bending forward, she added, "If I can just say one more thing, travelling is going to change you. You'll have experiences you'll treasure for the rest of your life."

Lyle dipped a finger in the milk container, pulled it out and flicked it, sending a light spray of milk toward his mother. A drop slam-dunked her orange juice. Another fouled right into one of her eyes. "Hate to break it to you Moms, but I want eggs."

Sally blinked hard but her eye stung with brazen pain. She was overcome with an urge to drop to the floor and howl endlessly. Lyle was so mean sometimes. Focusing her one good eye, Sally watched the drop of phlegmy milk dissolve and sink into the juice.

"Lyle, we don't have any eggs."

"And I don't want to travel."

He stood and swaggered toward the fridge. Ferreting through the shelves and compartments, he filled his large hands with cold cuts, cheese, butter and Nutella. Shoving the door closed with a large white foot, he returned to the table, a hunter with his gatherings. Grabbing the bread off the counter and a knife from the drawer, he sat down and proceeded to make himself a man-sized sandwich.

His legs, beneath the draping sheen of the synthetic material, bobbed up and down restlessly as he chewed, sending minuscule vibrations through the glass tabletop.

"No one regrets travelling," Sally stated, putting the lid back on the Nutella. She leaned back to examine her son. He was boyishly handsome with a mass of long wavy hair, so dense it sat on top of his head looking like it was waiting to slip off during extreme weather conditions such as a hailstorm or a hurricane. At twenty-two he was still filling in, soft hair darkening his chest and arms, although he seemed to be shaving his chest and legs these days. His eyes were gentle and intense, his upper body taut from lifting weights. Features skip generations, recessive and dominant traits fight a never-ending battle. Lyle is a whole compilation of dominant traits: brown eyes, unattached earlobes, and a tongue he rolls into a tube shape and sticks out when he wants to remind his mother that he's nothing like her. He bears no resemblance to his deceased father. Don was lean and bendable, with hair as thin as a baby's.

"You know I can't force you to travel. I would, however, appreciate it if you could explain to me why you exhibit dogged resistance to an opportunity that others in this world, including myself, would absolutely die for?"

"There more coffee?"

Sally poured Lyle a coffee, uncertain whether to ignore her son's bad attitude or demand he show some respect. Her feelings, when they weren't missing in action somewhere like socks or pens, easily clouded her judgment.

"Skim, not cream," Lyle insisted, wiping a crumb off his upper lip.

He took two sips, then examined his palms. In a rare act of openness he proceeded to share his thoughts. According to him, the whole world — every last fjord, alleyway and roundabout — was swarming with tourists with digital cameras, phones and laptops strapped to their undersized T-shirts and washed out camouflage shorts. "Nothing's authentic. Nothing hasn't already been stomped, leaned against, sat on, exploited or photographed to death. I got better things to spend my money on than pretending to be turned on by the Mona Lisa or other things I can see on my computer anytime I care to."

"Like what?"

Scratching his head, he answered: "Hills of Borneo. Landmines of Cambodia."

"I meant what better things do you have to spend money on?"

Lyle grabbed his chest with his hands. "I wanna get me a gun and go shoot people in shopping malls," he grunted.

Something needed tidying up. Sally's spine straightened. "That's not funny."

"There is somewhere I'd like to go," offered Lyle. "I'd like to drive down to Orlando and hang with Tinker Bell at Disneyland." Lyle smacked his hands on his thighs. "She's fairy hot!"

"Disneyland is in California. You could head down to Orlando. Then I suggest going around the Gulf through Alabama, across Mississippi, Louisiana, Texas, New Mexico, Arizona and into California."

"Tinker Bell hunting!" Lyle laughed, rubbing his pecs. "Finally, a reason to travel."

"You are so spoiled. You should be grateful for all you've been given in this life."

"I am. I'm grateful. Grateful I'm not German, or Australian. They're addicted to travel. I hear they're everywhere. Wandering materialists hoarding useless souvenirs. Taking pictures of statues and flower boxes and government buildings that they upload to the net with a narcissistic misconception that others want to view them. Mind you," Lyle paused emphatically, as if even he was taken aback with his edifications, "the Chinese are taking over. There are more Chinese tourists photographing the world than there are Chinese Canadians living in Canada, and look how many of those we have."

Lyle clasped his hands. "Moms! You know what's more spoiled than I am? Mother Earth. She's spoiled. Rotten. When you fly across the Atlantic you're putting as much carbon dioxide into the air as you do driving your car for a full year. So really, by not travelling, I'm protecting our future. I'm facing our bleak forecast for the pending and escalating destruction of soil, water and air, and have concluded that to minimize my carbon footprint, I'm better off staying put." Lyle picked up his cereal bowl and dumped his Mini-Wheats into the organics bin.

Sally closed her eyes. "Lyle. Just promise me you'll do something with your life."

Sitting back down, Lyle picked up a pencil and pressed the lead point hard into the square tip of his index finger. "Okey-dokey pokey."

Lyle drew a happy face on the front of his test. Thank God he isn't interested in the arts. It isn't in their genes. Best not to waste time like she had spending weekends painting faces of old men from *National Geographic*s. Her own mother had had a very misguided approach to early childhood education, telling young Sally that she could be anything she wanted to be, she just had to try harder.

Oh, precious time. Sally got up, grabbed the kitchen timer — a recumbent ceramic cow with the dial set into its side. (Fourteen years ago, Lyle, with Adele's help, had bought it for Mother's Day.) She positioned it between them, its blank stare gazing at Lyle, its round rump facing her.

"The first test is eight minutes. When I say so, open your booklet and start."

Lyle wiped pretend sweat off his forehead. "You got my thousand bucks?"

"Right here honey," Sally said, holding up the envelope.

Lyle nodded with approval. The phone rang.

"Don't get it," Sally shouted as Lyle stood up and answered it.

"Hello. Yup. Yah. Sure." Lyle handed his mother the receiver. "It's Adele."

Sally told Adele she'd have to call her back because she and Lyle were just about to start the Mensa home test. Adele said great, they'd both pass with flying colours, but she'd just heard something so funny and she had to tell her. Her friend Smith had heard this story about Margaret Atwood being at a dinner party and she was sitting next to a man who was a brain surgeon and he asked what she did and she said she was a novelist. *Oh really,* he said. *I'd like to write a novel some day.* Then she said, *Really ... well I'd like to perform brain surgery some day!*

"Hah! That's so funny," Sally said. "So clever ... so Atwood." There were a few oh's and yes's, and with a talk-to-you-later she put the receiver back in the cradle, sat down and turned to Lyle. "Your pencil sharp enough?"

Lyle tapped it on the table and saluted. "Adele written her book yet? *The In-no-cents,*" he enunciated with pleasure.

"She's getting there. Now let's focus honey." Sally stretched out her arms and breathed deeply. Carefully, she reviewed the sample questions with Lyle, then wound the timer. "Okay! Eight minutes for the first test. Ready? Now!"

As the minutes passed, Sally calmed down. She loved the questions that required finding patterns and similarities — the flower or the number that completes the series. The logical analogies: pear is to apple as potato is to ... banana, strawberry, peach, radish ... yes! Radish. (You have to get to the root of things!) The completion of passages using a choice of words for each blank was mildly challenging. Sally hoped she hadn't inflated her abilities. Lyle shrugged when she asked how he was finding it. "Smile!" she yelled as the camera snapped their faces between tests three and four.

After the fifth test Sally was fairly confident she was acing it. She decided they should take a minute to relax. "Come Lyle, stretch with me," she said, positioning both her palms toward the ceiling. Lyle grimaced and drummed his pencil on the table. Sally rotated her head left, right, then set the timer to twenty minutes. "Okay honey, you can do it. Let's go." And off they went. Until halfway through Sally noticed Lyle doodling on his booklet.

"Lyle honey, we're being timed."

He looked at his mother and dropped his pencil. Pointedly.

Except for the timer ticking there was silence.

Lyle reached over and grabbed his mother's booklet. "Let's see. You're doing well, Moms. Tell you what. Let's put the timer back a couple of minutes," he said, tossing the booklet in front of her. "And you can finish up."

"What about you?"

"I'm done. What's a pass by the way?"

"Oh for heaven's sake," Sally mustered. A small hiccup popped out. "I don't know but you better be near-perfect."

"Look Moms. Don't mean to spoil your fun but this isn't for me. However, I did earn my thousand ... and hey, you just saved yourself two big ones."

"I cannot endorse this behaviour."

"Why not?"

"I don't believe in quitting. In not doing what you said you would." Sally's face reddened and her mouth tightened. She slid the envelope that contained the money under her rear end.

"That," Lyle smirked, "is ridiculous. I said I'd do the test with you. I'm here aren't I? No one said I had to take it all serious like you."

A gnarly hiss escaped Sally's lower abdomen.

"Look," Lyle suggested, "give me the thousand and then take the other two and *you* go travel."

"With who?"

"I don't know. With yourself. With Adele."

Sally shook her head.

"Fine. Just relax okay? You can sit on your couch and read your *National Geographic*s." Lyle's voice was getting louder. "Whatever you want."

"I won't have you talking to me like that."

Lyle got up from the table and started laughing.

"What is it? Me? Am I funny to you?" Sally asked harshly.

Lyle gave his mother a hard look. She could hear his thoughts. He found her petty, irritating. And small — literally and figuratively. He rolled his tongue and stuck it out at her.

"Ahh," Sally screamed. "It's no use."

Lyle went to the fridge. In front of the cold white light of the open door he grabbed a carton of milk and downed three gulps. Returning to the table, he stood behind his mother, hooked his arms under her armpits and lifted her up.

"Still keeping 'em warm, eh?" He put her back down. "Let me know when them bills are about to hatch."

"That's enough." Sally socked a punch into her son's thigh.

"Hey," Lyle snapped, "lighten up will you?"

"You know, you *can* be nice. Other times, I swear something gets in that head of yours and your grey matter goes haywire."

Lyle put his hands to his head and swivelled it back and forth in jerky movements. "You're right!" he said. "It's full of haywire."

"Don't make me ashamed."

"Of *what*?"

The timer buzzed loud and rude. Startled, they both looked at it. Lyle stepped back and hoisted himself onto the granite countertop — his legs dangling and his wide shoulders looming over the room. His eyes hung open with a provoking insolence. Sally wanted to pound his bulkiness. Did he purposely want to disappoint her? His scrawny girlfriends, Grand Theft Auto, TSN? Was he really so dull? So incurious?

As a young boy all he ever wanted to do were chin-ups on the shower curtain rod. How many times had she pleaded with him: *It's not made for that. It could break. You'll be very sorry when you fall and crack your head open.*

"Tell me you're sorry," she pleaded, wondering why it had never occurred to her to buy him an actual chin-up bar.

"For what?" Lyle said, rubbing a callous on his middle finger.

"I'm sorry," Sally said.

A bit of silence held them together.

"What for?" Lyle asked.

"Is it too much to ask you to complete this test with me?"

"Why? I'm not good enough unless I pass your little

smarty test … is that it?"

Well matched, they glared at each other.

Lyle turned up the volume: "Look — you want me to travel?"

"Lyle, I want you to have a good life."

"You want me to travel?" Lyle yelled.

"I want you to do *something*. Teaching others how to shoot innocent animals is … it's intolerable."

"You want me to travel?" Lyle repeated.

"Yes," Sally admitted, loudly. "Just for a year. I would love that."

"Fine." Lyle leapt down from the shiny countertop. "I'll travel far away so you don't need to see my dumb face again."

"Lyle."

"I don't need membership in a club for social retards." Lyle paused. "You want it? Go ahead."

"Fine. But don't threaten me."

Lyle turned to leave.

"Please, please listen."

Lyle looked at his mother, his eyebrows raised defiantly.

"You never knew your father but he was a level-headed, graceful man. You've got that in you. But I want you to know you inherited something from me too. A little thing called intelligence. That's why I thought it might actually be fun for us to do this quiz together."

"Oh! Now it's a quiz." Lyle kicked Sally's stepstool, sending it skidding across the floor.

"Young man," Sally snapped as her son exited the room. "Come back here."

Heavy feet thumped down the hall and up the stairs.

Lyle's bedroom door slammed shut.

Sally climbed to the second floor and stood in the dark hallway outside her son's room. "Lyle," she yelled. "Can I talk to you please?"

The air was full of aftermath. Exasperation rankled her veins. She stood for a minute or two, until it was unbearable to be so still.

"Lyle, you don't know this but as an infant you cried all the time."

"I was so exhausted being on my own you can't imagine. I'd walk around with you in my arms and bump into things. You wouldn't stop crying, screaming. I used to wonder, what on earth was in your head? Was it life you hated, or me?"

Sally pressed an ear to the door. She could hear nothing. He must be listening.

"I tried walking with you, rocking you, swinging, singing. Everything I did made it worse. One night, at my wit's end — trying to get you to stop — I shook you. You started coughing. Your eyes went blank, you went stiff as a board, you stopped breathing. I panicked ... Lyle can you hear me?"

Her voice softened. "You started coughing and crying even harder." Sally gripped the door frame and continued, her voice unnaturally quiet. "I worried you were going to die."

"I rushed you to the hospital in the middle of the night. I risked intervention but I explained everything that had happened. I insisted on every single test possible. I stayed with you every minute, day and night."

Sally stepped back. Her eyes rested on the tarnished brass doorknob. "I just want you to know the truth. It has a name. Shaken Baby Syndrome."

"Also, you might be infertile ... Don's pituitary glands had an abnormality that affected his hormones. You were very hard to conceive."

"You can get tested," she added. "That's why I always tell you not to smoke or use drugs or wear tight underwear."

Lyle left the house an hour later with Sally running after him like a scorned lover waving the envelope of bills. She was anxious to see what Lyle would do next and shocked to realize that he was in fact old enough to leave home. And that he seemed uninterested in the $1000. Sally, she told herself, you did what you could. Just because you lost the battle doesn't mean you've lost the war. But oh my. All she wanted to know was where had he gone.

How startled she was when the door opened two hours later. He's back!

Proceeding as if his mother were not there, Lyle put a double deadbolt on the door to the basement. Sally counted two hours and twenty-two-and-a-half trips up and down the stairs as Lyle moved all his belongings to the wood-panelled basement rec room. Fitted with a small washroom and a bar fridge, Lyle wouldn't really need the rest of the house. But Sally had lost access to her washer and dryer.

Later that night, when Lyle was out somewhere doing something, Sally went into his room. It smelled thick with dust and traces of musk. He'd left something on the window ledge. A note with a three-pack of condoms placed on top. She read the note: *Don't talk to me.*

Don't call me at work. Don't write me any letters.

From that day forward Sally would hear him come and go. Every in and out through the doors to his subterranean hovel pained her. A couple of times she couldn't help herself and she called out his name but it echoed through the house like an unrequited noun, an incomplete thought, a lonely dependent clause. Lyle developed an uncanny ability to avoid his mother and other than the muffled sounds of his movements and being privy to the music he would play on his sound system, she was barred from his life. Sally, she told herself, just pray he hasn't bought a gun.

Two months later Sally pulled herself together and gave everything she had to the supervised test. Her IQ came back at 132 and the society offered her membership. She mailed in a cheque and called the director of her local chapter to enquire about the upcoming meeting. The director advised her to wait until the following month. Simple society procedure. Her cheque needed to be posted and cleared before she was officially a member.

Although the house contained few pictures and almost no mementos of Lyle's father, Sally and Lyle always acknowledged Don's birthday in some small way — just the two of them. As the anniversary approached Sally had a brilliant idea: Don had a favourite bracelet, a linked silver chain with onyx stones. She would have it enlarged and give it to Lyle. After all, this ridiculous estrangement was not going to continue forever.

On the day, Sally rose early and stood on guard near the back door. When her son emerged and slipped outside, Sally, tiny parcel in hand, ran after him — along the side of the house.

"Lyle, I know you don't want to talk to me, but please, I have something for you."

"Lyle, please." Out to the street and down a couple of houses to where Lyle's bike was parked.

"Please. I want you to have this. It was your father's."

It was as if she didn't exist. As if he couldn't even hear her. Lyle swung his leg over the leather seat of his bike and put the key in the ignition.

Infuriated at her son's mulish disregard not only for her, but his father too, she threw the tiny gift box at him. Lyle stared into his mother's eyes as a corner of the box crashed and bounced off his temple. He scowled, then kicked the box right across the street, put on his helmet, revved his bike and took off.

Too proud and too shaken to retrieve the box, Sally hurried back into the house. To her coffee machine and her morning newspaper and her classical music station. But she was restless and her mind kept wandering through memories — memories of Wayne, memories of Don — which played out like scenes from an old faded View-Master disk.

Wayne was big and bulky with a huge head and lots of shaggy hair that was often partially hidden under a baseball cap. Regardless of the weather he always wore cargo

shorts and T-shirts. As the lone photographer/reporter/
errand-runner for a downtown weekly newspaper, most
months he made a minimal salary; other months he re-
ceived coupons — to local restaurants and shops — that
were given to the publisher as bribery for free promotion.
Sally would often search out ads in the *Toronto Star* for
better paying jobs that matched his skills but he always
balked. She began to dislike his laid-back attitude and
realized that his agreeable mellow tolerance, which she'd
thought meant he was open to the world, didn't mean
that at all. He was stalled, closed, uninterested. The frustration grew more intense every time Wayne announced,
as Sally leafed through all their coupons, that he just
wanted to stay home. The marriage ended in 1975 when
divorce was no longer capable of arousing the pathos of
a tragedy but still tarnished most participants with a
dreary stigma of failure.

Just divorced and on a week's holiday from her job as a
data administrator, Sally took a trip to California. Everywhere she went she was aware of being alone. It was tir-
ing. In Venice Beach a bushy man named George, who
spent his days on a crate propped against a palm tree
reading human palms, told her she would have two
chances to get married. She didn't like the word chances.
She was not a determinist; she believed in free will. She
imagined she was invincible, like in that Helen Reddy
song, that she could roar in numbers too big to ignore.
She told George as much. George told her she wasn't a
spring flower anymore but that she had nothing to com-
plain about, she was going to live well into her nineties.

"But will I be happy?"

George tilted his crate back, let out a huge *ha*. Grinning, he displayed a sturdy row of nicotine-stained pearlies. "Learn to see your own reflection and you will be at peace."

George looked out at the mist coming off the aluminum-coloured Pacific waters. Turning back to Sally, he raised an eyebrow. "I am important and you are important. We're both people."

Sally was annoyed. This was not information she should pay for. She felt ugly. Everything felt ugly. George's fish-like eyes were too roaming for her liking and his big belly looked hard. He probably ate too much and had thyroid problems.

"Language makes thought possible. Thoughts make humanness possible."

Sally reached for her crocheted handbag. "You haven't answered my question."

"Discover the seeds of your destruction and you'll unlock many doors."

Handing him two one-dollar bills, she asked, "Do you know the seeds that are *your* destruction?"

"I keep my eyes open and I feed my heart."

"Well, I'd suggest you have your thyroid checked." Sally stood. "Oh fudge." She urgently needed to pee.

The public washroom was hotter than a sauna and smelled of urine and salty chips. A single light bulb hanging by a cord was burnt out. The latch on the stall door didn't lineup with the keeper. Sweat poured off her brow as she pulled the tab on her fly, pushed down her cut-off shorts, squatted (Sally never touches a public toilet), and released.

Of course, there was no toilet paper and the door kept bumping into her head. In the dim light she picked up her handbag. Rummaging for a tissue she noticed her bag was damp. Hunched over, her eyes adjusting to the dark, she twisted around. Two cigarette burns, the colour of George's teeth, were melted into the side of the toilet's plastic cover. Yellow liquid pooled on top, dripped slowly off one side. She gasped. Sally, you didn't open the lid.

This trip. Being alone. It was turning out to be so hard.

A few months later, things began to look up. Adele set her up on a blind date with a man she knew from the racquetball club. Don was old, he was forty-nine, but comfortably established as a jeweller. And owned his own house. "In other words," Adele had cooed, "he's a catch." Steady in manner, he was tall and very proper and had never married. The package was appealing. She could use a travel mate and she wanted to have a child.

Don had a tiny shop near the bottom of Church Street. He specialized in diamonds and promised Sally that they would travel to South Africa to visit his suppliers. Things weren't what they used to be a few years back when gold hit eight-seventy-five, but business was good and Don encouraged Sally to quit her job and assist him in the store part-time. "You're lucky," Adele told her. "Margaret Atwood says that you can only juggle two things: writing and a job, or a job and a kid. But not writing, a job and a kid. Once I get pregnant, I'm going to have to put my book away for awhile." She and Phil were planning to have a child and were working hard to save enough for a down payment. With mortgage rates continuing to slide down from an outrageous nineteen percent, they were itching to get into the market. "Oh, but I have a title for my book!" Adele blurted. "It's going to be called *The Innocents*."

"What's it about?" Sally asked.

"My life, this generation, our dreams, that sort of thing."

Newly married and second time lucky, Sally loved the way she and Don weathered storms and battles, as comrades united by what is right. They never paid full price if an experience was tainted with bad service, inferior quality, a missing button or a small stain. When their roof sprung a leak and Don discovered the company that had installed it had disappeared off the face of the earth, he wasn't discouraged. "Someone's responsible," he announced. Sure enough, it took six months of wrangling but the manufacturer was eventually identified and took responsibility for the cost of repairs.

One Saturday afternoon Don announced he was returning all the living room furniture to the department store where he bought it two years earlier. "You can't do that," Sally said.

"That's why people buy things at department stores," he said a month later when the new furniture arrived.

When Mrs. Muir came in to have the settings on her engagement ring checked and Sally found him replacing a pair of smaller diamonds with first-rate cubic zirconia, she told her husband that he was a thief. It led to a fight and then more fights about money and about who was the proprietor of what. Their sex life — normally sporadic because Don's pituitary gland was an under-producer — became more intense and frequent.

Suspecting she might be pregnant, Sally was sitting on the edge of the bed one morning writing out a list of books she was going to read to her baby. Don — assuming Sally would be interested — called out while towelling down, "Heavy day today, I need to start preparing the quarter's return."

Sally, you are married to a small-time criminal. She picked up a box of tissues decorated with yellow daisies and hurled it at her husband. Silently it sailed toward him as he walked across the bedroom, his skin still pink from the hot shower. A sharp corner pierced and ricocheted off the bridge of his nose.

Ethical accusations are one thing. So is physical assault with a box of tissues, so that evening Sally went to the butcher to buy Don his favourite cut: Black Angus rib-eye. I wish he would just die, she thought, as she examined the red, fibrous cuts, sinewy slabs and muscular sausages. To compensate for this horrible thought, when she returned home she tried to sound as excited as possible, calling out, "I have a surprise!"

But Don was splayed out in the living room, his irregular heart having twitched for the last time ten minutes earlier; his brain having fired its last instruction eighty seconds after that.

A week later, after the night of Don's interment, Sally ran into Wayne in a convenience store. The peaceful restlessness that accompanies a final goodbye prompted Sally to invite herself over to Wayne's apartment.

"How's my little girl?" Wayne asked the following morning as he grabbed himself a beer while inhaling deeply on a joint. Returning to the bed he ran a rough hand down Sally's naked back. His weight, his smell, seemed beastly. Sally looked at the mess of clothes, cameras and comic books: *Lone Ranger, Tomahawk, The Rifleman.* It was high noon and time to get out of Dodge. Politely, she fled.

That was the last time she'd seen Wayne. Lyle was born 36 weeks later.

As Sally sat in her kitchen, regaining her composure, the look on Lyle's face and the sight of him accelerating down the street on that death machine still startled her. She felt that old familiar pang of fear. What if one day Lyle met Wayne. Over my dead body, she thought, knowing that that was in fact a remote possibility.

She looked at her watch. Almost eleven. It was Don's birthday. Time to get a handle on things. She hastened to the front door and stepped outside hoping to retrieve his bracelet.

Months later Sally sat at her desk in the living room, which she'd furnished with a sleek laptop and wireless connection. She was attempting to set up an account with an online brokerage firm. The personal verification questionnaire required she declare her favourite author, pet, food and travel destination. She was torturing herself with the realization that unlike Adele, who had Atwood, Skippy, guacamole and Puerto Vallarta — she, Sally Snow, couldn't decide between Clancy and Grafton, had never owned a pet, had no passion for food and had definitely not travelled enough.

The phone rang. It was Adele. She was through the roof and over the moon. Her son Taffy was making a name for himself. His clothing line — THREADCARE — was getting noticed by the very group he had been trying to attract: eighteen-to-thirty-year-old hipster club kids and nouveau careerists. Demand was surpassing supply.

Adele explained that each THREADCARE item was imprinted with a seven-digit code on the inside of the garment. Purchasers log-on to the company's website using the code and register with a service called "You Help the World."

"You help the world?" questioned Sally.

"No, *you*. *I'm* too busy! Anyway, you can pick your preference: climate change, AIDS — those are the big ones."

"I'm not getting it," said Sally.

"Taffy's turning himself into a conduit for benevolence. Apparently it's the new way. You combine making money with enabling acts of social responsibility."

"Really!" Sally understood the concept enough to know that however sanctimonious it sounded, she would kill to have it be Lyle's. Cradling the receiver on her shoulder, she rolled up one leg of her jeans and started scratching. Something had bitten her in bed last night.

"So how does it work?"

"Well, after you buy a T-shirt or pants and register using the code, within seventy-two hours you receive a call from a social activism specialist."

"A what?"

"A twenty-year-old. You know, probably putting in time after Katimavik and before the ESL stint in South

Korea. He or she will talk with you — for up to nine minutes — recommend how you can participate on issues of global concern. The whole thing's pretty pretentious but hopefully he's doing more good than harm."

Sally was scratching vigorously. Her nails were not providing relief. "Ahh," she moaned. "And this is working?"

"I'm not sure he's changing the world, but he just bought himself an eighty-thousand-dollar sports car."

"Is this where I'm supposed to say, *You must be very proud?*"

Adele laughed. "Hey, is Lyle talking to you yet?"

"No," said Sally. It had been seven months since he'd moved to the basement. "I taped a birthday card on his door a couple of weeks ago. I put a cheque in it. The envelope has disappeared, he must have pulled it off, but the cheque's still not cashed."

Neither of them said anything.

"You know I've been thinking," Sally said. "I've raised a son. I worked for years at Birks. But I haven't done much else. So I've decided to do something really incredible. A couple I know from Mensa are sponsoring a twenty-year-old girl from Haiti. They're an elderly couple in their eighties, sprightly and generous. He's a retired professor and she's a marathon runner, both extroverts. We get along like nobody's business. Anyway, they live in a small condo and don't have room for her, so I'll be billeting her."

Adele was silent. "You serious?"

"There's more. She has a two-and-a-half-year-old son. He'll be staying with me too."

"Oh my God Snow," Adele screamed high and loud. "Can I write about this? I'll put it in *The Innocents!*"

Sally and Adele decided to meet for dinner the following week. Online, Sally searched out a Haitian restaurant but when they arrived at the address they found it had changed owners. It was now a Vietnamese restaurant. "I should have called first," Sally remarked, "these places don't last." Adele suggested a Congolese restaurant that was nearby.

Inside it was cozy with fewer than ten tables. Fragrant steam poured out from the kitchen and pictures of farmers in fields and women carrying bananas on their heads hung on the walls. Of the dozen or so customers, Adele and Sally were the only Caucasians. "Authentic," whispered Sally.

"Food must be good," said Adele, whose face was open in eagerness.

When they couldn't figure out what they wanted, Sandi, their waiter, suggested the peppered fish in banana leaves and the goat stew. Sally thought his eyes were the most beautiful brown imaginable. His face, in profile, looked like a figure from an Egyptian painting. They agreed to follow his recommendation. "Very very good," he said. "I will bring you some bread too."

"Can we have a bottle of house white please," Adele said. Sandi bowed. "This is so amazing," she said as Sandi briskly walked away.

Sally stared at a picture of an exotic okapi that was underneath the glass table top.

"Know what this is?" asked Sally.

"An okapi," said Adele.

"Right! How did you know?"

"From the *What am I?* books. I used to read them every night to Taffy. They're fantastic. I'll get a couple for your house guests as a welcome gift — they'll be perfect for both of them to learn English. Books never hurt."

"That's for sure."

"Margaret Atwood says the only thing all writers have in common is that they were readers as small children. Anyway ... enough about Margaret, tell me about Ruth and Joseph. Those are their names, right?"

"I hope I know what I'm doing," Sally admitted.

She began her story about Harold and Mildred Norman, the couple she had met through Mensa. How they'd worked for years as United Nations Peacekeepers and how Ruth had worked for them briefly as a housemaid. They had been trying for almost two years to bring her and her son to Canada. They had invested an enormous amount of money and effort but perseverance was in their blood. "They are wonderful old-stock liberals. God bless them, they joined Mensa in hopes of staving off dementia and believe you me, it's working! Good minds on those two."

"You have to understand," Sally continued, "this is an amazing opportunity for this young girl and her son. Haiti is the poorest country in the western hemisphere. Imagine a land mass half the size of Nova Scotia, with a population nearing nine million despite AIDS contributing to a high infant mortality rate. That's Haiti."

After several toasts and questions ranging from what does she look like (pretty but an old soul) to why does she want to leave (it's a volatile country full of upheaval with little opportunity compared to Canada — gosh just look at our Governor General), Adele declared it was all absolutely wonderful.

As the arrival day approached, Sally figured enough was enough, it really was time to have a conversation with Lyle. One night she stayed up late and when Lyle came in around midnight, she called his name. Either by divine intervention or because he momentarily forgot his resolve, Lyle stopped in his tracks. "What's up?"

Sally explained about Ruth and Joseph, that they'd be living in the house for a year or so, and that she was sure Lyle would like them both.

Lyle looked puzzled. "Have you met them?" he asked politely.

"No," said Sally, "but I've seen lots of pictures and I know a great deal about them from their sponsors who I know through a social and cultural group I'm involved with."

"Anything else you wanna tell me?" asked Lyle.

"Just that I hope we get to see more of you," said Sally. Lyle rapped the door frame with his knuckles and ducked down to the basement.

A lot can happen in seven months. Lyle seemed a little more serious than Sally remembered. And he'd grown a funny looking tuft of hair on his chin that seemed out of place. It was fuzzy like a steel wool soap pad and shaped like a woman's pubic hair. He frightened her a little but the moment he disappeared she longed for his presence.

The day before the scheduled arrival, Sally did a final check through the house. It was the week before Christmas and with Adele's assistance the house had been decked out in full yuletide regalia: door wreaths, stockings, a seven-foot tree with coloured lights, Santa candles scattered about and Sally's grandparents' wooden nativity set had claimed its usual perch on the mantle. The reds and golds of the old gilt paint still held on. Baby Jesus took centre stage and two sombre wise men (one had been missing for decades) knelt with the parents, watched by four sheep and a cow.

Harold had put covers on the outlets and safety latches on the lower kitchen cupboards. There was ample food in the kitchen, which Milly had bought, including rich rice, plantains, avocados and bananas. Milly had even written out a list of basic Creole words for Sally to learn. A highchair for Joe was next to the table. Lyle's old bedroom was set up with a single bed for Ruth and a crib for Joseph. There were empty drawers, hangers in the closet, towels laid out, a small desk with a chair, a reading lamp and an English dictionary. "Lord," she exclaimed to Adele, "I've been going like a bat outta hell. But I'm so excited. It couldn't be more perfect could it? A week before Christmas!"

Harold and Milly wanted to pick up Ruth at the airport. When Sally suggested Harold shouldn't be driving at night, his hale stubbornness put the brakes on that idea. "This old coot's still got plenty of mileage," Harold said emphatically. Sally asked if he was referring to himself or his Honda Accord. Harold laughed so hard his big wing-like ears turned red.

The night was cold but dry. With the paperwork in perfect order, Canada's two newest residents and their sponsors cleared customs and made their way to the Snow residence where Adele, with a camera around her neck and a notebook in her back pocket, had just finished hanging a banner across the kitchen that said:

Welcome to your new life. We love you Ruth and Joe.

"*Bonswa, bonswa,*" Sally screamed as they entered the house.

The first couple of days were absolutely hectic. Sure enough, Ruth didn't speak very much English, but she smiled a lot and was gentle and obedient. Sally orchestrated how they spent every hour and she could feel herself blooming with her newfound authority. Everything was important and had to be named. Just making a *cof-fee* in the *cof-fee pot* was exciting. Pantomiming the difference between *off, stay,* and *a-way,* on the alarm system was as much fun as playing charades. Sally surprised herself with her patience, assuring herself that naming everything and talking *slow-ly* to *e-nun-ci-ate ev-ery syll-a-ble* would pay big dividends in helping Ruth integrate to her new country. When baby Joe — as everyone had taken to calling him — cried, Sally would put her hands over her ears, peer into his face and whisper, *qui-et.* Life was imbued with vibrant significance. Rinsing out the sink with the swivel spout and vegetable spray on the kitchen faucet would send Ruth into peals of laugher. Discussing that there was shortbread, but no — there was no such thing as longbread, made everyone light up. And baby Joe was a pure delight. He loved to dance and scream "*manmi, manmi,*" and clap his hands. On the third day, Harold came by to take Ruth and Joe out for an afternoon. "Sally, you need a break," he announced. When he brought them home he had nothing but praise. "I don't know what you've done, but Ruth couldn't stop telling me how happy she is to be here."

That night, Adele came over, and she and Sally sat up drinking wine and debriefing about the past few days.

"Where's Ruth?" Adele wanted to know. Sally ran upstairs and urged her to join them. Shyly, Ruth came downstairs and accepted some wine. She asked how Adele and Sally knew each other. Sally explained, as simply as she could, about the regional spelling bee finals in Grade Seven. How she was eliminated on guacamole, and Adele, flush with confidence that she could win, but her body so full of fright, turned her back to the audience. There was some *con-fu-sion*; it was hard to hear her. According to the stage monitor, she spelled it right — b o h e m i a·n — but still to this day, only Adele knows for sure if she truly deserved to win.

"Sally's very *com-pet-i-tive*," explained Adele.

"Can you spell competitive?" Sally asked Ruth, but Ruth just shook her head and laughed, so Sally let it drop.

In the final days before Christmas, Sally took Ruth shopping. In the mall, she walked through the busy corridors with Ruth beside her, pushing Joseph in his stroller. They bought a tablecloth, candles, presents for Harold and Milly, Adele and Lyle. "Psssst," Sally said to Ruth, inside the toy store, holding up a set of Baby Einstein DVDs. "These are terrific. I think Santa needs to get a couple for baby Joe!"

Ruth was agreeable, offering smiles, saying "*désolé, désolé*" when she didn't have the right words. Their shopping excursions were full of purpose and fun and they never seemed to come home with less than a dozen bags. Sally worked hard to widen Ruth's experience by teaching her that Old Navy was the *least* expensive, the Gap *mid*-range, and Banana Republic the more *ex-clu-sive*. At one point they ended up in a store that was so dark and confusing, Sally lost her shopping companions. After a minute of absolute panic she discovered them at the back of the store where a screen was showing a live web-cam feed from a beach in California.

Back out in the light of the atrium, Sally's temper didn't even flare as she explained to Ruth, who was looking slightly drawn in the mouth, that California was approximately 3,500 kilometres away. By comparison, Haiti is less than 3,000. They bought a little Canadian flag from a street vendor. The bright colour seemed to perk Ruth up and she insisted on attaching it to the front grate of Sally's old Volvo.

"I'm happy," Ruth said, as if it were an observation.

"I am too," Sally exclaimed. And she was. She loved having someone listen to her. She loved having so much to share and teach and give. Watching other shoppers scurry in and out of stores, mindlessly clutching their bags and tearing off in search of gifts that the recipients could easily purchase for themselves, Sally experienced a rare sense of superiority. She, Sally Snow, was helping the world. In one small way.

They stopped to treat themselves to two large, non-fat eggnog lattes with a shot of caramel. The indulgence was well beyond Sally's routine but she pretended it was normal. Sitting on couches inside the coffee shop, with baby Joe in his stroller sleeping, Sally noticed a middle-aged man in a suit, smiling at Ruth, and it occurred to Sally that a beauty like Ruth was easy prey. Buoyed by

knowing her companion provided her with a certain ca-
chet, Sally began to explain a little about life in Canada.
She warned Ruth about the easy way of relations here.
How hard it can be to find someone with whom you can
be together through life. That in this part of the world
we no longer think of marriage as being forever. That
men expect women to protect themselves against diseases
and pregnancy. Sally was aware of other customers
watching them. She kept her eyes focused on Ruth's magnificent face with her large humid eyes and the darkest
of deep red lips. Looking at Ruth, everything felt astonishing, like at the beginning of a love affair.

Ruth asked about her son in the basement.

"Oh Lyle," Sally said. "He wants to be *in-de-pen-
dent*," she explained, "so he keeps to himself."

"His father?" Ruth asked.

Sally, feeling particularly interesting, almost fascinat-
ing really, told Ruth about how Don died, very unexpectedly, before Lyle was even born. Ruth asked if Lyle
looked like his father.

"No." Sally daintily took the wooden stir stick and
swirled the milk foam in the bottom of her cup. She
could feel how intensely Ruth was listening to her, how
much the moment itself called for some kind of intimacy.
A disclosure that could seal their connection. "To be perfectly honest … I was very fragile after I lost Don. In a
moment of lapsed judgment I had a very small indiscretion with my first husband. Sometimes I look at Lyle and
he looks more like him, than he does Don. Oh, it's probably just my mind playing games, or my guilt projecting
itself." Sally touched Ruth's hand. "You know what I
mean, don't you?"

The next morning, Sally woke with the worst kind of hangover; the kind you get from too much talking and not enough drinking. Over and over, word by word, she replayed her conversation with Ruth. *Fragile, lapsed judgment, indiscretion* — no way, no way Sally told herself. Ruth couldn't possibly have grasped what Sally was confiding.

When she entered the kitchen, Ruth, dear sweet girl, was at the table, a baby cloth over her shoulder, burping baby Joe. The room smelled of baby powder and the sweet dustiness of Arrowroot cookies.

Sally climbed atop her stool and opened the freezer door.

"Good morning, Sally," Ruth said, as she patted the back of her son's head.

"And good morning to you," Sally replied, reaching for the Dark French and Colombian decaf. Quietly, Sally made coffee, chose a yogurt from the fridge and sat down to concentrate on what was ahead: baking, cleaning the bathrooms, reading the newspaper with Ruth.

Sally watched Ruth's hand gliding back and forth across baby Joe's back. She's a good girl, thought Sally, but what a long road she has ahead of her. She needs to improve her English and find a way to make a living and she needs to stop breast-feeding, Sally thought, scooping out the last of the yogurt from the single-serving container.

"You know what I think?" Sally said. "I think you could be a very good personal caregiver, or maybe even a nurse. But first, we need to get Joe onto *for-mu-la*."

"He's two-and-a-half," Sally said to Adele, later in the day. "She has to stop or Joe's going to be developmentally impaired."

Adele asked if she'd discussed it with Milly or Harold. "No," Sally shook her head. "I know them. They'll attribute it to cultural differences and tell me not to worry — that it will take care of itself."

On Christmas Eve, as Ruth sat on the couch with baby Joe for his before-sleep feeding, Sally sat next to them and explained that in Canada, most mothers usually stop within the first year, and all mothers by two. Life is busy here. "We can't afford that kind of *in-con-ven-ience*," Sally said. "Next year you'll be enrolling in a number of skills training courses and English lessons, so we need to wean Joe off breast milk." Ruth apologized but she was smiling so contentedly, Sally worried she wasn't convinced, so she grabbed her own breast and urged, "no more sucking." Ruth stroked Joe's head and nodded yes, and was about to try to conjugate the verb *try*, when low and behold, who walked into the living room but Lyle, carrying a present which he put under the tree.

"Hi Mom," he said with a wave before approaching Ruth and extending his hand. "Hi. You must be Ruth. I'm Lyle."

As Ruth offered her own hand, a large wet nipple popped out of Joe's mouth. Sally couldn't take her eyes off it. Ruth's breast was enormous, dark, magnificent, with a trickle of warm milk leaking out a long, swollen nipple. For a moment Sally thought she was in a *National Geographic* photograph, until she realized it was Lyle, her own son, kneeling down and offering baby Joe his index finger. Joe grabbed it with a smile. "Hey big fella," Lyle said.

It's Christmas Eve. Sally is overwhelmed to be here with Lyle, Ruth and baby Joe, but Ruth's large breast is tipping the scales. There is something rough and loutish about it. It is too big and intrusive.

"Ruth, cover yourself up," Sally said in a commanding tone, before getting up to see what needed to be done in the kitchen.

Christmas was a delight. Exhausting but full of love. Adele came by in the evening, with her camera and notebook. While helping Sally load the dishwasher, she said, "Everyone has one good story in them. Margaret Atwood says a writer has several. Thank you Sally Snow, for giving me this story."

Later in the night, Sally listened as Adele explained to Ruth what *fem-i-ni-sm* means. That it includes equality of rights: legal, workplace, abortion.

"Have you ever heard of Angela Davis?" Adele asked. Ruth shook her head no.

"Alice Walker?" Again, Ruth shook her head.

"Oh Snow," Adele said. "What an innocent."

Snow came the next day, and Lyle, who seemed to have turned a corner with his mother, offered to shovel the walkway. Afterward, he and Ruth went outside to catch snowflakes on their tongues. As the days followed and everyone got used to one another, Sally became increasingly overwhelmed with the amount of milk and bread and juice they were consuming, the loads of laundry that needed to be dropped off at the laundromat (thank God Lyle had agreed to do a few loads for her in the laundry room) and the unbelievable way things ended up in the wrong place. On New Year's Day she told Adele she could not ever remember being so tired; it was more exhausting than when Lyle was a toddler. The house was always full of smells and there was so much to do. "Ruth's good but she just doesn't understand the standards here. A 24/7 effort is required. Progress is being made but I think I've had the stuffing knocked out of me."

"You are like baking soda," Adele said, pulling out her notebook.

"What?" said Sally.

"You suck it all up and absorb the stinky odours while doing magic with the baking and then you scour around and clean up dirt and stains. You must be exhausted."

Ten days after Christmas the sky was a dark mauve colour and snow started falling again blanketing the air with a quiet hum. Sally went out to pick up more groceries. On the way back home it had warmed up and the streets were starting to get soft and sloppy. She couldn't believe it had only been two weeks since Ruth and Joseph's arrival. So much had happened. Tonight, she'd start to take the decorations off the tree and maybe make a little hot chocolate for everyone. It occurred to her that Ruth and Joe had probably never tasted hot chocolate with marshmallows! Sally made a detour to a convenience store to pick up a bag of fluffy marshmallows.

As she stepped in the back door she felt the warmth of being home. Taking off her coat and boots she noted that the furnace was set too high for this milder weather. As she turned down the dial she became aware of the music downstairs. Joe was sitting in his highchair in the kitchen, banging his bottle of milk. Bits of tea biscuits covered the tray, his mouth and his hands. He put his head to the side, gave Sally a smile and said, "Ally."

"Hello," she said softly, stepping over to peer up into his face. Baby Joe easily hit Sally's head with his bottle, banging it against her temple. He squealed.

"Ouch," Sally said, moving away. "That thing's a weapon." Her hand on her temple, she padded over to the downstairs door. Standing in front of it she heard Ruth and Lyle's voices over the music. She turned slowly, hoping the floor wouldn't announce her presence. Then it occurred to her that this was her house. That Ruth was her guest, that Lyle was her son, that she was not a burglar and she did not need to be tiptoeing around. And guess what? The door wasn't locked.

"Hidy ho!" she called out as she stepped down the stairs, one after the other. Two heads snapped in her direction fast, like mousetraps. Lyle, in his boxers, was standing behind a completely naked Ruth. His outstretched arms enveloped her and they were both holding a large rifle with the barrel aimed at a poster of a polar bear tacked to the wall. Strange enough — to revisit a room one knows every square broadloomed inch of after almost a year, but this wildlife adventure, this flesh and blood travesty, this black and white naked statue was enough to make her not only stop fast in her tracks, but back up a step. A moment later she let out a universal cry for help: the primal scream. Lyle, holding on to Ruth, stared at his mother while he lowered the gun. Ruth averted her eyes. "I will have absolutely none of this," yelled Sally as she turned back up the stairs, slamming the door behind her.

Upstairs she sat in the living room, stewing. Baby Joe started to cry. It was that time between day and night when the lights on the tree were programmed to come on. They lit up and started blinking at her. She hated them. As far as she was concerned she never wanted to see Christmas lights again. Or her son. Or Ruth. How obvious. How banal. She stood and walked to the tree, pulled out the plug, headed to the front foyer where she grabbed the box that the decorations lived in the other eleven months of the year. She pulled the balls, bows and tiny sleighs off the tree and started chucking them into the box. It occurred to her how pathetic it all was. Just what, pray tell, was her son thinking? Getting his jollies with a poor refugee girl. He must be Wayne's son. He probably doesn't think he can get her pregnant. But Ruth, what does she know exactly? And what does she want? A free ride? How dare she stand naked like that with her child sitting all alone in the kitchen playing with crumbs, while I decorate and undecorated, make another meal, clean, do laundry, go shopping, try to steer my son right, try to help someone less fortunate, try to do some good. It's all supposed to amount to something productive or understandable. My son. And Ruth. "Ahhhh," she screamed. Baby Joe screamed back.

The back door lock clicked shut. Sally threw the box on the floor and sat on the couch. A shuffling noise approached. It was Ruth.

"*Désolé*," she softly whispered.

"For what?" Sally demanded.

"I trouble you."

Joe was wailing in his highchair. Ruth put her hands over her ears and offered Sally a tiny smile and whispered, "qui-et."

Sally got off the couch and walked by her with such force Ruth had to reach out to steady herself. Sally filled the kettle, put it on the element and turned on the heat. She opened a cupboard, reached for a tea bag, put it in a mug and stood firmly footed, staring at the kettle. Joe wailed a little louder. Sally looked at the floor, sticky with apple juice and covered with graham cracker crumbs, bits of gift wrap, cereal flakes, and flour. She lifted her feet, up, down, up, making the rubber from the bottom of her slippers tap out a ticky-tacky sound. As the kettle came to a boiling whistle, Sally grabbed the oven door handle and started howling long and loud. She couldn't stop. She thought she might go deaf from her own shrieking but it didn't matter. Nothing mattered. She was too tired to care. Ruth stepped forward, turned the element off and put her giant hands gently on each of Sally's shoulders. Sally screamed louder, turned to face Ruth, whose thundering size made Sally explode with a rage that was part breakdown, part heartbreak. Sally plunged her childlike fists into Ruth's stomach. Desperate for strength, she pounded her superficially and then deeper and deeper into her abdomen. Sally stop, she told herself, but she couldn't.

"She seduced my son. She's using him to get pregnant."

"Sally, you don't know that," Harold said, looking frail.

"Neither do you," said Sally.

"They are consenting adults. That's not the issue here."

"All I did," explained Sally, staring hard into Harold's navy sweater vest, "was hit her lightly a few times. I was overly tired and wasn't thinking. It's been hard on me."

"Sally, you should have come to us if it was too much," Harold said, sinking into the cracked leather upholstery of his chair. "We could have helped."

"This isn't my fault."

"Sally," Harold warned.

"No one's blaming anyone here," said Milly.

"She's probably given my son AIDS."

"I don't know where you acquired this information and I don't believe it's accurate," said Harold. "But we need to deal with the fact that you assaulted Ruth."

"I will have absolutely none of that. That girl's as responsible as I am."

On the drive home from the Norman's it was already dark. Sally, sitting atop her cushion, her feet attached to the pedal extensions, tried to concentrate on the road. She wanted to play it safe so she drove slowly. Cars kept honking at her as they passed. Even cars passing from the other direction were honking. "Go to hell," she shouted, feeling neither fully inside her life nor fully outside of it. Sally was part spectator, part performer. The line between fact and fiction, reality and fantasy, was unclear. Was this really Sally's life? This series of misguided hopes wrapped in guilt and remorse. She wanted to open up her chest, pull out her heart, wash it, pat it dry, dust it with talcum powder, put it back with a pious gentleness and continue on. She glanced at the snapshot tucked into the rubber seal of the car's front windshield — her and Lyle during the Mensa home test — a relic from another life.

As she parked her car behind her neighbour's van, she realized her lights weren't on. Sally'd been driving in the dark. All the way home. She flicked them on. The little flag was still there, with the two bars and maple leaf, the colour of a beating heart on a white background.

POOEY

"WHAT ARE YOU snooping around for?" Leona's husky voice bounced off the living room walls.

"Nothing," Jackie shouted into the cold air of the refrigerator, thankful she was here, knowing, always, there were plenty of reasons to check on her mother. Most pressing of which was no one else did. And then there was the issue of food. If we are what we eat, Leona was oxidized, fused to the vegetable crisper, ripe for fruit flies.

"Did I tell you Margo died?"

"Mom, you have nothing edible."

"Eh?" Leona called out.

"Everything in your fridge has gone bad."

"Honestly. Something gets a little mouldy and you get all worked up."

"Who's Margo?" asked Jackie, thinking she ought to know.

"Margo was my maid of honour."

Water rushed from the taps and burbled down the drain. The sliders on the vegetable drawer screeched, the old heavy refrigerator door sealed shut. Jackie slipped into the living room.

"Oh Leona, shut up," said Leona, propped up with

cushions in her wingback chair, her *terra firma*, a TV tray at her side, tall stacks of newspapers piled around her. "Your daughter has better things to do than listen to your palaver about the dying generation." She knocked back the last of her drink and gave an encouraging shake to the ice cube sliding around the edges of the foggy glass. Peering into the tumbler, she puckered her lips like a child upset at the thought of eating vegetables.

Jackie couldn't watch. She stared instead at the fossilized footprints on the broadloom from where the chaise longue and the player piano had exited with her father a quarter century ago.

"Do you have something to report?" Leona asked.

Maybe, thought Jackie, remembering that Roman had dumped her. And that while he'd dumped her he thanked her. Thanked her for being in his life, thanked her for everything she had taught him — as if they were on *Sesame Street*.

"I'm single."

Her mother looked at her, unblinkingly.

"Again. Actually it's been a couple of months, so it's hardly worth reporting." Jackie picked up the vacuum attachment of a haircutting kit on the loveseat, put it on a heap of old manila files strewn on the side table and sat down. "Remember he went on that week-long retreat?"

"That way out thing."

"Yeah, well he came back to the city saying his brain was burning with synapses. Apparently he's an indigo child."

"A what?" Leona sounded annoyed.

"An indigo child," Jackie shouted. "They have superior intuitive and spiritual powers."

Leona tsked with disapproval. "He's a bit of a nut, isn't he? All those lemonade washings."

"Cleansings," Jackie said. "Anyway, whatever, I'm not getting any younger and I want to have a child."

"Why? Your brother has two little brats and he's always tired. You give children everything and then they reject you. Get a cat."

"Do you wish you'd had cats?"

"I'm allergic."

This was the usual pattern of their conversations, they inched forward like cattle grazing on hillsides.

"What he considers he knows today, come but tomorrow, he will find misknown," Leona said, raising her empty glass before putting it on the TV tray. "Oh pooey, darling daughter, I don't mean to kick a gift horse in the mouth."

"You're not, Mom."

Grateful for any hint of approval, Leona's face softened, but only momentarily. "Jackie," she said sternly, as she pulled at her oxygen tube, yanked out the nasal clip, poked a cigarette between her lips, flicked her lighter and inhaled. "Your mother had an accident last week. Bit of a mishap."

Through the smoky swirls in the shadowy room, Jackie checked for bruises or swelling.

"So much piles up," Leona said, avoiding her daughter's eyes. "I was sifting through the mess to find my Medigas bill and I managed to knock over the Hentschel. The mirror, the glass broke. God bless Ronnie from next door. He took the damn thing away once and for all."

"Are you all right? It was against the wall. How'd you knock it over?"

Leona inhaled with an all-consuming whoosh. Smoke streamed out her nostrils and up past her nicotine-stained eyeballs. After putting her oxygen assembly back in position, she stood up, butted her cigarette and took two steps toward the window. With both hands down the back of her pants, she looked out at the street and scratched. Jackie watched the sweatpants inch down, revealing two flat buttocks that looked like pizza dough hung sideways.

The room was too still, too quiet. Gone was the constant moral tick tock — an existential anthem — that had marched through the house: time's passing, nothing's happening. Which wasn't true. Things did happen in this house.

There was the night Jackie left the bath running upstairs and part of the ceiling caved in. The day her brother, dressed in a Superman cape and underwear, let a couple of Jehovah's Witnesses into the house, then broke the nose of one with a baseball bat. The night the dog brought home a freshly killed muskrat and dropped it at Leona's feet. Leona kicked it under the avocado-coloured auto icemaker refrigerator. It shrivelled and hardened and occasionally Jackie would find her mother face down on the linoleum, peering into the darkness to make sure it was still there. Probably still is.

"Mom, why don't I take your car and go to the store. Get you some things. Juice, bread, fruit, cottage ..."

A panicked, thumping scurrying erupted from behind the wall.

Jackie shrieked. "What the hell is that?"

"Probably the squirrel."

"What squirrel?"

"Eh? Squirrelly, the squirrel. Lives in the wall."

"Jesus!"

"If you're going to go out and get me some things you may as well pick me up a pack of cigarettes." Leona's hands came out of her sweats and were reassigned to scratching duties above her bellybutton, then underneath her large bobbing breasts. "Oh, and a chocolate bar too." Leona smiled. "With nuts for my friend, Squirrelly."

Jackie pulled the arm of the loveseat forward. "You can't live with squirrels, they're very destructive." She reached down, banged a fist on the wall.

"Could you also nip into the liquor store and get me a bottle of Ballantine's? I seem to be all out."

Jackie stood up. Coughing from the dust, she backed into a tall stack of newspapers, which slowly tipped over, knocking the TV tray and Leona's empty glass into the air. As Jackie lunged to catch the tumbler she slipped on a glossy flyer and fell to the broadloom.

Leona looked at her grown daughter lying on her side and held out a twenty. "Is this enough?"

"I'm glad you decided to come, Mom," Jackie said, looking at her mother, nestled in the white bucket seat of her Coronet. It was late March, late afternoon, and garbage pickup was late. Coloured bins decorated the sidewalk.

"I really think you should let me drive," said Leona.

"No. I never get to drive. Let me drive you."

Three streets later, Leona was sure Jackie forgot to lock the front door. Jackie assured her she did not forget.

"Oh to hell with it," said Leona. "They can take what- ever they want." As Jackie slowed down, a car behind them honked furiously.

"Go go go," yelled Leona.

Jackie stiffened. Attempting to parallel park, she backed the car up onto the curb and jostled the car be- hind her. Leona gasped. As the honking car tore off, Jackie lurched her mother's old car forward and fit it into the only parking space, which just happened to be in front of the liquor store.

"Well this is a good spot," Leona noted. Jackie watched the little ball of skin on her mother's eyelid, perched fragile and stubborn, like a wingless butterfly.

"I didn't sleep the last two nights, that's why I'm slow today. Lied awake worrying. I feel absolutely sick. Go get the groceries and my cigarettes. I'll wait here." Leona turned to face her daughter. "Maybe I can hobble into the liquor store with you when you get back. It's ... oh listen to me. You're tired too, aren't you? You look awful."

"I do?"

"Honest to goodness you look at the whole kit an' caboodle and I don't have the answers." Leona coughed, then peered into her hands.

"Answers to what?" Jackie snapped.

"To what it all means. Ecological disasters. Political tyranny. Why does no one like semi-colons anymore? Oh progress ... pooey. Man's distinctive mark alone, not God's, and not the beasts'. Really, darling daughter, it's good you don't have children. Not in this miserable world."

Jackie slammed the car door shut and stomped up the street. She hated the subtle undercurrent that linked her in some fatalistic way to her mother, as damaged goods. You are very special but look at your mother, Roman had said, warning her against having children, and declaring no, he would not give her his sperm.

Jackie scowled at people she passed. She scowled at a little dog tied up to a fire hydrant. She scowled at her thoughts. Scowl and the world scowls with you. It was her protection. It fit her like a lead-lined vest — the kind you wear while having your teeth x-rayed.

Back at Leona's house, Jackie put the purchases away.

"I can't stand to think about it," announced Leona.

"Then don't," Jackie said sharply as she washed her hands, reminding herself to buy a pregnancy test on the way home. She took a deep breath. Pictured her apartment with little shoes everywhere, tiny fingerprints on the walls and a fridge covered with crayoned drawings. But three strikes and I'm out, she told herself, imagining the jokes she would make one day, bouncing her child on her knees, about how the stuff in those vials had been more expensive than Beluga caviar.

"And the little baby. It's absolutely dreadful."

What the hell was her mother talking about? Jackie, announcing she was going home, headed toward the door.

"Get this out of here." Leona frantically waved a section of the newspaper.

"What is it?"

It was the front page of the *Life* section, featuring a staged picture of Jackie's father, looking ponderous, taken through the window of his car. His daughter, Tabitha, was sitting beside him looking far too grown up.

Unknown woman in red Beetle saves family

COLIN LAVOIE SPECIAL FIRST PERSON FEATURE

It was a beautiful Saturday morning. I was driving my daughter Tabitha to her dance class. I opened my window and heard the distinctive five-note warble and twitter of a white-throated sparrow. Then the frightening sound of a prolonged horn. Fear gripped my spine. From the oncoming lane, a dark blue Toyota 4Runner turned right in front of me.

The driver must have heard the horn too because he sped up and careened in front of us. As providence would have it, I slowed down.

We missed each other by inches.

As I pulled over I saw a bright red VW Beetle drive by with a woman in it. I realized she was the driver who had seen the nightmare about to unfold and sounded her horn.

That was two weeks ago but I can't get it out of my head.

I think about you, the woman in the shiny red Beetle.

I wish I could let you know how much I thank you every day. Perhaps the best way to do this is to let you know the poignant details of one life you saved.

"Oh puke," Jackie said, tucking the newspaper under her arm. How cruel, that Leona had discovered this inside her beloved newspapers. She kissed her mother goodbye. The softness of Leona's cheek and the little ball of flesh on her eyelid filled Jackie with a teeny tiny sense of absolute terror that she had forgotten to say something.

Walking up the street she passed the garbage truck. The threatening noise of the diesel engine and the creak and moan of the packing panel filled the street. A bald man and a tiny woman wearing bright orange jackets hurled containers and insults at the smelly beast — its big gaping mouth gorged and belched as it crawled backward in lurching starts and stops. She wondered if the Hentschel was inside the hopper. The old clock had been her paternal grandmother's but through some oversight of her father's it had stayed with her mother. In the years following her parents' separation, her father — when he checked in on Jackie and Dave once a year — would always inquire about the clock, asking, "How is the old tempus fugit?" Jackie was never sure if he was referring the clock, or Leona.

On the subway, Jackie opened up the paper and continued reading.

I contribute to society. I'm a motivational consultant. If I had died the world would not fall apart. However, where I can't be replaced is with my family.

Tabitha is on the cusp of womanhood. She has been studying dance for six years. I am not convinced it will be a career but you have ensured she can carry on without injury or tragedy.

My little one, Lily, is fourteen months. Already we see similarities between her and Tabitha. Sometimes it's only Tabby who can put her to bed, although other times nothing can please her except watching *Max and Ruby*.

My wife Kiki and I have been through a great deal. We lost our first child twenty-three years ago to blue baby syndrome. Kiki is only forty-four but she has cancer. She said she needed to hold on until Lily turned a year old. Now that that's passed she credits me for giving her the strength to continue. By saving me you permit me to offer her this support.

You are probably not a firefighter or a lifeguard, yet I wish I could give you a medal. Instead, all I can give you is my thanks. In fact, I can't thank you enough. Words don't do it justice. But I hope they reach you wherever you are.

Two days later Jackie's period came. Her insides felt like a big heavy car battery that had been discarded and left to ooze and corrode. It put her in a horrible mood so she called her brother to check on directions and to vent.

"And I love this part. I contribute to society. What? Like the rest of us don't?"

"Enough okay? Nobody said you had to read it," Dave reminded his sister through the hands-free microphone.

"What? It was in the paper."

"I don't get what's bothering you."

"Did you read it?"

Dave didn't say anything.

"Okay, I know it's stupid but it's like we're pariahs. He's our father too."

"Guys, we should leave now," Dave shouted.

"That's all you can say?"

Dave told her he was in the car now taking Nicole and the kids to Sissy's baby shower and wasn't she supposed to be going too and he didn't have time for this bullshit.

Jackie looked at herself in the mirror. The pointy white slingbacks and pink crinoline dress with spaghetti straps and frill flounces had been a Value Village score. She applied her lip gloss, smacked her lips, looked at her pale face and screamed — for running late, for looking stern, for feeling uncomfortable in a dress and pantyhose. And for being a needy little girl who still wanted Daddy's attention. She hobbled to the kitchen table, sealed up the card, stuck it under the bow and tried to remember why she'd thought it was a good idea to go to this shower. Sissy was Nicole's best friend, but Jackie hardly knew her.

Dave and Nicole's little girls, Bryce and Dusty, answered the door. "Who are you?" they shrieked.

"Aunt Jackie," she said. They screamed, jumped loose and gangly in their platform heels and slammed the door in her face.

"She's dressed like Barbie," Bryce yelled when a slight and graceful woman named Prue came to the rescue, opening the door and introducing herself as Sissy's aunt.

"Come in and make yourself at home," Prue said. "Nicole's around here somewhere and Sissy's in the dining room."

The foyer was appointed like a developer's model home, clean and functional with a well-polished antique table displaying a spring bouquet of flowers. In the living room, light streamed through the windows and bounced off yellow and purple balloons floating along the ceiling. There was a fresh potpourri of citrus and lavender, or maybe that was Prue.

A few women near the entrance turned and scanned Jackie, head to toe, as if she were a massive piece of candy floss. Hadn't the invitation said to dress up? She brushed against a banister and tried to give off the impression it was as comfortable as a chair.

The room was filled with conversations. There was a prodigious moan of approval for designated parking spots for moms and tots, and agreement that people who don't have children have no idea that you don't have time to chat on the phone let alone see movies. One woman has a boy with an eating disorder (refuses carbs); another has a daughter who sports a third nipple; but a woman named Liz seemed to be the clear winner: her son has an LD.

"What's an LD?" Jackie asked.

"Learning disability. Ben has trouble with math," said Liz.

Jackie nodded. The couch in front of her had a pattern of brown acorns and green leaves. She figured the design repeated itself every thirty centimetres or so, she couldn't be sure; she's always had trouble with math.

"You've come as Doris Day!" said a tiny voice attached to a woman Jackie recognized as Sissy's mother.

"Hey, great getup! There's some punch in the kitchen. Here, I'll take that," Nicole said, reaching for Jackie's gift.

In the kitchen, two teenage boys eating ice cream from a cardboard carton asked if she was the fairy godmother because one of them needed help — seriously — he's addicted to gaming and crack.

"I forgot my wand," Jackie said, as she poured herself a glass of punch. She headed to the dining room where Sissy, looking particularly rabbity in a pale blue turtleneck with fluffy pink trim, was surrounded by an admiring bunch crowding around her like teens in a mosh pit. They all resembled Nicole — healthy and Nordic like cross-country skiers, with large teeth, pale blue eyes and that particular kind of blond hair that can turn grey unnoticed.

Jackie caught Sissy's eye and smiled with a congratulatory nod. Sissy pointed at her massive *with-child* womb, rubbed it like it needed a polish, then stuck out her tongue and crossed her eyes. Being preggers has made her weird, thought Jackie, as she stepped back, knowing sure as her pinched feet were throbbing that she won't be anything like that. She wobbled sideways and knocked something that felt like a sack of potatoes. Immediately it began to scream.

A woman shot Jackie a look of horror, held up her hand like a stop sign, then scooped up the plump toddler.

"I'm so sorry," Jackie said.

Over the child's cries the woman cooed: "Did the woman hurt you? Let Mommy kiss it better."

"Awww," a loud explosion rang out around Sissy. "I felt it. I felt it. It kicked!" A couple of women clapped.

Jackie went back for more punch. The feral teenagers with ice cream had disappeared. "Just a few more presents then we all have to guess Sissy's waistline!" someone announced. Astonishing really, Jackie thought. How insipid these women are, so smug, so happy with themselves and their spoiled children with their special problems. These are women who spear you with their yoga mats and block store aisles with their strollers, then smile at you like you'll be happy about it.

"Jax!" Nicole called. "Sissy's opening your present."

"Coming." Walking into the dining room Jackie's foot disappeared. "Ahhh," she cried as she buckled over, collapsing onto the cherry hardwood, the cranberry-coloured punch shooting out of her glass and splattering Prue's white pants.

Jackie limped up the stairs to her apartment, took off her dress and grabbed a beer from the fridge. She thought about how ridiculous she must have looked. How Prue had flat-out refused to take any money for dry-cleaning. "Stain-resistant blend," she had insisted, through clenched teeth.

Sadness wanted to devour her. She got all dressed up and didn't have a good time. She never had a good time. She was like her mother. She thought about Roman. Part of her missed him, but a bigger part was glad to be free of him. His judgments. His healthy habits. His my-body-is-a-temple crap. She went to the fridge and grabbed another beer.

The following month there was a phone call from Dave — a rarity — telling her the name of the palliative care facility where Kiki was now staying. Two days later Jackie visited. Kiki was lying still, all bones and soft skin, her heart partially shut down, mechanical beeps and rings keeping her breathing company. The smell of urine and tasteless food filled the room.

"It's true," Kiki managed to utter. Her words

sounded like they were coming from a tin cup. "My days are numbered."

Jackie nodded. She reached for Kiki's bony hand and held it in hers, aware of how loose her wedding band was. Kiki's long fingernails dug into Jackie's palm, sharp as thumbtacks.

Two weeks later Sissy gave birth to an eight pound two ounce boy. "Perfect," everyone said. Her husband had filmed it and put it on YouTube. Jackie watched the clip, slightly repulsed by their need to share. But it reminded her, she needed to find a midwife. Her second attempt was going to be successful, she was sure of it.

The next day was not a good one. Jackie's period arrived, rust-coloured and thick, staining her hopes, and Leona had a small fender-bender on the way to buy a card for the new mother.

"Mom, just take cabs or let me drive you," Jackie anxiously urged.

"I'm fine. Someone has a little accident and you get all worked up," Leona said.

Jackie couldn't even imagine how Leona actually drove.

The following month Dave called again — Kiki had passed away.

At the service Jackie didn't recognize anyone until she spotted Bryce and Dusty swinging off a coat rack in the side vestibule. "Thank you for coming," her father said to her mechanically, as if he didn't quite recognize her. "I'm so sorry about your mom, it's good to see you," she said to Tabitha who was sitting with two friends. Tabitha all but ignored her. Halfway home it occurred to Jackie that her half-sister probably didn't know who she was. It had been years since they'd seen each other.

A few weeks later Dave called yet again. Evidently something was changing for him. Perhaps all this life and death alchemy made him want to cultivate a kind of familial loyalty or love. Whatever it was, the son who never remembered his mother's birthday had decided they should have a party. He was even a little worked up. "It's her seventieth! I'm tired of playing games. Mostly, I resent having to worry about *her*. So I want to have a party," he added, clearly irritated. "I'm thinking Oisi's a week this Friday."

Jackie was to bring Leona. Dave and Nicole would come with Bryce and Dusty. Colin with his two: Tabby and Lily.

Jackie arrived at Leona's, looking forward to the night. After two strikes in a row she was feeling third time lucky. "Are you sure you don't want to consider intracervical or intrauterine insemination?" the counsellor had asked. But Jackie didn't want her baby conceived in a clinic aided by strangers wearing latex gloves, so two weeks ago, hips held high in the comforts of her own bed, she'd slipped the syringe in and pushed the plunger. The thought that right now at this very moment she could well be pregnant had put her in a terrific mood.

"Hi," she called out as she let herself in. There were no lights on, but it wasn't quite dark enough to be spooky. The blue eyeshadow and the red lipstick were promising but the stillness and the smoke were fair warning.

"Well hello, gorgeous daughter. Don't you look wonderful?" Leona let out a laugh that was potentially menacing, like a missing front tooth. "Your father will be happy to see you. I know I am." Leona slapped her thigh. "Someone's turning seventy. We're all, gonna have, a party! If I were any happier, I'd be a balloon. Not to be mistaken for a buffoon. Or the sanctimonious old arse I married."

Enthusiastically she continued.

"I'm ready to strut, like a peacock. Fly through my smoke rings. It's going to be as fun as all get out." She pounded her fist on the armchair.

"Do you think your father will sing? *Canto ergo sum.* That would be so healing for us all."

"What's going on?" Jackie asked.

"Now what's with you, little sourpuss?"

Jackie turned away. Her heart quickened. Who's idea had this been?

"Oh," Leona said. "Is this too Eugene O'Neill for you?" Abruptly, her voice changed. It sounded sober and thoughtful. "I was aiming for Noel Coward but I just don't seem to be that gay."

The ice cubes in Leona's glass clanked like loose marbles. "Oh pooey." Crouching forward to stand up she added, "I've got a brand new canister."

Jackie stared at two crusty brown cigarette burns in the carpet and her breathing constricted. It was the thud that alerted her that her mother had fallen.

"Everything's under control," Leona stated as she rolled onto her knees and propped her glass on the armrest of her chair. "Let's get the show on the road."

"All the world's a stage." Colin's voice boomed across the elegant room.

Dave stood up. "Everyone, curtain's up, our star is here."

Leona stood back from the table, hesitantly, and let others come to her. Nicole was the first. "Hi Mom!" followed by Dave, "Hello Mother," and Tabby, "Happy Birthday." Bryce and Dusty danced around Leona ceremoniously as if she were a maypole. Colin, kneeling on one knee, kissed her hands.

"I have been so looking forward to meeting you," said an extremely handsome woman Jackie didn't recognize.

"Why?" Leona asked.

"I'm Linda," the woman replied. "Colin generously invited me here and it's an honour."

"Matriarch and Queen of Rigamarole," said Leona, holding out her hand.

"Jackie, lady-in-waiting, chauffeur, oldest child."

"Happy to be your friend," said Linda to each, in turn. Her smile displayed a beautiful set of teeth upstaged only by a pair of playful blue eyes. "Colin and I met through most unusual circumstances. And we both love birding. But another time. Please, let's carry on."

"Leona, Jackie, what can I get you?" asked Colin, beaming.

Jackie noticed her father's long grey ponytail was gone. He'd shaved his head. A delicate bristle softened the fine angular bone structure.

"Double single malt please," said Leona, as Jackie pushed her mother's chair in and parked the canister beside her.

"Red please," Jackie said, thinking her father looks amazing. Handsome and well-aged. He has the self-assurance of a man who believes only time and practice prevent him from being the very best at whatever he turns his attention to. It made her feel proud, and completely insignificant.

Drinks in hand, they perused the menus. Leona announced that she hated sushi and asked what they were doing in a restaurant that had the gall to charge money for seaweed. Dave said *I thought you loved sushi.* Leona pouted. Jackie suggested she have the chicken teriyaki. Nicole agreed that was an excellent choice and Linda said there really was no better choice. *Have it Mom, and I will too,* Jackie said. Colin said he was up for the sushi boat. Tabby said she wanted the shrimp tempura because Adam told her to have it. Linda leaned forward and excitedly asked if Adam was her boyfriend. *Dating's stupid,* Tabby said calmly. Dusty said Bryce had a boyfriend. Bryce said *shut up or I'll say something you don't want me to.*

Orders were taken. As the waiter dashed away Linda piped up saying she hoped she wasn't being too forward but she'd like to propose a toast. "To Leona Lavoie. May your heart, and your plate, always be full."

Leona looked at her drink, downed it, and said *to be,* or *to me,* no one was quite sure. Then she stared at Lily, asleep in her car seat on a chair next to her ex-husband, and frowned.

Colin explained that he didn't know where it came from but his kids were the best. "You see," he said, shooting a wink at Leona, "some people are happy just to survive. Not my brood. Jackie knows food retailing like no one's business, she manages Fresh & Wild in the Bloor West Village. Dave's building one of the largest house painting businesses in the city. Tabby, as you know, is going to be the next Karen Kain, and little Lily is perfect. Nicole is a President's Club Realtor. And our fabulous grandkids are on their way to being musical prodigies. You should hear them on my old player piano."

Conversation broke into smaller pockets. Jackie kept an eye on Leona who switched her focus to her hyperactive grandchildren. At Bryce's urging they were attempting to reenact a scene from *Charlotte's Web*.

Linda explained to Colin and Dave that there are five steps to living a long and successful life. The first step is to believe in yourself. The next is to believe in the opportunity to make mistakes. The next is to believe in the future. "I hope the future includes an opportunity for me to get to know all of you better. I just love this family." And with that she raised her glass.

"Wait wait wait," said Dave. "That wasn't five steps."

"Ha! Aren't you the smart one. To be successful you have to take the steps two at a time!"

"Didn't see that coming," said Colin with a grin.

These three are made for each other, thought Jackie.

"Tabitha," Leona said, cutting through the revelry with enough force to create an awkward pause around the table.

Leona pulled a pink envelope out of her purse. "I

never knew your mother, but I know it must be very hard on you. You're in my heart, dear."

Tabby took the card with a nod to Leona.

"Now," Leona bellowed. "I need a washroom. If it's downstairs I'm gonna wring someone's neck." Jackie stood up to help and Leona scolded her. "I'm fine on my own, thank you very much." And with that she headed to the back of the restaurant looking both tipsy and club-footed as she leaned on the rolling canister for balance.

Linda, sensing the moment was appropriate, looked at Jackie and announced: "I'm in the middle of menopause and wish to pose no threat to your family."

"Then don't," said Jackie. Turning to Nicole she asked how Sissy and the baby were. They were great.

"Listen," her sister-in-law said softly, "Dave's think-ing we should sell your mother's house. She's not doing that well. We're worried, no air conditioning, all those newspapers, she can't keep going. Dave was so upset about the Hentschel. I can handle the listing for three percent. I'd do it for nothing but the buyer's agent takes two-and-a-half so I think that's fair."

Jackie downed her glass of wine, asked where Leona would live. Nicole said they didn't know but there were places. "Anyway, Dave can get a crew in there and get the place painted before it goes on the market. Just thought I'd mention it." Out of the corner of her eye Jackie saw Dusty slip under the table. Next to the va-cated chair, Bryce, in homage to Leona, had stuck the ends of a single straw up each nostril. When the food came Jackie excused herself. She found Leona splayed out on the cold tile in front of a toilet.

As Leona and Jackie returned to the party, father and

son were sharing tips about the best desk workouts. Dave loves armchair push-ups; Colin — pleased that Dave's finally got his business to the stage where he can work from an office — was demonstrating the tush-toner. Linda cheering them on, put her hand to her heart. "My secret? A combination orange, pomegranate and cranberry juice every morning."

Jackie announced that unfortunately they had to leave.

"Jax, where's your mother? Please stay," Colin pleaded. "It means a lot to me."

"No. We really should be going."

Leona moseyed by, muttering that it was too late for little kids to be out eating octopus.

"What about the cake?" asked Linda.

Colin insisted that they at least take their meals — and the cake, Linda added. Colin summoned the waiter to the table, ordered him to wrap up their food, told Dave to walk them out. Jackie made the rounds, leaving her dad for last.

"Good to see you, Dad," she said, as she gave him a hug.

"It's good to be seen!" Looking at Leona who was waiting at the door, Colin added, "I'm sorry your mother does not have more stamina. Please tell her how wonder-ful it was to see her."

In the parking lot, Dave seemed to have forgotten Leona was there.

"Drinking?"

Jackie looked at her brother. "What?"

"She was drinking?"

Jackie stared back in silence.

"Drive carefully," he said tenderly. Then he raced around the car. "Mom, I almost forgot, I have a present for you."

Tucking Leona into bed, Jackie leaned over and kissed her forehead. The smell of hair spray was so intense she sneezed. "Don't ever marry a man ten years your junior," Leona said. "Even if he does make a wicked martini and makes you feel so happy you don't care about anything else."

Jackie stroked her mother's hair. Her fingers lingered on the crown of her scalp where tiny scabs felt as rough as tree bark. She brushed them lightly but they were hard and stubborn.

"I'll bet Linda drives a red Beetle."

"Where does that come from?" asked Jackie.

"My brain."

Hours later Jackie lay awake staring at her bedroom ceiling. She wondered if Leona was lying awake, too, thinking everyone's just waiting for her to die, all alone, like abandoned roadkill. The thought was too much. Something inside her broke. Into pieces. Pieces of sadness. She thought of everything she knew about her mother. It was only little pieces — shards of goodness and misplaced servitude. There was the Master of Arts *summa cum laude* graduate. The looker who turned down three marriage proposals. The multitasking housewife. The obedi-

ent cuckoo who agreed to let 100 volts of electricity —
no more than what a standard household outlet carries
— charge through her brain. The divorced drinker. The
worrier. The thoughtful giver of cards.

Jackie couldn't stop crying. Remembering Leona at
dinner, her legs barely able to hold her carriage and her
thoughts so easily soured, there was only one thing that
seemed to mean anything in this world: protecting her
from misfortune, injury and sadness.

Just before dawn Jackie realized she'd never told her
mother that she loves her. Even though she loves her
more than anyone in the world.

The next day Jackie knocked but there was no answer.

"Mom," she called out, turning on lights. The house
was deathly quiet. "It's me. I'm here." Noisily, she
dropped her knapsack and keys on the floor. She approached the bedroom.

Standing in the doorway her eyes adjusted to the light
as they travelled the room. The bedspread was dishev-
elled, the nightlight on, an open book was on the bed
next to a lumpy body. There was a glass of something on
the nightstand and the bowed ash of a cigarette, burnt
in its entirety, was delicately balanced on the edge of an
ashtray. The air was warm and sour.

A head turned and looked at Jackie with such fright
she felt like a ghost.

"Where'd you come from?" Leona's gravelly voice
moaned. "What are you doing here?"

"Nothing," Jackie said softly. "Do you want to sit
up?"

"No. What do you want?"

"I dunno … can you get up?" She approached the bedside.

"It's early isn't it?"

"I'll wait for you in the living room. Call if you need help," Jackie said, reaching for the glass and the ashtray.

In the kitchen she poured the drink into the sink, emptied the ashtray, cleaned a few dishes. Leona hobbled into the living room and turned down the dial on her oxygen compressor just as Jackie was taking a puff from her inhaler.

"What's gotten into you?"

"My asthma," Jackie said, wheezing.

"Try living here," Leona grumped.

Jackie navigated the piles of newspapers and sat on the couch. "How was last night? Was it okay? Seeing Dad and everything."

"Pffffffff," Leona shrugged. "What choice did I have?"

"You always have a choice."

"Nonsense," Leona said with a grunt, nestling into her chair. "Empire builders like your father and your brother have choices. They're ready to solve the problems of the world. Probably because they don't have any of their own."

"You left this in your car last night. Dave's present."

"Well. What munificence," Leona said, raising an eyebrow as she ran a finger along the edge of the scotch tape.

It was a book. *The Upside of Down.* "I won't take it personally." She rubbed her hand across the cover and read aloud, *Catastrophe, Creativity, and the Renewal of*

Civilization. Tapping it hard, she said, "Imagine that!" before releasing a huge cough from an earthy cavern seven decades deep. "Dave bought a book. Maybe there is hope after all."

Later that day Colin called Jackie, proof positive an odd movement was afoot within the family that, at minimum, involved people calling people. Jackie liked the idea although it made her a little uncomfortable. She remembered how Roman used to say, *we've been through so much shit together* — as if it were a privilege.

Colin told Jackie how wonderful it had been to see her and gallantly told her he had a favour to ask. It was the nanny's day off on Sunday and he and Linda were hoping to get out of town. People had seen ospreys in the Kawarthas. In fact there were about 200 nesting pairs around Rice Lake — all thanks to a ban on DDT. They were anxious to see if they could spot a family of these fabulous, majestic birds. Could she look after Tabby and Lily? She could have Kiki's car if she wanted to take them somewhere. He'd fill up the tank. Lily's car seat was in the back. Tabby's plenty old enough but having lost her mother so recently he didn't want her to be alone for long.

It was such a shock to receive a phone call from her father, Jackie reacted as if she'd been bestowed with a tremendous honour. She even expressed interest in their outing. "So how long do ospreys nest for?"

"To the Falls," Jackie called out, suddenly seeing herself as someone with means and credentials enough to be in charge of two minors. The day felt magnetic, as if the vanishing perspective of the wide grey road was pulling the heavy vehicle forward. The luxury SUV was new enough that the leather still had a carnivorous, musky smell. Or maybe these gas guzzlers have a time-release deodorizer.

In the rear-view mirror, Jackie could see Lily in the back seat, her head bent to one side as she gazed out the window with an intense curiosity that suggested she had a great deal to contemplate. So do I, thought Jackie. She told Tabby she was sorry they'd never hung out together, adding, "I'm really looking forward to today." Tabby, buckled up in the passenger seat reading a magazine, didn't look up.

Her half-sister looked a lot like Kiki. She had her shiny black eyes and hair and creamy smooth skin. She wore big loopy earrings, silver bangles that clanked, flared jeans with fancy stitching and tight layered tops that revealed breasts that sprouted unnaturally high, Jackie thought. There was a loud blast of horns. Tabby looked up as Jackie swerved back into her lane.

"This is a big car," she said, gripping the steering wheel, aware that the hot sun through the windshield was making her drowsy. She looked at the dials and wondered how to control the temperature.

Seeming to read Jackie's mind, Tabby pushed a couple of buttons and turned a knob. Cool air immediately flowed from the vents.

"Thanks," Jackie said, thinking she could really get used to a car like this. And speaking of cars, "Hey, does Linda drive a red Beetle?"

"Yeah," said Tabby.

"Do you like her?"

"Why wouldn't I?" Tabby asked, sounding non-plussed.

"I don't know," said Jackie.

They coasted through acres of greenbelt dotted with wineries and single story buildings with businesses that sell tubs and bearings and heat-resistant castings. Jackie pressed a couple of buttons and the radio came on low. A few songs later traffic turned heavy and everything slowed down.

"You must miss your mom," Jackie said to Tabby, who was slouched against the passenger door.

She nodded.

"If you ever need to talk you know you can call me."

Tabby pressed the lever, lowering her window and spit a large goober onto the highway.

Now that's adorable, Jackie thought. She looked at her half-sister's tiny waist and fluorescent nail polish and felt such profound envy at this little flower, set to bloom, she almost hit the car in front of them. Tabby was getting used to it and kept quiet.

The Falls were magnificent. Shimmering smooth on top like blown glass. The drama was in how it all gave way, rushing over, thundering down and foaming contentedly at the bottom.

At a lookout perch she gave Tabby some change to look through the observation binoculars. Tabby returned unimpressed. "They're dirty."

Lily, strapped into the stroller, began to squirm and fuss.

"I'll take her," said Tabby knowingly.

They searched out a washroom with a baby-changing station and Jackie let Tabby do the dirty work while she pulled out supplies from the tote bag.

Back on the main drag they strolled past the tacky amusements, then stopped at a rooftop patio and ordered mini burgers and fries. Tabby put Lily's bib on and fed her pureed vegetables from a Rubbermaid container.

"Wanna play a game?" Tabby asked, holding up her magazine when they were waiting for the bill. "I show you a picture, okay, and you say right away fabulous or hideous."

"Fabulous," Jackie called out at a picture of Anna Paquin. An ad for medication for genital herpes: "Definitely fabulous." A close-up of a needle injecting Restylane into a woman's upper lip: "That's gross, I mean hideous!"

Tabby laughed.

"Look," Jackie said, peering over the railing and buoyed by Tabby's mood. "A Hollywood wax museum. Let's go."

Inside it was stale and cheap like a funeral home. Stars, stiff and startled looking, were trapped under glaring floodlights. Tabby took exception to Reese Witherspoon who was totally wrong; she looked like Alicia Silverstone. Michael Douglas looked like Viggo Mortensen. Jackie said Tabby knew a lot about actors. Tabby explained that she and her mom used to watch movies together.

The further they trudged through the passages the

danker it became. "Come on," Jackie urged Tabby as they stood at the opening to a dark crypt. Tabby shook her head — she'd had enough, she'd wait outside. Jackie watched her leave, then rolled the stroller into the dark tunnel. She waited for her eyes to adjust, then moved forward. Noisy jets of cold air exploded and shot down her back as haunting howls shrieked from skulls embedded in the walls. On and on, it would not stop. Lily released a deafening wail as Jackie, heart pounding, backed into a surly teenager. "Get a life, bitch," he snarled.

She pulled Lily from the stroller and rocked her until she calmed down. Holding Lily, she pushed the stroller through the back door, which opened, into a colourful souvenir shop. She set Lily down on the counter underneath a sign advertising wax hand replicas and rubbed her plump back. Lily's face and eyes were reddened and her head rolled from tiredness, but she grabbed Jackie's arms and said, "Tappy, Tappy."

Tabby was standing just feet away, in front of a display of giant pens with big red buses on top of them. "Just a sec, sweetie," Jackie said, giving Lily a kiss on the forehead. Walking up to Tabby, Jackie gingerly peeked around her long hair. A pearl-shaped tear was rolling down her cheek. Gently she rubbed Tabby's arm. A shriek and a flurry of commotion erupted.

As a fast-acting employee pulled Lily from the vat of wax, hot paraffin dripped off her. A thin layer masking her from head to toe hardened before their eyes, coating her like a freshly wrapped spring roll. Tabby and Jackie dashed to the counter and splashed cold water on Lily's skin.

There were no first-degree burns on her soft body but it was stiff with terror as she wailed. Assisted by two tacitly efficient employees, Tabby peeled off the wax. In a trembling voice Jackie announced she'd be right back. Exploding with nerves she ran down the street and into a clothing store where she grabbed an infant's set with a cartoon of a man in a barrel above the words: *I survived The Falls*. "Please hurry," she begged, "my baby fell into the hot wax." The cashier looked at her suspiciously before handing over her purchase.

"Good thing she kept her mouth shut or you wouldn't be so lucky," the first aid attendant said as they applied medicated lotion to her exposed skin and changed her clothes.

As the road out of Niagara turned into a highway, Jackie pressed the gas pedal aggressively, burdened with the reality that this big eight-cylinder monster could never get the two in the back, or her, home fast enough. The transmission leaped gears and revved menacingly, like it too was angry at her. Wound up tight, her thoughts accelerated. She looked in the rear-view mirror. Tabby was sitting next to Lily, an arm around the car seat. Everything so promising just hours ago was now reduced to an experiment that had proven without a doubt that she was an abject failure. There was no way to deny this catastrophe. Thank God Lily was all right. It happened so quickly. It was only seconds. The attendant said there was nothing wrong with her. Thank you thank you thank you.

But you? Jackie thought. You're a dangerous offender with no talent for motherhood. An understudy. No good reason to exist except to return these two beings to their rightful owner. Maybe Roman was right. She imagined telling her mother what had happened. *It's good you don't have kids*, she'll say. *Not all it's cracked up to be, believe me, they leave you exhausted, feeling ... pooey.*

Hours later Jackie sat at her kitchen table. Her father hadn't raised a fist or even his voice, but he'd chided her that she had a hell of a lot to learn about handling responsibility. It left her feeling unmanageable and grubby, like a juvenile delinquent. She unwrapped the aluminum foil containing a piece of Leona's chocolate birthday cake and shoved it in her mouth in three spongy pieces. Her throat couldn't keep up and she started to cough. Part of the cake went up her nasal cavity and slid around down to her trachea, making her cough even more. Gasping and wheezing, she reached for her inhaler. She shook it, took a puff, then flung it across the room. Bewildered and shamed, she downed a triple vodka and went to bed.

In the morning she went to the bathroom. Obeying the post-it note she'd stuck on the mirror, she reached for the yogurt container and peed into it. She took the plastic test stick out of the pouch and dipped the absorbent tip into the container. Someone was calling her. Ignoring her phone, she held the stick steady for twenty seconds, then put the cap on it and sat on the edge of the tub, waiting.

In the kitchen, she put the test stick down and poured herself a glass of orange juice. Her hands were shaking. She reread the instruction sheet. *You should see your health care professional who can advise you on what steps you should take next.*

She checked her phone. It was her mother who had called.

Slithering out from underneath the slurred words was a message, loud and clear. "Dave called to share the wonderful plan you've concocted. Well I'll have you know, the upside of down is I'm not going gently outta here until you kids stuff me into a coffin." She sounded angry. And deeply wounded.

Jackie pressed END on her handset. She sat down at the table, an anxious sludge of worry in the pit of her stomach, and dialed her mother's number.

"Oh, it's you," Leona said. "What do you want?"

"Just wanted to tell you something." Jackie's throat tightened.

"Yes, I heard you had a bit of an accident yesterday."

Jackie was quiet.

"I'm not going to wax poetic, just want to say it's good you don't have children. It's not for everyone. Oh pooey, I don't know what I'm trying to say."

"I love you Mom."

"Eh?"

"I love you." And with that Jackie hung up.

She stared at the + in the result window. *Over 99% accurate.* Sitting back, she took a deep breath and smiled.

Pooey.

A small laugh escaped. It made her wheeze. She retrieved her inhaler from the floor. A mousy looking clump of dust dangled from its mouth. She pulled it off, shook the canister and took a puff. Sitting back down, she breathed deeply and exhaled, then spun the stick like a roulette wheel. It whirled across the table away from her. A wild and disobedient thing.

"Holy shit," she said, laughing, unable to stop and unable to figure out what, exactly, was so funny.

THEORIES OF RELATIVITY

I

LAST YEAR, on his sixteenth birthday, Chris set the bathroom on fire. At least that's how the family refers to the event, as an obvious rite of passage for a teenage boy — falling somewhere between a dallying addiction to Internet porn and the delayed shock and awe of drinking and driving.

I know teenagers — his father John says, endeavouring to bond with his clients. *My sixteen-year-old set the bathroom on fire.*

Ours set the bathroom on fire — his mother Julie shares, on the subject of teenagers.

He sets bathrooms on fire — his sister Mel warns her girlfriends who think Chris is cute.

Uncle Mike was there the night it happened, leaning on the kitchen counter, talking about the time he was in Playa del Carmen during a hurricane. Rescued five dogs stuck in a second floor apartment after the staircase blew away. Julie, tearing lettuce, said, "I've seen what dogs in Mexico look like. Couldn't you have saved something better? Like a tourist?"

Detecting more than the skunky, dense odour of cannabis, Uncle Mike was the first to react. Actually he was the only one to react — but that's not too surprising given that he's a fireman. He slammed his beer on the counter and bounded down the stairs to the basement. Took him no time to put out the fire and damage was minimal, but the whole thing put such a damper on the night this year Julie's decided — come hell or high water — that Chris's birthday is going to be a happy occasion.

"The family that smokes together, stays together," she announces, leafing through a magazine for a recipe she's sure she saw for quails cooked in a Thai basil and coconut black bean sauce. "Chris, would you be able to get us a couple of joints?"

"Julie!" John looks across the top of his reading glasses. "It's *his* birthday. Don't make him buy his own. I'll take care of it," he says, nodding at the baggy mass on the couch.

"Ah! Here it is." Julie folds the corner of a page, flaps the magazine shut. Looking across the room she tries to discern what her son is reading. Looks like an old Hermann Hesse novel that used to be John's. He must have found it in the basement.

"Make sure it's grass, not hash," she instructs as she heads to the hallway.

Exasperated by his wife's need to over direct everything, John shakes his newspaper, folds it, shifts his attention to the TV. To images of business people in a Parisian suburb sifting through what's left of their stores. Thousands of cars torched by youth gangs. Police officers being shot. "Thank God that couldn't happen here," he says.

"They're crazy over there," Julie says, peering out the front door.

"Are we eating or what?"

Julie turns, faces her daughter's eyes that are rimmed raccoon-like with black eyeliner. Combined with her artificially tanned skin, she looks like her aspirations reach no higher than being an occasional setter on a bouncy, all-girl beach volleyball team.

"Come help me heat up the tuna casserole."

"Don't you, like, just put it in the oven?"

Julie ignores the mocking tone but recognizes her weakness. She'd rather be lightly bullied by Mel than run the risk of having her only daughter share less of her messy emotions, or, God forbid, move out on her own and get into all kinds of trouble. "How's work?" she asks, pressing the buttons on the oven's digital timer.

"This guy comes in every week, never tries anything on. Like hello?" Mel's dancing around the table and spinning the cutlery.

"What's that about?"

Mel inspects her reflection in the microwave. "Work can be so boring," she whines, reaching for the oven mitts with the cat whiskers. She slips them on. Then bats her hair over her shoulders. Hisses, "*Pissu hedena sanda*!"

Another phase, another language. Julie wonders if it's Sinhalese. Something Fanny and Nirasha, Mel's newest BFFs have taught her.

"Hon," Julie holds out four plates. "Can you put these on the table?"

Mel holds up each plate and checks her reflection, before placing them on the table.

John presses the red button on the remote. Leans back in his chair. He's had enough news, enough of allegations of racism and states of emergency. All his life he's held on to one belief: there are many cultures and religions in the world but underneath it all people, everywhere, are essentially the same.

Thump. Thump.

Chris's feet, pushed out of their loosely laced runners, dangle off the couch.

"How was your day?" John asks.

"Good."

"Hey! How about a Leafs game? A week Saturday against the Pens. Malcolm gave me tickets."

"Take Uncle Mike."

"You sure?" John tells himself he should know better. Chris has always preferred the open-endedness of baseball to the swarming combat of hockey.

"Yup."

"What are you reading?" he asks, hiding disappointment with curiosity.

Chris's long thin arms hold out the cover of a paperback so his father can see it.

"What's it about?"

His son's eyes are so clear. His face so ready to receive, store and share information. John has the feeling Chris is going to explain something to him.

"It's your book."

John laughs, unable to recall anything about the book.

He watches Chris return to his reading, admires his son's ability to be so fully absorbed by a book. It's a luxury, reading. One he wishes he could afford but he never seems to have the time what with needing to keep pace with technology that's changing every season thanks to the digital revolution that's putting a finish to photo finishing. Used to be you could charge more for a one-hour turnaround; now that's standard. For anything longer, like three whole hours, you need to offer a discount. He might be his own boss but the boss of what, exactly, he wonders, and the anxiety he felt at work today seeps back into his body. If anyone knows how to set up and shoot a family portrait he does. But this afternoon, crammed into his tiny studio, there were two sisters, two husbands, and a combined brood of twelve children ranging from a colicky four-month-old to an uncommunicative teenager with shoes as massive as Chris's. Trying to arrange all these people, with whom he could barely communicate, he began to panic. Sweating profusely in front of the backdrop of the CN tower, he leaned over, asked a little girl with mistrustful eyes: *Who's your daddy?* and immediately felt like a pervert. He stood up, drenched with self-loathing. He was ashamed at his lack of charisma and his inability to relate to people who come from a world so different from the only one he knows, and disturbed, because not only do these families insist that no one smile while the pictures are taken, they're certainly not much for saying *please* or *thank you*.

Aware that his optimism for life is slipping and worried by the possibility it might never return, he rubs a pale hand along the nap of his black Levi's cords and feels the burden that comes with knowing that nothing's certain anymore. Not in this brutal economy and not with the United States riding high with a colossal, unsustainable debt. It's all about real estate. But what exactly is the value of the space he takes up? A 1,200 square foot box at the far end of a shabby strip mall full of crappy food places and carpet outlets. Not much, that's for sure. But the property managers could decide that a Second Cup or a Quiznos would make a more viable lessee than an independent photo studio and he'd be gone faster than he can get his Punjabis to say *paneer*. What then?

He stares at the blank TV screen. How the hell are they going to afford university tuition for Chris? The kid gets high marks, maybe there's a chance for scholarship money, although he'd be competing with Chinese and South Asian kids.

He chucks the remote onto the padded ottoman and reminds himself to keep at it. When you have kids you need to practise what you preach and that means trying new things (once again), like offering photocopying and fax services. What a disaster — to be interrupted for a twenty-five-cent sale.

The oven timer beeps. John listens as his daughter pleads that she needs her shots. Julie suggests Thursday. His daughter announces that they can go to Starbucks on the way — I love Sumatra! Julie warns that coffee isn't a good idea. "I'm not giving blood, I'm getting vaccinated in case I want to travel next year," Mel whines. John closes his eyes, aware that everything tires him. Mel's so demanding; Chris so secretive. They were so much easier to love before they became creatures of the outside world.

Julie, standing in front of the kitchen sink, looks out the window. It's dusk and leaves flying off the maple tree are whipping themselves into a frenzy of flight patterns. Everything feels temporary, idling between summer and winter. It's been a strange year with a long hot summer stretching full into October and the trees appear confused. Some have lost their leaves; some are still regaling in full foliage. She wishes she could get a shot on Thursday too — one that would protect her from the exhausting ravages of parental responsibility. Yes, it's normal for teenagers to be distant and detest their parents, but the look Chris gave her last week when she asked him why he came home at three in the morning is like a foreign toxin swimming in her blood. His silences are torturous. When did his thoughts become so impenetrable? How can a single look make her feel so irrelevant and stupid?

Her feet hurt. She looks down at her Diesel runners with cowboy boot detailing that Melody had declared "genius." Julie has to admit (but only to herself) that she bought them to impress her daughter and no, they aren't very comfortable. "Mel hon, can you please tell your father and brother that dinner's ready?"

"*Ka na vaa*!"

With Mel's holler still ringing in the air, everyone takes their place at the kitchen table, underneath the dusty old Tiffany lampshade.

"Lance Mackenzie is coming home next month," Julie announces.

"He's a doorknob," says Mel.

"I know you think he's odd but really he's an incredible young man. He excelled at school. Went to Centennial College and earned a communications diploma."

"What's that?" Mel asks.

"I'm not entirely sure," Julie admits. "I think it has

to do with writing and language and the web and such."

"My understanding is," says John, leaning toward the centre of the table, "it's becoming more and more valuable in business. People are forgetting the basics of writing and speaking clearly. Young kids today can look up anything on the Internet and copy facts but they can't put forth an idea, can't argue a point of view. The sad thing is — they can't think."

"Well, Lance reads a lot," suggests Julie, "and he knew he could either be a couch potato or do something. So he went to Africa to teach English as a second language."

Mel rolls her eyes. "Last time I checked people in Africa need food and water, not a foreign language."

John nods. "I won't argue with that."

Julie watches her son eating in his efficient and graceful manner. No messy prodding, mashing and sculpting like Mel. If only he'd stop working at that depressing hellhole of a restaurant.

"People are all too happy to play saviour and run off to these war-torn countries when often we can do a lot more from here. Working to coordinate supplies, drum up donations," John explains.

"Maybe, but I want to work in the third world," says Mel. "Remember the DART people who helped during the tsunami? Disaster Assistance Something Something. I want to work with them."

"They're part of the military, sweetie," says Julie.

"Oh."

"You'll have to join the forces."

"Forget it then. No way am I going to let someone tell me how to style my hair."

"Speaking of hair," says John, "Can you see what

you're eating Chris? Honestly, I don't think I've seen hair like that since *I* was seventeen."

Chris ignores his father. Waits for the *what goes around comes around* line he uses to claim knowledge or authority. It doesn't come. Instead, John stands up, excuses himself, and runs down to the basement. Half a minute later he reemerges wearing a buckskin jacket he's had forever. It has red wine stains down the front and smells of dirty socks.

"Oh please. Anything but that," Julie says, getting up to put the kettle on.

Mel's removed all the peas from her casserole and is sliding as many as possible onto the prongs of her fork. John tousles his long but very thin hair. Bursting with boldness, he picks up a spoon and starts singing into it.

"Almost cut my hair. Happened just the other day. It was getting kind of long."

Mel waves her fork back and forth like the pendulum on a wind-up metronome. She's managed twenty-three green peas, stacked in rows.

"But I didn't and I wonder why … I feel like letting my freak … flag … fly …"

"Is your father misbehaving?" Julie enquires, wondering if this demonstration of her husband's will become a memory her children store away as evidence that their parents are pathetic clowns.

"Affirmative," Mel says.

"Okay, I'm a middle-aged fool but I love that song. It's from the 70s."

"Like, we care?" says Mel.

"You should. That song was written by one of this country's greatest treasures. Neil Young."

Taking off his jacket, John sits down wondering how much longer he can pretend to know something his kids might find interesting. When will they finally shut him out? Completely.

"I thought it was David Crosby," says Julie.

And back and forth they go. *Neil. David. I'm sure it's Neil. David. It's Neil singing. No it's not.*

John stops. He wants to pound his forehead and pull out what's left of his hair. Julie tells him it doesn't really matter and deep down he knows she's right but he so very much wants *something* to matter. "Regardless, it's a brilliant expression of tormented hilarity. Impassioned irony!" he yells, hoping to sound enthusiastic. "A classic stoner declaration of the incomparable joy of remaining true to oneself."

The kettle whistles. Julie gets up to unplug it.

Chris's chair scuffs the floor. He grabs his plate, walks to the sink, turns on the tap and the garburator, and scrapes the leftovers down the noisy vortex. His father's hopeless. He loves movies with men who smoke and drink and play cards. Always says his big dream is to shoot craps in Vegas. His mother took early retirement last year because she doesn't handle stress well, so now his father insists they're watching their money. What a brilliant excuse. If his father truly wanted to go to Vegas he would. It's not another galaxy! Lightly placing his plate in the sink, Chris shuts off the water and heads upstairs to the sanctuary of his room.

"Chris, honey," Julie calls out as she puts the teapot on the table, "don't you want some dessert?" But there's no response.

In his upper bunk, three feet from the ceiling, Chris stares at the familiar patterns in the wallpaper. The antique cars make him feel like a child caged in a world of miniatures. He puts his hands on his chest. The memory of his body vibrating from his classroom exit is still inside him. He remembers Paganelli's words: *Before the story begins there has to be a separation. The hero is removed from the ordinary world of his or her life.* Now *that*, it occurs to Chris, is irony, unimpassioned. Being told exactly what to do while the teach drones on about the call to adventure. How you have to listen carefully or you miss it. *Tell me something I don't know.*

He's read the course material twice. Something is stolen and needs to be returned. Money. A ring. Three gold hairs.

It's what he wants, he knows it absolutely, instinctively. Paganelli explained that the hero is often spirited away from an attempted murder and reared by foster parents in a distant country. Well, not everything should be taken literally. Chris often looks at his parents and although he has his father's quiet reserve and his mother's close-set eyes, they are aliens to him. He has a hard time believing he comes from the same DNA — that once upon a time he came out of his mother. He feels closer to his fellow dishwashers at work. With them, everything is full of possibilities. All you have to do is reach out and grab it. Jerrick wants to open a laundromat; Bailey's going to be a teacher. Motherless, fatherless, they are reinventing themselves, guided by strong morals and the right attitude: work hard, help others, only steal what won't be missed.

Pounding of a drum. Riffs of an electric guitar. Music crashes off the walls. His father's brought out the vinyl.

He's on a nostalgic bender now. He hears his mother yell to turn it down. The screech of the guitars fills Chris with contempt for something he can't name — a kind of debilitating melancholy he has to escape. Here, and at school.

Jordan's such a dink. When Paganelli started talking about Luke Skywalker, Jordan kept poking Chris's back, shuffling a note under his arm, until he finally took it.

I've got a boner

Chris turned it over. Wrote back.

Go see princess lay ya

And slipped the paper back on Jordan's desk. Jordan pretended to be all surprised. *What's this?* he exclaimed loudly, holding up the note to show Chris's writing.

Paganelli wasted no time. Told Chris to come sit at an empty desk at the front of the class. *Take the force with you*, Jordan had whispered as Chris packed up his books.

Walking to the front of the room it occurred to him that he could continue walking — right out the door. And walking never felt so fucking good as it did at that moment. With every step he felt it — how his future is far beyond the groping ordinariness of getting off, or getting high, or getting by with as little effort as possible.

"Where do you think you're going?" Paganelli had asked.

Lockers, doors, water fountains — as he passed by, everything slowed down. Every move felt weighted with wonder until he could no longer hear, until every step he took was like a beam of sunlight shining through every dull bogus cliché about how we're supposed to live life.

He rolls over onto his side. His father's turned down the volume but it's impossible to block out his singing.

"Gonna join in a rock and roll band. Got to get back to the land and set my soul free."

II

Inside the Crock Pot, it's the calm before the storm. Winded, Chris runs in the side door. Lori and Amy are wrapping cutlery in napkins with colourful maps of the Caribbean, which will, in turn, be rolled inside plastic bibs sporting the Crock Pot slogan: *Use your forks or your fingers but leave satisfied.* The place has always had a reputation for being different, tasty, not too expensive. Used to apply to the food. Since Rick's taken over, it refers to the waitresses.

"Hi, sunshine," says Lori.

"Hi!" Chris replies, before he swings open the door to the kitchen and steps into the fluorescent industrial glare. Jerrick and Bailey are standing by the sink. Bailey's hosing down the bus boxes.

"Hey!" he blurts, unable to hide his excitement. "You're both here."

"Special night tonight," Jerrick says. "Boss man's second anniversary. I'm just hanging, staying outta trouble."

"It's you and me on tonight," says Bailey.

Chris hears Rick holler at Isabelle to come to his office. He heads to the back and changes into his Crock Pot shirt. As he washes his hands old lady Isabelle does a once around the kitchen and announces that they're closing to the public at nine-thirty. "Don't get too excited," she says, with a sarcastic look.

By seven the place is its usual simmering mishmash of disorder. Rick's in a ripe and ready mood. "Junior, move move move," he shouts as Chris clears a table at the back. "And put those fries back in the serving bin," he adds. "Fucking ass monkey," he sneers as Bailey unloads the dishwasher. "Hurry this shit up," he yells at Steve who's using every inch of the grill. "Not paying you for that," he snaps at Jerrick who's decided out of the goodness of his heart to take out the garbage. At 9:40, the sign for Private Party goes up and the door's locked. By ten, the last of the customers has left. A platter each of jerked chicken, plain rice, ribs and beef barley stew are brought out and Isabelle lines up three bottles of house red — a homebrew that Rick's brother makes.

Bailey blesses his food. Steve insists there's no deer balls in the stew. Rick tells everyone that's a bloody disappointment because deer balls are tastier than cow rumps and they're cheap — two of them under a buck! Amy announces that the toilet in the woman's washroom is plugged. Jerrick heads off to fix it.

"Okay, the most number of rattlesnakes someone's ever held by their tails, in their mouth?" Bailey asks. Everyone underestimates. Chris catches Bailey's eyes to let him know that he gets it — incredible things are possible when we're not distracted by mediocrity.

"Let's get it on," declares Rick, after Steve turns up the adult contemporary R&B mix he loves. Jerrick returns, toilet's fixed. Bridgette and Amy argue about whether or not some customer named Spunky is married. Steve advertises *he's* not, then props his mouth open with a mint-flavoured toothpick. Jerrick gets back to the business of explaining to Chris how pool forces you to respect the laws of physics regarding motion and nature. "You have to learn how to overcome chaos. Thing is, way to overcome chaos is not what everyone thinks."

"Right," Chris agrees, shaking vinegar on his fries. "Can't use too much logic."

"Yes, my man! Chaos feeds off too much thinking. You're not separate from the cue, the table, the balls. You gotta break down the line between you and every-thing else."

Chris throws his head back with a whoop of laugh-ter. He can feel his cheeks on fire. "I hear ya!" he shouts, waving a fry in the air.

Jerrick completes a schematic he's been drawing on the back of a napkin. "There," his says, passing it to Chris and Bailey. "One hundred and forty seven points. A perfect break."

Bailey stares at it awhile. "If you start with the free ball, then a black," he says slowly, marking up Jerrick's drawing, "then the reds, followed by black ... One fifty-five. That's your score."

Lori leans toward Jerrick, her piercing blue eyes dart back and forth across his face. "I think you just got snookered."

Jerrick grins.

"Wanna teach me how to put a ball in the pocket?" Lori's voice is smoky but the dimples that bookend her cheeks make her look wholesomely cheerful.

As Jerrick sits back to consider, Lori starts telling him that her roommate has a convertible they take up to Wasaga Beach. Rick interrupts, whistling at her like she's a dog trotting off in the wrong direction. "Okay little Miss Sunshine, my office," he orders.

"You can ignore that," Jerrick says.

"Shut up, toilet boy," Rick warns. He orders Isabelle

to get him another bottle, walks behind Ginelle and whispers something in her ear, then hoofs it to his office with the bottle. Ginelle follows him.

Lori stands up, winks at Chris as she wobbles slightly. Leaning across the table she throws Jerrick a pack of Crock Pot matches. "Have my people call your people."

Chris watches her move towards Rick's office, aware that it's not the wine that's given him a buzz. It's Bailey's facts, Jerrick's laws of physics and the sleazy wink Lori tossed him — all in equal part.

"Hey, where're you going?" Rick yells from his office, as Lori misses Rick's office door and heads toward the side door.

After a small struggle with the deadbolt, the door's ajar.

"See yah later, alligator," Lori calls out, stumbling over the threshold.

"Isabelle," Rick shouts.

"I couldn't live without mine even though they don't know I exist," admits Malcolm, sitting across from John, a bottle of scotch and a baggie of pot between them. "By the way, this stuff's a lot stronger than it used to be. Don't smoke it like a cigarette." He looks around. "Where's Mel?"

Julie, unloading the dishwasher, says she's out dancing with her girlfriends.

"Is she still wearing kimonos and eating with chopsticks?"

"No!" says John. "That morphed into a Russian phase."

"Very tragic time," explains Julie. "She memorized a poem by Pushkin. Something about the year that brings my death."

"Now it's all things South Asian. She irons her hair and speaks in Sinhalese."

"Still going with that French fella?"

"Yeah," says John. "*Monsieur sous chef*. Always working. I don't think they're serious but Mel's never that serious about anything."

"Not like her brother," suggests Malcolm, flipping through Chris's well-worn copy of *Heart of Darkness*. "He's probably got the head for law you know, if it interests him. Anyway, better get home. Please give my regards to the birthday boy."

After escorting Lori to her apartment, Jerrick, Bailey and Chris, loud and full of affection for each other, head off to scan the parking lot on Overlea for unlocked cars. No twisted coat hanger or broken window shit for them, and when a door opens they comb it over for the usual: coins, CDs, a bag of Licorice Nibs. Bailey is talking about the speed of light and how we're viewing the past when we look at the stars. Jerrick's whistling and drumming on the car hoods. Emboldened by this fraternity, Chris feels he can do anything.

A door opens. He stands, momentarily stunned. "Got one," he yells.

Bailey and Jerrick run over. "Alright!" Jerrick bellows.

"Huzzah," says Bailey, pulling a few folded bills out of a cup holder. "Done good, little hoody." He hands the thin wad to Chris and looks at Jerrick who's scanning the far corners of the lot.

"Fucking fuck," breathes Jerrick.

Bailey slaps Chris's back. "This way," he yells, as the bossy shape of a police car drives right at them, diagonally, across the lit pavement. Panic gives flight to their feet and they head for the ravine, racing for their lives, the cool air filling their nostrils and exploding in their lungs, every muscle in their bodies electrified with purpose.

John announces he's going to hit the hay. Julie says she's going to watch a movie.

Waiting up for the kids, thinks John. Upstairs he lies in bed excited at the idea of Chris going into law. But how many years is that? Does he have the patience or the tenacity? He's so young it's hard to imagine him out in the world. Kids grow up quicker nowadays although they don't leave home as early. The world his kids live in is tougher; things are more expensive everyone says, or maybe it's just that money's more important. Oh, who's he kidding? Everything *is* more expensive. And competitive. He can't believe he's carrying a second mortgage on the house just to finance the business. If Mitsubishi ups the service contract on the self-serve kiosks he's in deep trouble. How the hell could they ever even consider the cost of law school for Chris? Thanks to him, and his self-indulgent dream of being a great photographer, the days of each generation doing better than the next are over. When you have kids you realize the horrible consequence of being selfish. It rots you to your core. What is it Julie says? — it's in giving that we receive. Well, that would be great if they actually had something to give their kids. All the things they took for granted that their kids would have access to — good public transit, education, health care — are now in jeopardy, deteriorating, threatening to disappear. If only he had more money he'd worry less about how brutally tough the world's become. There'd be a buffer between him and his family, and the nagging depression he feels on his morning commutes as he drives his car along Danforth and all the little shops appear to be struggling to survive one more day because everyone's gone to Walmart and Costco to buy pastries, balloons, contact lenses, figurines and scanners at bargain basement prices.

John gets up, mad at himself because he can't sleep. Shouldn't have had that third scotch. Sitting on the edge of the bed he rubs his hands together, aware that these days he feels more and more like he can no longer compete. Like all he's really good for is taking passport photos and shooting the odd wedding. His movements are less coordinated, his hands ache with the seeds of arthritis, he's short-tempered when customers touch his cameras. People used to have more respect. They used to actually come into the studio and ask his advice about film speeds or camera lenses. They never used to touch his equipment so he doesn't know if his own bad behaviour is because his nature has started to sour or because he feels a greater need to protect what's his. He can't stop feeling he's only thinly sheltered from another world, one that's encroaching on his own, one that lives and breathes civil disobedience and natural disasters. One that's harsh enough to leave bodies in fields, roadsides and rivers in the aftermath of earthquakes, floods and wars. He's an Anglo-Saxon — not exactly an endangered or a tortured species, but a disposable one. He's a Gordon Lightfoot song. He's a tiny northern bobwhite singing obliviously about the days when dark verdant forests were silent and the rivers flowed clean with pure baptismal water.

How pathetic is he?

He lies back in bed and pulls the covers up around his neck.

His son will probably scowl at the idea of law. And his too impressionable daughter, three years since she quit high school. She's not going anywhere working part-time at the Gap and pretending she's Sri Lankan. At times like this when he's not sure about his business, his career, his place in the world, just thinking about Mel makes him unsure whether it's her or him who's out of touch. He resents her trials and tribulations, the capacity she has for experimentation. He knows she's only trying to find her way, although the ethnic explorations do contain a whiff of rejection.

In the kitchen, Julie pulls out the quail recipe, reads it again and checks the cupboards for rice vinegar and cornstarch. Adds star anise to her shopping list. Returning to the living room she asks herself, is she too lenient or too protective, too trusting or not enough? Is it just the nature of teenage boys, that they're vulnerable and tough, wise and stupid? That they smoke dope and play with lighters? Just because they always seem to be on the verge of danger doesn't mean they are. Chris has always been the steady one. The smart one. The one they've never needed to worry about. She drops her favourite movie into the DVD tray.

I just wanna be a good mom, a decent person, a good citizen, she hears, as she dozes off.

Chris slips in through the front door and heads upstairs. "Where've you been?" his mother's groggy voice asks.

Don't talk to me like I'm an idiot, Julia Roberts's voice demands coolly.

"I gotta go to bed, Mom," Chris says quietly.

As he lands on the top bunk, he hears his mother creaking around — she loves stories of real-life heroines who, against all odds, fight monumental crusades to defeat villainous giants. That movie, *Erin Brockovich,* she watches it at least twice a year. Always claps at the end, exclaiming, *What a story!* Why watch movies, Chris thinks, if you don't actually take them to heart and try to live by the principles that excite you?

His door opens. The sound reminds him of all the years he's spent in this room. "Tomorrow's Thursday," his mother whispers, "you have to go to school, sleep tight."

He waits for the door to close before he turns on his side and looks out the window. She would have absolutely no patience if he told her what he was, deep inside. She'd tell him his ambitions were interesting but that life's actually more ordinary than everything he's filled his head with. If he protested she'd chastise him for having a superiority complex. His parents, like most people, love rebels and whistle-blowers and freedom fighters, but only when they're neatly packaged and not living in their house. And Mel's just like them. What she really wants is to get married and do everything their parents do, only better — decorate better, eat healthier, have a more eclectic music collection. He closes his eyes, reminds himself you have to be smart to escape from the big boring lie about how you're supposed to live your life. His face relaxes into a grin. Eight! A guy once held eight rattlesnakes in his mouth.

III

The sign on the door has been pulled off leaving bits of yellowed and hardened sticky tack on the green door. A white sheet of paper is taped up with a message:

As of October 1, this clinic will be closed

"That's strange," says Julie. "This place has been here for years."

Mel stares at her mother. She looks pale and colourless under the fluorescent lights. Her mother's mouth opens and words come out: "I can't believe they don't put where they've moved to. Or the closest clinic nearby."

Mel holds her Vanilla Frappuccino tight, looks down the hallway and sighs. Her mother will need to commiserate with her father about this. They always feel mortally wounded when yet another old haunt falls off the face of the earth.

Julie insists on checking the directory by the front door. The listing for the clinic is gone with no trace or explanation. The lobby is wretchedly airless and nothing is listed for the entire second floor except a Dr. Upfield, foot specialist. Lots of signs everywhere about a Filipino social club, a number to call if you're new to Canada, free flu shots in room 108 and guitar lessons to explore your creative self.

"Let's use our heads. Let's not go and get all upset," Julie says, motioning that they should leave. "We can call Dr. Bramer's office tomorrow and see where they recommend we go."

"Yeah yeah," Mel says, looking across the street. "Can we go shopping?"

"Do you need to get a present for your brother?"

Mel looks confused.

They step into the daylight.

"Let's go in there," Julie says, pointing to a South Asian grocery across the street. "I need some star anise for the black bean sauce."

"You learn something new every day," Julie says on the way back to the car. "I had no idea it looked like that."

"You mean like a star?" asks Mel, checking her reflection in a store window. The man behind the counter must have wondered what their connection was. Especially when she said *s tu ti*. He probably thought she was adopted, which is excellent.

John, wandering through the bedroom zone at IKEA, decides on a solid pine queen-size bed from the Leksvik series. It not only has a storage box underneath, but a discreet compartment, with lid, in the headboard. He sits on the bed wondering what his son will stash in that clever little hiding place. He can't quite figure out his son's proclivities, but then he himself hadn't really experimented all that much until he was in his twenties. That's when he and a lot of guys he knew discovered *The Story of O*.

The nakedness of it had spoken to his vague sense of the delicate line between love and obedience, fear and desire, pain and pleasure. He was convinced he understood it all, although he wouldn't have been able to explain what *it* was. But he knew *it* was something primal. And truthful. Like that weekend, in his studio, back when he was in an old drafty industrial loft. He and Julie had been fantasizing about their future children with a bottle of red wine and a joint and John was staring at the water pipes that ran along the ceiling. Energized by a sudden and crazy inspiration to tie up his future wife he jumped to his feet, coaxed her out of her clothes and warmed her white skin, rubbing it delicately with patchouli oil. "You must never cross your legs," he said. "It's forbidden." He draped her in a silk scarf left over from a photo shoot for Reitmans. They swooned in unison as he called her his silky mistress and attached her left wrist to the hot water pipe with one of her socks. They laughed together as he called her his happy whore and wrapped her right wrist to the cold water pipe. "You are free to leave," he said, understatedly, barely opening his mouth.

"I'm cold," Julie murmured. He kissed the top of her pubic hair and then her soft and warm labia, aroused by its dark woody scent. He brought over a small space heater and let it blow on her, the warm air making the scarf undulate against her flesh like a gentle whip. After strapping his camera around his neck, he waltzed around her in big strides. From the dusty turntable came the sounds of a dulcimer and a duo singing about a marauder, whatever that is. With every shot John became more excited. Julie looked like a beautiful martyr in bondage, hung naked, drenched in submissiveness and candlelight. Was she made of stone or wax? His daring made him sweat. He knelt in front of her, worshipping her openness, and started shooting upwards between her legs. Then he heard an unmistakable sound. Julie crying. Quickly dropping the camera, he bolted up and hurried to untie her. She buried her runny nose in his sweater and whimpering between gasps, pounded her fists into his shoulder blades. He dragged her over onto his ratty pull-out couch, covered her with an itchy wool blanket, then took off his camera and clothes and lay beside her, vowing never again to attempt such ritualistic play.

A voice over the speaker system calls out the licence plate number of a car with its lights on.

John stands up, writes the model number on a piece of paper and heads for the customer service counter thinking nothing's more important than being a parent. Julie and I work hard. Ours is not a slave and master dynamic, errant knight and lovely maid. It's a partnership. Life's too fragile for sexual heroics. I'm frontline marketing and fifty-one percent shareholder; Julie's better with organizational issues, backroom production and operations. No couple ever gets it exactly fifty-fifty. Always best if one person has final say on how many kids and what kind of mortgage to get.

A car slows down. It's trailing his stride. Chris picks up his pace. The car does too. Fists clenched, he throws a look over his shoulder.

Shit.

"Hey, headed my way?" John shouts, eagerly. "I have

to pop into the drug store. Why don't you drive?"

"You want anything?" his father asks as Chris expertly maneuvres into the only available spot in the parking lot. "A lottery ticket? Vitamins? Maybe some condoms?"

"Are you talking to me?"

"It's your special day!" His father laughs. "Be right back."

Chris sits waiting. The feeling of being held captive is excruciating. His father means well but his attempts at bonding are embarrassing. If he wanted some condoms he'd buy some. Yeah he likes getting sucked off but without a condom. Lots of guys do and just because they do it to each other better than girls doesn't mean they're fags. Really, if you want to be anything special in this world you have to care about grander things than getting your bagpipes blown. Chris reclines the driver's seat. Closes his eyes. Even though his birthdays are often a little disastrous, his parents do try to make them special.

When he turned eight his father took him to see *Apollo 13*, explaining that when *he* was eight, JFK was President and said we *choose* to go to the moon and we *choose* to do other things not only because they are easy, but because they are hard. The world of moon missions full of crackling silence seemed outmoded to Chris, but at the end of the movie his father had cried. Chris sat watching the credits, unsure what to do.

One year, on their way to pick up a Baskin-Robbins birthday cake, he and his mother were nearly sideswiped by a car running a red light. His mother slammed on the brakes and they skidded into the middle of the intersection. After a momentary hush, other drivers began a chorus of honking. His mom kicked the gas pedal and the car rolled through the intersection. As the tires beached to a wailing stop against the curb she began sobbing uncontrollably — her nose and eyes a bright, sniffly red. Chris told her not to cry. "But it's your birthday," she choked.

The passenger door opens. Chris sits up. His father falls into his seat all excited. "Look what I found," he shouts, holding up a DVD with a special discount sticker. "Apollo 13!"

IV

"What is it you want to be then?" his mother asks, hoping they might finally be able to pin down which universities he should apply to.

"Myself."

"You know what I mean. A career. We all need to make a living."

"I don't want to make a living."

"Then what do you want to do?"

"Be challenged. Know things."

"What things?" asks his father, trying to sound sympathetic.

Chris has no patience for this. His mother may have taken early retirement but she still has a primary school teacher's desire for all things to be easily explained. For the circle of life to revolve with nothing more complex than primary colours and twenty-six letters keeping the big wheels turning. And his father isn't much better. He's always been so afraid. Afraid of strangers. Afraid of the world. "Look, I'm just going for a walk," Chris says. "Going to pick up my paycheque. I won't be long."

The elm trees hiss in the wind, the leaves skittish and blackened. The air is cooling and carved pumpkins, some happy some sad, are beginning to appear in windows. Chris walks fast, propelled by a sense of his own destiny. His parents went on and on about his new bed but it's a little late. Another ten months he'll be long gone. Somewhere. Living. Exploring. Hitching, hiking, squatting.

Near the intersection where the restaurant is, Jerrick and Bailey are standing at the side of the convenience store. Chris detours toward them and notices Jerrick bouncing back and forth, on his toes, punching the air, his hands wrapped in gauze. His heart starts to race with his legs. He trips over a pop can and picks up speed to keep his balance. "What's up?" he asks as he knocks into Jerrick.

"Wazzup is bad," says Bailey. Seems last night there'd been a grease fire on one of the grills. No one reacted except Jerrick who doused it with baking soda and threw pot lids on the grill. He put it out but burned his hands something bad. Tonight, he'd come in and Rick told him to get lost.

"Asshole wouldn't have a restaurant if it weren't for me," says Jerrick, kicking a garbage can. "Bastard calls me the dish pig. Almost two years I've been cleaning his grease trap, pulling intestines out of his prawns and that fucker fires me because I burn myself saving his ass." His eyes are wide and wet. He keeps hopping back and forth on his toes. "I can still do something. Fucking fucker owes me money and he won't give it to me. The bastard knows I'm not legal."

"Have to do something," says Bailey.

"What are you gonna do?" asks Chris.

Jerrick kicks the side of the building.

They stand silent for a while, except for the sounds of Jerrick pacing and Bailey inhaling a smoke. "Guys." Chris shuffles his feet. "Just stay here. I gotta go pick something up. Don't go anywhere."

"Got nowhere to go," Jerrick says as Chris stuffs his hands in his pockets and dashes off.

Uncle Mike arrives carrying a six-pack and a small present wrapped in paper with brightly coloured balloons. "Smells good in here! Where's the birthday boy?" he calls out.

Julie wipes her hands on a tea towel. "He's just a little late. Went to get his paycheque."

"Hey Mel," Uncle Mike says, "you're looking lovely."

Mel's been experimenting with her tanning lotion, applying it with greater concentration and her skin is acquiring a more natural, dark glow. With her new brown contact lenses the overall effect could be described as saffron and ecru. She's relaxed and feeling good in her new jeans and shirt that she got at Mendocino — a sheer cotton pullover with loose sleeves and a tiny brocaded pattern up the front. Her father thought it was a hippie shirt and told her so, along with his *what goes around comes around*.

Uncle Mike opens himself a beer and begins regaling everyone with a story about this guy who for years dressed up as a firefighter, showed up at all the big fires and train wrecks. "Apparently the guy was a big hero during the Mississauga train derailment. But the guy could never go legit because he had a record from way back, possession for purposes of trafficking." Julie, rubbing moisturizer into her hands, says, "How unfair is that? Especially considering our drug dealer's a lawyer."

Uncle Mike laughs, grabs another beer. "So Chris is seventeen, eh? Let's hope there're no catastrophes this year. Remember the year he was born? Gretzky was traded to LA."

"If I remember correctly," says John, "a guy named Bush was President, there was a war in Iraq and record deficits were being racked up in the US. Need we say more?"

Chris peers through the little round window on the door to the kitchen. That's prize, he thinks — Rick's got Isabelle cleaning off the grill. The door to the boss's office is open. Chris walks in, breathes the familiar odour of stale smoke and musty carpet. "Chris, my boy!" Rick butts out his cigarette, slides around his desk and leans on its edge. "I need you to work a bit tonight."

"Why? Don't Bailey and Jerrick have things covered?"

Rick shakes his head. "Jerrick got himself into a little trouble last night and Bailey's taken off so I need you to help out." He sucks on his cheeks, flexes them until they knead themselves into the shape of a lopsided smirk. He pushes himself away from his desk and approaches. Rick's hairy, monkeyish body disgusts Chris. His warm thick paws land on Chris's shoulders and turn him around until they're both facing into the restaurant. Talking slow and steady, Rick outlines the plan. His hot breath, menacing and barbaric, smells of garlic and whiskey: "Go on out, do a shift ... then come on in here. I've got your cheque and for all your trouble we'll have a little celebration. Just for you. Check those girls out ... tell me which one you like. Jenny's on tonight. And Bridgette. Both great. Nothing like it, your choice Chris."

Chris swallows. His head is spinning, his body throbbing. To him they look like Barbie dolls, battle-worn and bruised, their heads ready to be pulled off. They've spent too much time answering to a crass prick who treats them like dirt. Jerrick's never going to get paid, even if Rick hires him back next week. He takes two deep breaths, clenches his fists, turns around. "Thanks boss. I'll go take care of things."

Isabelle is no longer in the kitchen. Must have stepped out back, probably having a smoke. The door is propped open and a breeze billows in. He looks back through the restaurant. Steve's stretched over the bar looking for something, probably Bridgette.

Chris walks into the storage room and uses a stool to reach the lighter fluid. Back in the kitchen he opens the cap. His thumping heart makes his body vibrate. Holding the bottle up like an elixir, he points it at the grill and squirts it across the flatness of the stainless steel. Breathing hard, he digs in his pocket for his Zippo lighter — the one with the Playboy bunny engraved in the brushed chrome finish that his parents gave him a year ago for his sixteenth birthday. The one he was playing with when the bathroom caught on fire.

After checking on the sauce, Julie calls the restaurant but no one answers. She decides not to leave a message. John suggests he could head out in the car and try to find him. He can't be that far away. "But," he thinks aloud, "the kid likes his freedom. Might get upset if it seems like we're out driving the streets looking for him."

"You're right," Julie says, looking at the two joints she taped (using the removable stuff), on the sappy card John picked out at Shoppers. "Maybe he's just hanging out at work for a bit. Maybe they're having a cake for him."

Chris strokes the hinge of the lid before flipping it open, then rubs the flint wheel with his thumb. Panic opens up loud and certain like a mouth hungrily calling out *"now, now."* He flicks the wheel hard before he tosses the lighter onto the grill. Flames roar, hot and yellow, faster than the speed of light. All is luminous.

UNDERWRITING LOSS

LEE KIM HAD operated the convenience store for twenty-seven years. In all that time he only pulled out his baseball bat five times. A sixth time probably would have saved his life and that's the irony, people said. Someone asked, "Was that irony or tragedy or plain old bad luck?"

"I can't believe there isn't people that seen it or know more than what they're saying," said local resident Danny O'Neill into the big, black microphone held in his face by a woman from the news. "He was good to the community. Whatever it was, he didn't deserve it."

"I know someone knows something," said a man who didn't want to give his name but had come by to place a sunflower near the rusty, padlocked security grate in front of the store. Flowers kept piling up. Some in glass jars with water. Some freshly bound in paper wrapping. All of it fading and stiffening in the summer sun.

Leslie stood up, took off her headset, leaned over the top of the cubicle divider and searched the top of Ida's head for signs of a natural scalp. Ida's copper-coloured hairpiece was called Electra and it was made of real hair. It had cost a fortune but Ida said it was money well spent because it saved her time to do other things, like read the city's four newspapers and watch *Entertainment Daily*. Today Electra appeared a little off-centre, like it too was suffering some of Ida's excitement.

"Don't stare at me like that," Ida scoffed. "I didn't do nothing. I just share good news. This one's number forty-six. Eight more than last year." It was coffee break time and she was soaking up every sketchy detail. "Says here he was getting ready to retire. He was gonna sell the store. Can you believe that? That's bad timing."

Not for a second does Ida believe statistics cited by the police to prove the city's safer than it has been in forty years. Every workday morning she steps off a sleek elevator, waves at the company security camera and announces the date and the city's year-to-date homicide tally.

Leslie peered over her friend's shoulder.

"If we could all just share our toutons a little more, wouldn't be so much woe and heartache." Ida's from Newfoundland and resents having to lock doors and stand in line to pay for things.

"Oh my God. I knew that guy."

Ida gasped. "Holy smokes." Her voice crackled from the deep pockets of menopause, cigarettes, alcohol and capped teeth. "You knew him?"

Leslie peered closer. "Yeah, I lived around there years ago."

"You knew him. Holy cripes."

"Well I didn't *know* him."

Ida pointed a finger at Leslie. "Too close for comfort. Way too close. What I wanna know is why'd they have to stab him five times? Once or twice would have done it." Ida read slowly, her index finger underscoring each word: "According to police reports, Kim was stabbed in the abdomen five times."

"Oh my God," Leslie said as she leaned against the cubicle wall, her shoulder blade pressing into a clipping about a grandmother who was hanged on her clothesline by a gang of girls. The floor beneath her seemed to move, almost imperceptibly, as though she was in a revolving restaurant. "Why would someone do that?"

"You don't wanna know," Ida cautioned as she closed and folded the paper. She leaned back and raised an eyebrow. "You look like a movie star today."

Ida was obsessed with the grisly turns of life, but she was a cheerleader at heart and thrilled that Leslie was having an affair. At least that's what Leslie had called it, one day, sitting in the noisy food court eating combo number three from a Styrofoam container.

"Cripes Les, you been holding out on me," Ida had said, pushing a cinnamon bun into her mouth. "Who's the lucky fella?"

"Brian McKinnon, Business Valuation, nineteenth floor."

Ida'd whistled through the puffy dough, her eyes growing large like bingo balls. "Holy annuities. A married actuary."

Leslie sat in her living room and watched a TV show about an unsolved crime, followed by a TV show about an unsolved crime. Then the news. During the segment about Lee Kim's murder the reporter talked endlessly about everything the police didn't know, then posed questions to people on the street. Questions about who and why, questions no one could possibly answer — at least not to a big black microphone held by a woman from the news. Leslie remembered the cautious way Lee Kim would eye the door and the round convex mirror that hung from the ceiling, then smile at her. She pressed her fingers into her stomach and tried to imagine exactly what kind of pain one feels — sharp or broad, numbing or unbearable — each time a knife enters your flesh.

The next morning, as she hunted through her drawer for a clean pair of nylons, she wished it was Friday. However odd or sad it might seem to others, Friday nights at the bar with Ida were the anchor to her week. She loves arguing with people she barely knows about how swimming in a lake is better than the ocean, a vasectomy is better than getting one's tubes tied, and that it would take more than money for her to sleep with our current Prime Minister, or his wife for that matter. I think I'm getting in touch with my baser self she tells Ida, who tells her it's about time.

Ida lives with her brother Ralph — a Presbyterian minister with big bushy red sideburns and a voice to match who preaches pragmatic messages of tolerance and charity. Ralph writes his sermons on Friday afternoons then comes home to recite them from his third floor study. Ida finds the echoing homilies about trusting in the guidance of the Holy Spirit a little too strong for the end of a workweek. If I hear it before Sunday it feels like cheating ... like I have insider information, she says. Anyway, there's no real honesty in reciting *Forgive us our trespasses,* if you don't get out into the world now and again and see what a trespass looks like — up close.

So every Friday they meet at the bar, where sloth, lust and pride sit happily on the bar stools and wooden chairs, nicely lubricated, arguing, pontificating and sharing jokes. Until around midnight. After that the scales start to tip from the power and the glory of human connectedness to the neediness of gluttony, anger and greed. The rule was they leave at three beers or midnight. Whichever came first. A rule they usually forgot somewhere between the second and third round.

As Leslie walked to work she wondered why she and Henry, in their twelve years together, never went out much and almost never to bars. Henry was lovely but their life had been claustrophobic; he always needed to know exactly where she was even though he himself was often not fully present. He was overly precise, hated whimsy or silliness and wouldn't ride in cabs past nine at night for fear a previous customer might have thrown up.

Henry would never understand why Lee Kim's murder sparked a sense of loss in her — not that she understood either, exactly. But she respected her feelings. If Henry were still around he would insist she was being stupid and sentimental, appropriating others' misery in order to find meaning in her own life. His own heavy, smouldering moods always made him want to protect her or rein her in. Especially after the miscarriages.

After the first one, Leslie had been home, watching *Oprah*. The guest was a woman who had been born with a heart defect into desperate poverty. She never knew her father and her mother died of an overdose. The girl was put in foster homes where she was abused. She ran away and lived on the streets while she put herself through high school working at minimum wage jobs at night. No one knew she was homeless. After earning a doctorate in kinesiology, she developed a technique called *Bendomonics*. It was simple yet sophisticated and used only one's own body weight to strengthen and tone, with emphasis on balance and alignment. In less than two years she'd become the most sought-after trainer on the planet. Even Gwyneth Paltrow said *Bendomonics* was better than Pilates. When Leslie shared the story with Henry, he said it was all scripted bullshit. That none of it was real.

"How do you know?" she asked.

"Oh please," said Henry, whose heart did not beat for anything that smelled even slightly of fairytale or miracle. He had little use for books, gym memberships or churches. His was a pragmatic universe of tempered limestone and poured concrete. He worked for the transportation ministry. Every day he was responsible for dispatching crews to go out into the city and fix fences. Wooden fences, chain-link fences, aluminum fences — fences that kept people from wandering out on to busy highways or stumbling across train tracks, or that prevented children from falling through openings and down hillsides and tumbling into swimming pools and drowning.

After the second miscarriage, a social worker at the hospital gave them a brochure titled *Healing with the Truth*. Truth was Leslie had an incompetent cervix, which meant it was adept at letting fetuses slide out. "Should you wish to attempt again," the social worker said, "you're going to need complete lack of physical activity."

After the third one, a counsellor explained that she'd need to deal with her feelings of guilt and that she and

Henry both needed to talk to other people — separately. "You're like two people who have been blinded at the same time — trying to teach each other Braille. Reach out to others." Her name was Helen. She reached out and took their hands in hers and clasped them together. Leaning forward she whispered, "Eventually you will learn acceptance and your marriage will reach a new level of intimacy." As Helen let go, Leslie could feel Henry's eyes admiring her professional empathy.

"I didn't like Helen," Leslie said in the car heading home.

"Why?"

"She talks like she knows everything. Like she can just log onto our lives, measure a few heartaches and predict our future."

Henry was silent.

"Do you have anything to say?" Leslie asked.

"No."

"No?"

"I don't care," said Henry angrily.

Leslie looked at Henry, his hands gripping the steering wheel, but the look bounced back. His mouth and lips were tight and turned inward. He had that white-collar criminal look. Leslie knew there was nothing more to say. Once someone like Henry stops caring there's a little pause; it's hate lining up and stamping its feet, getting ready to march in and take over.

Leslie waited for Brian, as she did every Thursday night. Every Thursday night he asks her to close her blinds, then presents her with a Leonard Cohen CD. They sip wine and talk about music and work, eventually making love on the couch or the floor, but never in the bedroom. He has supplied her with the entire collection, chronologically, so they are now recycling back through, but listening to the lyrics this time.

Brian McKinnon, star of the actuarial pool, is known for his energy and his ability to remember names. Leslie, star of the customer care centre, is known for her ability to handle customer complaints with just the right mix of patience and logic. In fact, it earned her a Personal Achiever Award last year and that's how they met. As an executive sponsor of the employee awards program, Brian had presented her with her certificate.

The doorbell chimed.

"You won't believe what happened," Brian said, closing the door behind him.

"Ask me what happened," he begged, lifting Leslie off the ground and twirling her.

"Leonard Cohen has a new CD?"

"I got a $30,000 bonus," Brian said, as he returned Leslie to the ground.

"I think we should offer policies for unborn babies," she suggested, later. They were sitting on her couch — or rather he was sitting on it with Leslie straddling him — discussing a contest run by the marketing department called *back-of-the-napkin*. Employees were to suggest new product ideas and if marketing deemed yours worthy of consideration, you won $1000.

"You mean life insurance for fetuses?"

"Yes," Leslie said.

Brian opened his eyes. "Fetuses aren't individuals with determinant yields. How would we measure risk for little Leslie junior?"

"If people like the idea and can afford it, they'll buy it."

Brian laughed. "As an organization, we strive for profitability and security. The caveat is that our products need to be vetted in accordance to their strength to mitigate loss."

Leonard was in the background but couldn't be ignored.

And you think maybe you'll trust him
For he's touched your perfect body with his mind.

"Can't you analytical wizards just come up with a formula for it?"

"I don't think we want to encourage a market segment of lowlifes who take out coverage, get knocked-up, then self-abort to cash in."

There are heroes in the seaweed
There are children in the morning

"This is stupid," Leslie said.

"What is?"

"Everything," she said. Knowing she meant the way they pretend to need each other. Brian telling her he was desperate to touch her; Leslie fucking him like there was no tomorrow and telling him, when it was her turn to provide an amorous declaration, that she loved his sense of humour. He didn't have a sense of humour. She hated the fact that Brian felt free to talk about un-born children he had no interest in fathering. She missed Henry. He may have been frustratingly rigid but he wasn't vain and self-satisfied. And he didn't need music to stir up emotions. Even pretend ones.

"You should go home," she told him. After an hour of pleading and arguing, Brian left, telling her she'd never find another man so in love with her. She slumped to the floor, worn out. She missed being someone's wife. Being accused of spending too much money, then being warned not to eat the jalapeños. Having someone confident enough to be angry at you, and then protect you, all in one habitual minute.

The next evening, after she washed the wine glasses and threw out the Leonard Cohen CDs, she checked her email. There was a message from Brian asking if he could come over. She deleted it and changed her clothes, thinking about how great having a beer at the bar with Ida was going to be.

As she approached the bar she saw something taped to the windows — a notice, official and uninviting. *Thank you to all our customers ... is now closed.* She frowned, pulled on the brass door handle. It moved only a sliver before the metal of the deadbolt clanked. She froze, confused. A man walked by and looked at her.

"It's closed."

"Why?"

"Don't quote me," he said, "I heard it's going to be a Tim Hortons."

"A what?"

"I heard they secured a long-term lease." He glanced at a notice. "Franchises are safer. Insurance rates are cheaper, mitigating risks, that sort of thing."

"Thanks. I won't quote you."

"Ida," Leslie yelled, spotting her comrade trundling up the street. "They've closed the Winchester."

"What?" Ida shouted.

"It's closed. Closed up."

"Why?"

"It's going to be a Tim Hortons."

"Holy cripes. That's sacrilegious. This drinking hole is older than me."

The two of them stood staring at the notice taped on the door, both expecting it to change into something else. A notice about a film shoot, or a passing grade from the city food inspector, or a failing grade.

Ida put an arm around her. "Let me buy you a coffee."

"Sometimes we have to move on," Ida said, emptying a third creamer into her coffee. "Things change. Always have. Always will."

"Well there's change and there's wrong," said Leslie, looking out the window at the Winchester.

"Les, it might not be the best time to tell you this but I'm no good at keeping secrets."

Leslie bit into a double chocolate. It was doughy and tasteless.

"Ralph is moving back to the Rock. I think I'm gonna go with him." Leslie stopped chewing.

"It won't be till next year. But I can retire in Newfoundland. If I stay here I'll need to work another five years."

Leslie's eyes and nose filled up at exactly the same time. She breathed in deeply, hoping it would subside. "Sorry," she said.

Ida pulled out a small package of tissues and handed one to Leslie. "Ralph's church has been sold to a developer. They're gonna make lofts out of it. It's what they're doing with a lot of the smaller churches."

Leslie chucked the rest of her donut into the paper bag. "That's awful," she managed. A small spittle of brown dough flew out of her mouth and attached itself to Ida's coffee mug. A fluorescent bulb overhead hummed loudly, then flickered and adjusted itself to a half-glow.

"I'm gonna miss you terrible," Ida said. "But there's phone. And email."

"Who wants to live in a church?"

"People who never go to one," said Ida.

Early Monday the news is announced. During the afternoon, awareness events are held and information packages distributed. Relocation options are generous but participation is, of course, at the discretion of each employee. The key message is: *Due to redundancies created by a recent executive oversight it is time to leverage advantages that require the rationalization of resources. We are proud to announce that as part of the company's moving forward initiatives, Client Services will be moving to Calgary.*

"Guess your timing couldn't be better," Leslie said.

Ida looked at her. "You okay, honey?"

"Be back in a minute."

On the nineteenth floor, Leslie walked down the hall and into Brian's office.

"Did you know about this?" she asked, holding up the bulletin.

No, not really, and why? he asked. Eventually he admitted he did, but only theoretically. Then he told her that in actual fact, it would probably be a really good way for her to start afresh. She tossed the package at his head. "I'd rather be a drunk in a midnight choir."

Outside the convenience store a man with holes in his sweater was sitting on the edge of the sidewalk feeding a newspaper through the sewer grate. Leslie crossed the street and placed twenty-seven red roses next to an empty beer bottle with a dandelion in it. A few men were standing around smoking and keeping an eye on the woman from the news who was wondering if she had enough footage.

"Excuse me, miss. I see you've brought a generous bouquet. I'm with City News. We're here to film a segment about the reward the police are offering for information regarding the brutal, senseless murder of Kim Lee."

"Lee Kim?" Leslie asked.

"Yes. I'd like to ask a couple of questions. Did you know Lee Kim?"

"I didn't know him well," she said, as a streetcar rattled by drowning out her words.

"What brought you here today?"

"I just wanted to drop off some flowers. Out of respect." She looked at the reporter who smiled and nodded.

Leslie's nylons were an abomination in the hot afternoon sun. It was the third day in a row she had worn the same clothes. Another small act of insubordination. A drop of sweat fell between her breasts.

"Do you think the thousand dollar reward will help find his killer?"

"I wouldn't know."

"This is the city's forty-sixth murder victim this year. Do you think the police should be doing more?"

"I have no idea. What *are* they doing?"

The reporter held steady. "What do you remember about the victim, Lee Kim?"

"I told you I didn't know him. I just came to the store sometimes. Or used to. I used to live nearby."

"Do you feel safe in this neighbourhood?"

"I'm here, aren't I?"

The woman dropped the microphone. "Great. Can we get a shot of you placing those beautiful roses you brought in front of the store?"

Overcome by a pungent smell that was either the flowers in the sun, or the newswoman, or her, Leslie moved back, and stepped off the sidewalk. A car screeched and honked. She dashed out of the way and hurried to the other side of the street.

Wedged between an overflowing garbage container and a small maple tree, an assemblage of used goods was being merchandised: clothes, kitchen stuff, videos, books. Leslie stopped to have a look. "Hey lady, what you need?" said a woman who sauntered over, sizing her up through colourful thick plastic glasses. "I got some nice clothes. You a size six?" She bit into an apple, chewed, shot Leslie a piercing look.

"This book and a couple of cigarettes?"

The woman scowled.

"And a lighter. How much?"

The woman whistled through her teeth. "That's a tall order. Jussa minute." She shuffled over to a couple of men sitting on a brick ledge. One of them was painting a bicycle. A short discussion took place and the woman came back to settle. Twenty dollars later, Leslie walked away with two cigarettes, a matchbook with two matches, and *The Acquisitors*, by Peter C. Newman.

She headed across the grass to an empty bench. A few people, with bags on their shoulders walked by, no doubt heading home from the downtown core. She sat on the bench, lit a cigarette and inhaled deeply. It was stronger than Ida's brand. She leaned back. A helicopter noisily whirled overhead in the blue sky, fading from sight as quickly as it appeared. Probably heading for a hospital, thought Leslie. Number forty-seven?

She rubbed the cover of her new book, wondered why the company would bother moving her. Lots of people could do her job. Must be cheaper in the long run for them to relocate staff. She thought about Henry and wondered if he missed her; she thought of Ida and already missed her.

As she finished the cigarette she noticed a man in the distance swinging his arm as if conducting an orchestra in slow motion. He was wearing a green velvet jumpsuit. His shoulders and back had sharp angular edges. He was walking sideways smiling into the sky and had a string coming out of his hand, like a marionette. Leslie walked over.

"I couldn't see it," she said when the man turned and grinned.

"You want to try it?" he said.

"No."

"It's easy."

She stood there awhile, trying to figure out if this guy was trouble. He looked like a tiny James Brown.

"Come on. I'll teach you." He handed her the string.

She was surprised at the strength required to hold it. The kite was small and dark against the sky. "How high is it?" Leslie asked.

"Two hundred. Light years," he said, laughing. "Don't stand too still. Just keep movin' it gently … back and forth. And let the string out slowly."

"It really pulls," Leslie said.

"Yeah, that's it. Just keep movin' a bit. Watch out for the landmines," he said pointing to a fresh mound of dog excrement.

"You got it now. I'll be right back."

And with that he skipped over to a couple in the distance who were sitting cross-legged, looking into a plastic cup. Back up in the blue sky, thin clouds were coming in from the north. A few seagulls were catching the breeze below the kite.

There was a rhythm to it. Mesmerizing and freeing. Like an exquisite slow dance with a beautiful stranger. Leslie let the kite out a little more.

A few minutes later, a smell entered the park. It was dire, tinged with mischief; something was burning. Made you want to breathe deeply but then it cauterized your lungs with a crispy stench. Bits of black paper started happily falling out of the sky. Big pieces. Little pieces. Where were they coming from? She looked around. It was impossible to see the source. A film of smoke continued to sail into the park. A fire truck's siren, then another, pierced through the air seeming to contain all the fear and uncertainty of the city. She looked around but Tiny James Brown and the cross-legged couple had disappeared.

She wondered if she should start to wind up the string. How do you ensure a smooth landing? Didn't every kite eventually crash? She imagined it nose-diving, no doubt just as Tiny James Brown bounded back into the park. Where was he? More bits of paper floated down. A breeze pushed on her back. The sirens wound to a sudden stop, close but not in sight. She scanned the horizon again. No sign of Tiny James Brown. Across the street the news crew had gone and so had everyone else, leaving just the flowers bunched up along the storefront.

She let the string out a little more, counted to forty-six and released. The kite kept moving, pulling itself up, willfully, among the blackened smoke and bits of paper. Higher and higher it fluttered like a murdered man's soul giving one last wave goodbye.

THE DRY WELL

THE FIRST TWO months would be the hardest. That's what everyone said. Even friends who'd never bought a house. Hopefully they were right because as soon as Heather and Keith took possession, the dark two-storey wasted no time revealing its deficiencies: roof leaks, there's fleas in the floorboards, roaches in the pipes, fireplace has no chimney, dishwasher's broken, and noise travels effortlessly through the single plaster common wall that separates them from their semi-detached neighbours.

"Classic first-home tragedies," Keith says in response to it all, scratching his legs. Heather — the one who advocated for home ownership, then pushed for this one because it was the ugliest house on the street and therefore a good investment — has taken to releasing loud screams. And being emotionally enthusiastic about doing laundry in the middle of the night while watching home reno shows. "Yes!" she shouts, when a voice-over asks: *Isn't it time you had the beautiful bathroom you deserve?*

Weekends begin with a list of chores. On their third weekend, as Keith sprayed the baseboards with an insect growth regulator, Heather tried to bleach the stains in the toilet bowl, then scoured the backyard for the best compost location. The thought of worms and ants and bacteria moving and decomposing through clods of earth and waste so reminded her of her own mortality, she looked down at her hands and touched them. They appeared small and needy and in that moment she decided they needed to celebrate.

"We own a house, " she announced. "Let's have a dinner party."

The following Saturday she drove around displaying good posture, exceptional driving skills and a love of attending to errands. Everything — from the whiter than white of the dry cleaners, to the clanking cacophony of bottles at the liquor store, to the sanguine thick meat at the butcher's — seemed like a reward. She owned a home and someday she was going to have a beautiful bathroom. As she breezed by others in the shops, she played it all with gusto — *throw in the gizzards too they'll be good for the composter!* Her red lipstick glistened. Her curvaceous body appeared to want to pour out of her clothes. For fun sassy reasons. Good times.

Searching for an extension cord at the Depot, she spotted a display of doormats. There were two: *Go Away* in bold red letters; *Welcome* in a black cursive font. She contemplated her choices. *Go Away* was rather impertinent considering they were still getting used to the sounds and smells of the place, still pretending it had been a good idea to skip the home inspection. But *Welcome* was too corny, like rice pudding or light switch plates with windmills and tulips.

"Turn it over." A voice called out.

She did.

One side said *Go Away;* the other *Welcome* — a

double-sided compromise. She couldn't resist.

Heather jostled her shopping cart to a checkout and wondered how her strikingly handsome, silver-haired husband was doing. Over the rattling caster wheels she pulled out her cell and called him. He was twelve years older than she was, with a sketchy work history and no savings, but he'd finally landed a contract with a company whose rules of conformity suited him: dogs, music and pool tables are encouraged in the workplace and the bosses understand that the tattoo on his forearm — Ethel Merman in *Annie Get Your Gun* — denotes a permanent state of mind. He's gorgeous and fun. And he's kind. And even though they've only been together two years, Heather can't imagine life without him.

"I'm sorry." Keith sounded frustrated. "I have to work late."

"Don't worry, my love. Just do me a favour. At lunchtime, can you pick up a key lime flan from that place on King Street?"

"Will do."

"Great. Get home as soon as you can. I can hardly wait to see you. I love you."

"Cash or charge?"

Heather handed her credit card to the cashier. Becky was written in black marker on her orange apron.

"Sixty-one twenty-nine."

"Are you sure? That's too much."

"Sign here," said Becky. "We have a six-month no-pay credit card," she added, handing Heather an application form. "Customer care is at the other entrance."

"I wouldn't worry too much about the leak in the roof," Allison said.

"Get it fixed once it warms up," said Bill, as the front door slammed and Keith rushed in with a swirl of cool air and an apology for being late.

"Hey strangers," he said, circulating the room with hugs.

"Missed you," Heather whispered into his ear. "I put your dinner on the counter."

Keith headed to the kitchen and popped his plate into the microwave, thinking it's nice to come home, to be home, to have a home. The place is warm, perfumed with butter and herbs and the scent of fresh flowers. And a faint whiff of Minwax cleaner.

Beep. He opened the microwave and plate in hand, glided out of the kitchen.

"It's a big conspiracy," Heather declared. "Once upon a time knob and tube was state of the art. Why do we have to make it the enemy?"

"It's not like lead pipes that can give you cancer," Allison insisted. "But it is dangerous. That's why you can't get insurance."

"You need a lawyer," said Bill.

"My brother had urea formaldehyde. That's something to worry about."

"And termites."

"Oh, listen to us!" Allison punched Bill's arm. "Don't listen to us. We don't own a house. We have a kid. We can't afford it."

Keith sat down, admired his wife. She was stunning, as always. As a piece of chicken entered his mouth, a perilous shriek escaped her mouth.

"What is it?" yelled Allison.

Heather, stiff and rigid, pointed to the floor behind Bill. "Mouse. There's a mouse."

Keith grabbed the salt shaker and hurled it full-force. The tiny rodent, darting along the baseboard, just narrowly escaped the trajectory of the wooden missile. A couple of inches of thin tail graced the floor as it took shelter under a bookshelf.

"Sabrina's not doing her job," commented Bill.

Keith's eyes narrowed. He raced upstairs and returned holding the white longhaired feline, her legs dangling like fur-covered wind chimes. "Okay killer, do your stuff. Remember, keep it clean." He lowered her to the floor. "Pressure constantly, connect, make it count." The cat rolled over and scratched herself. Fending off fleas must have left her worn out and disillusioned, Keith thought.

Heather stood, her hands gripping the table. "I can't handle mice. It's the *one thing* I really can't handle."

"It's rats you need to worry about," said Allison.

"Come on, champ," Keith coaxed, and eventually Sabrina rose to the task, darting and batting at the hole between the slope in the floor and the baseboard where the mouse had disappeared.

"I'll put a fiver on Sabrina," said Bill, getting up for a closer look.

"You ever seen a kitty with such a powerful left hook?" Keith's nerves were energized. Compared to this, dessert won't even matter. "Hold on to your hats," he said as he excused himself, hoping Bill and Allison would keep reassuring Heather that a mouse is only a mouse.

"What's this?" Allison asked excitedly, when Keith returned to the dining room holding a tray above his head.

"Yours to pick. We've got Kinder Eggs and gummy snakes and worms."

Heather closed her eyes. He forgot dessert. The only thing she asked him to do and he couldn't even remember. She prepared to announce that she is going to have an aneurism. Or maybe a massive heart attack. Right in the middle of this horrible shitbox.

"Bill, leave the cat and mouse alone," Allison said. "Come have a gummy," she urged, patting the chair next to her.

Bill and Allison left, insisting everything was fabulous, superb and great. Heather, moving from chair to chair, consumed whatever wine was left in the glasses before moving on to the dregs in the bottles. She and Keith debriefed. There was Allison's infatuation with the Dalai Lama and Bill's hair loss, but no matter how Keith tried to amuse her, Heather was still mad that he'd forgotten dessert. Keith tried to make up for it by washing the dishes.

"People don't really eat dessert any more. Everything was perfect," he insisted, changing the water in the sink. Should have done the glasses first.

"It was not," Heather argued.

"Was too."

"Was not."

"Okay you're right," Keith said. "It was disastrous."

"Thank you."

"You're welcome. Sorry about the dessert. I need bigger post-it-notes."

The house creaked around them. Heather, drunk and

exhausted, leaned into her tall paragon of male beauty. He smelled like the season: cedar branches and Woolite. She stared up, amazed at how gorgeous the view is from beneath his nostrils. "Will the mouse be back?" she asked. Keith didn't answer. He wanted his other wife back. The one who can take charge and isn't scared.

"Hold me," Heather moaned. She put her arms around his waist, melted into him and hoped her lovey-dovey act wasn't too suffocating.

Keith rinsed the glasses, remembering he never wanted to buy a house. Too much work and worry.

"Kiss me," Heather said, wondering when she was going to officially explode from so many gummies.

Keith turned around. Let the sudsy water from the sink run down his arms onto the floor.

"Fuck me," Heather said.

Keith slid his hands into his wife's and led her in a waltz across the kitchen. There was a bad smell. "Yuck. How can you love me?" Heather moaned. Broccoli. Always gives her egg farts.

Keith let go, took two steps back, fell to one knee. His arms swung wide as he looked into his wife's eyes. They are stage lights, baiting and illuminating. In his larger-than-life, musical theatre baritone he belted it: *"It's bet-ter than be-ing a-loooooooooone."*

Sabrina ambled in. Dropped an almost dead mouse at Heather's feet.

They got a little smarter after the first month and decided to keep a bucket under the leak in the bedroom. On weekends they spray the baseboards and change the cheese in the traps behind the appliances and under the kitchen sink. "I think we're getting somewhere," Keith says. Heather isn't as sure but is still practicing highly inflamed exuberance: "We can get a heated towel rack!"

One morning, week five, her sneezing and sniffling woke her. Allergies she thought, rolling over to sleep a bit longer. The thought startled her. She didn't suffer from allergies. And something stank.

She reached for her housecoat from the back of the door and creaked down the stairs. The smell was stronger on the main floor where she grabbed a flashlight from the kitchen drawer. She pressed the sticky pushbutton switch for the lightbulb above the landing. Five steps down she noticed it.

"Fuck," she said, to the pool of water. "Fuck."

She sat on the cold step and shone the flashlight along the walls. The furnace started up, its motor clicking before the fan belt churned, then clanked to a halt. Heather aimed the light beam at a spot along the back wall where a quiet stream was emptying itself through a piece of untrimmed wall. Fear seeped into her — things were shifting too far. Somewhere between the ceiling and the foundation the house was going to collapse. She and Keith were just biding time before being buried beneath a mound of bricks and rubble where they will die with their roaches and rodents and broken dishwasher.

The furnace tried to start again but failed. Heather sneezed. It was a swamp down here.

"Hello?" Keith tiptoed down the stairs. Sat on the step behind Heather, a leg on either side of her.

His presence was a trap. Those long legs boxing her in, pretending to provide protection but they're just a couple of legs. Useless, except for running away. A Styrofoam chip from the packaging for the wardrobe they purchased because the house didn't have enough closets floated by, then spun slightly and drifted on.

"Holy toledo," Keith said softly.

Heather tied the bottom of her housecoat around her waist and waded in. It was several inches deep and numbingly cold. Thank God they didn't have much down here. Mostly junk piled onto two old rusty metal shelving units. A couple of cardboard boxes were stacked beside the shelves. Heather inched forward to the centre of the room and ran her toes along the rough surface in search of the drain. Yuck — her foot bumped into something. She fished it out of the water with her foot. It was a T-shirt of Keith's. She squeezed it into a ball and threw it at her husband.

He caught it with both hands. A splatter of cold drops stung his face. His throat ached. He felt ill-suited to life. Cursed. A week ago he lost his job. He'd been sent away with two weeks pay, a letter of recommendation and a gentle warning that the market was saturated with people with his skills. Most of whom are twenty years younger than me, he'd thought, furious that he had worked so hard dedicating hours to mastering style sheets and colour tables and tags and attributes, and as fiercely as he devoted himself to the webbed world, it had rejected him. Apparently being fired had nothing to do with him and everything to do with the industry being good at using its own resources — readily available source code, pre-made templates, drag and drop site building — to sting itself to death. Like a scorpion.

Heather lifted one of the boxes and moved it onto the washing machine. Water's moving, Keith thought. That's good. Means the drain's working. Heather's feet must be freezing. Much to her displeasure, Keith often likened her to a bison. She was strong-shouldered, wild and thundering. But her mental acuity plummets when she's upset. Angry Heather loses things like the keys to her car, sometimes even the car, but mostly, she loses her mind. He hoped she wasn't going to lie down and play Ophelia.

Heather swished her feet in the oily water thinking how stupid houses are, and about Dutch and Gloria next door, who told her that the root from an old tree of heaven worked its way in under their foundation a few years back and burst the sewer pipe. They describe it as if it were a Greek tragedy, using words like monstrous and heinous, always providing concluding comments such as, *But on a scale of one to ten life is now a forty.* Keith calls them a couple of yappy Pomeranians. Heather thinks they're like Thing One and Thing Two, calling out: *look at us, look at us!* They need to prove a kind of homey superiority. She was beginning to seriously resent them, along with their precocious nine-year-old, whose protests at bath time would lead one to believe her parents were preparing to boil her and turn her into soup.

Daylight was shining through the two small basement windows. Heather had a big meeting at work. The thought made her feel exhausted.

"You want some help?" asked Keith.

Heather picked up the second box and put it on top of the dryer. "Please don't trouble yourself," she said, before pounding her fist into the side of the washer.

Keith put his arms around his knees. He knew Heather expected him to react to domestic strife and financial constraints with more fire and brimstone, but it's just not his style. It's a leak; it's fixable, isn't it? She pressed her hand on his shoulder as she passed him on the stairs. "Excuse me. Some of us have to get to work." You don't need to rub it in, he thought, telling himself that it's not that he doesn't have passions — that most demanding of modern life's assumed necessities. He does. There was Irving Berlin, Gilbert and Sullivan, and Stephen Sondheim. Once, there were magic tricks. Recently it was cascading style sheets. But each time, his failures meant he moved on. And each time his ability to let go grew stronger than his determination.

Heather squirted the contents of a blackhead onto the bathroom mirror and asked her husband if he would be capable of calling Gloria and asking for the name of whoever they used when their sewer pipe burst. Keith nodded, gripped with an old familiar sadness that the only thing he really and truly had ever wanted to do was be a musical theatre genius, and rolled the lint remover across his wife's shoulders. "Don't worry," he told her. "I'll mind the candy store while you head off to fight the war."

Music came in through the walls. It was 9:40. Keith called Gloria who was terribly excited by all their troubles. "How high's the water?" she asked three times. Keith insisted it was no big deal. Asked what the music was. Gloria explained it was a Professional Activity day and Trinity was home, working. She may only be in Grade Five but she loves to make music mixes for Mario, their friend who does a little DJing at special events around town. Keith blurted that's hysterical and he'd love to see her set-up.

"Why don't you come over?" Gloria suggested. "It'll give me time to look up Gerald's number and you know kids, they love show and tell." Keith imagined bonding with the little music mixer as he brushed his teeth and fed Sabrina.

Gloria was cheery, like Mary Poppins, calling out, "Trin Trinity, someone wants to see you."

But Trinity was perfunctory and suspicious. She maneuvered through a few windows on her computer and played a beat. It was a Spanish rap mix with the *ka-ching ka-ching* of a cash register in the background. Keith listened, asked her what she thought of a DJ whose work he liked.

"He's okay," Trinity announced, swinging on her chair and looking out the window. "He blends good and drops a load of hard funk. Mixes it with house." She went on to explain that she was creating her own sound by adding a beat to some early Ellington tunes. "I have an ear," she added.

"Wow! Can I hear some?"

Trinity was a little put-out but played a song.

"That's awesome," Keith said. "It's great."

Keith watched Trinity scroll through her music library. "Where'd you get all this stuff?"

"The Internet."

"You buy it?" Keith asked.

"I'm nine."

"Well, you're a very talented little girl."

Trinity pursed her lips and let out a sigh.

On his way out, Keith thanked Gloria for Gerald's name and number, then mentioned how terrific Trinity was. "She's talented! She's got an ear. But I think she's doing a lot of illegal downloading."

Gloria smiled. "It's called sharing."

Gloria's sunny manner clouded his thoughts and he wanted to behave badly. He wanted to be nine. He wanted to scale Trinity's inflatable rock wall that rose above the backyard privacy fence and lie on top of it all day. Instead, he pointed himself toward his own front door and wondered how to tell Heather that the furnace is definitely bust and that mice seem to have moved upstairs to the bedroom.

Gerald arrived at the front door with a tired slouch but ready for business. A clipboard in one hand, Bic four-colour pen in his shirt pocket, thick blond hair cemented back with gel, he stretched out his hand, thick and dry. He seemed familiar, like a golden lab. Keith liked him. He looked like an honest, hard-working kind of guy. The kind of guy whose favourite book as a boy had been *The Last of the Mohicans* and who is comforted daily by one belief: true heroes are not upwardly mobile.

"Never set out to be a contractor," he told them, "but I took a few odd jobs after high school and low and behold, thirty years later, got a truck full of tools, a bad back and a phone that keeps ringing. Just a minute."

"Hello," he said, into his cell.

Gerald wasn't rushed. Didn't ask a lot of questions. He was obviously more comfortable making eye contact with houses than with people. While staring at the floor he devised a plan. He went to his truck and returned with a drywall saw. Cutting out a good-sized hole in the wall, he commented, "Look at that, you don't have any insulation."

"Should we?" Heather asked. Gerald ran his hand up and down the cinderblock between the studs like he was feeling around in the dark even though the lights were on.

Keith tried: "Would it be good to pull down the whole wall and put it in? While you're at it, that is, assuming it's not too expensive."

"Put in what?"

"Insulation."

"No," scoffed Gerald. "I wouldn't."

"Why?" asked Heather.

"Don't need it," he insisted with a shrug. "I'd pull the deck apart though. It's rotting."

"It is?" Keith and Heather asked simultaneously.

"Yup," he said, leading the way back upstairs. He lifted a board and flicked his thumb across the wood. It crumbled, like feta cheese. He put a few pieces on his pad of paper and offered it up. "Believe me, you're better to just rebuild this. You could save some of the boards but you'll be replacing the whole thing again in three years. If it was me, I'd just throw it away and build myself a good, solid new deck. Depends on how long you're going to stay here, though." Keith and Heather searched the deck looking for answers.

"Leave it like this, you're asking for termites."

"Lucky you called me now," the golden lab said as he lifted his weight into his pickup. "I had a job, real big one up in Markham. A rich lady wants me to redo her kitchen. She's got four Dobermans. One of them's having babies. Big litter, you know. Doesn't want to disturb them. Normally I'm booked right up but I just happen to have this one week open. This is perfect for me." And with that he turned on the ignition. His foot, a little heavy on the gas, caused the well-worn cylinders to cough and choke.

"Hey," Keith knocked on his window. "You know anything about roofs? We got a leak upstairs."

"Best to call a roofer for that," Gerald shouted through his window as he quickly pulled out into the street. "Pleasure," he called out with a wave.

The plan was that Gerald would be back a week Monday to rip out the wall in the basement, remove the deck, dig a hole along the side of the house, apply sealant, install a membrane, refill and do a little grading. Inside he'd do a quick power wash — nothing fancy. Five-six days tops. Twenty-one hundred plus four hundred for materials. "You won't do any better," he'd warned, pointing a finger at them. "Just disposing of the drywall and all this rotten wood's over three hundred."

"Good thing he knows what he's doing," Keith said as the dusty truck disappeared from view. "Since we don't."

"Speak for yourself," Heather said. "Who do you think's paying for this?" She wanted encouragement and gratitude. She wanted Keith to thank her the way a head of state does when motivating troops for war. Or the way a doctor thanks terminally ill patients enrolled in a clinical trial.

"Thank you," said Keith, wishing he'd taken industrial arts instead of theatre arts. The bison stampeded by him. He looked down the street, felt depressed in a way he worried would never leave him. He was never getting back on stage. When exactly did this happen? He'd been the star of his class at the National Theatre School. Now, he wasn't even an actor. Not even a web designer. Just a guy with a volatile wife and a house he had no business owning. *We learned everything the hard way too,* Dutch was always saying to him. *We had a big tree of heaven. It was right here.* Blah blah blah. He looked at Gloria and Dutch's garden beds. Namby-pamby rows of yellow tulips, manicured hedges lining imitation brick pavers. He felt disdain. And a little bit of envy.

That night Heather couldn't sleep. Anger stormed around inside her with no way to exit. In the morning she'd tell Keith that she expected more from him. He should be able to do something about the roof. Do some research on the Internet and get up there and fix it. What was wrong with him? If it wasn't so expensive to sell a house, she'd hide the evidence of its faults and just sell the place from right under his feet, and hers! She looked at Keith, leaned over him. She couldn't stand the way he slept through the night with his mouth open. She got up, went downstairs, warmed her hands over the stove element telling herself that it was early May and therefore technically fine that they didn't have a functioning furnace. As the chill left her hands the mouth-watering thought of Hickory Sticks made her boisterously hopeful. She'd taken to keeping a stash in the bedroom closet for stressful nights but had raided it earlier. Ten before midnight — just enough time.

The streets were quiet. She was alone save for one car in front of her, which slowed down, without warning, in the middle of the intersection, then decided, ever so gradually, to make a right-hand turn. Heather slammed her breaks just in time, lightly tapping his rear bumper. In the glow of her headlights she watched the driver step out. He inspected his car then gave her the finger before driving away.

Walking the aisles completely frazzled, she bought the family-size bag, which was good because there was still some left when she arrived back home. She poured what was left in a bowl, took it up to the bedroom with a spoon, and sat on the bed shovelling orange sticks into her mouth, delighting at how her saliva moistened and mashed the salty, crunchy wad.

"The deck." She shook Keith's arm, then put her hand to her mouth to prevent more stuff flying out of it. "We forgot to ask about the deck. Gerald never said anything about rebuilding it."

"You didn't ask," said Gerald, when Keith called him the next morning. "I assumed you didn't have enough money. I can do that later, or I bet you could do it yourself although materials are about two-thirds the cost so you won't save that much."

Keith asked him approximately how much. An arm, a leg, one of each? Of course they didn't have the money but he didn't tell Gerald that. He told him he'd think about it, taking pleasure in the thought that Gerald believed that he knew how to build a deck.

"My, my. This is very weird," said Gerald, after he'd dug a trench at the back of the house. "Can't find any weeping tile."

"What's that?" asked Heather.

"Weeping tile?"

"Do we need weeping tile?"

"All houses are supposed to have it," said Gerald, stretching his neck. "For drainage."

"Is that a problem?"

"Might be, but you'd need to get a big company in here with an excavator and a crew. Up to you if you want to go that route. Thing is on these old houses, they've been here for a hundred years. Maybe you'll be okay."

Gerald did what he said he would. Heather paid the bill with the remains of her savings and that day, as if to prove there is supreme order to the universe, Keith got a job at Ace Insurance. Bill helped him get it. He was to input data and format policy documents. It wasn't exactly *Les Misérables,* but it was something. They'd landed on their feet again. Summer was on the way. The backyard was a mud pit but it was their mud pit.

Three weeks later, Keith celebrated his first pay by purchasing an inflatable pool suitable for six children up to age ten. Skinny dipping under the stars in the warm night, he and Heather drank until they were pleasantly drunk, then they drank some more until Keith needed to sing.

Anything you can sing, I can sing louder. I can sing anything louder than you. Heather took her role: *No you can't.*

Yes I can, Keith retorted. *No you can't,* Heather replied.

Yes I can. No you can't.

They sang their hearts out through several verses until Heather rolled on top of Keith and planted the wettest, hardest kiss she could on his soft mouth. They kissed like crazy. Like they used to. Like all they are and ever have been or will be is pure sex. Like stopping would mean death.

Heather broke the spell, pulling away, her face flushed and breathless. Sitting up she grabbed a roll of flab on her stomach. "I'm fat." There was no doubt, she was getting chunkier. Keith liked her that way but since she didn't, he urged her to try his favourite synchronized swimming move — the Jell-o eggbeater. Heather watched his demonstration. She wasn't amused. Even her thoughts felt fat, but eventually she followed his lead. They spread their legs wide, rotating one clockwise and other counterclockwise, rotating faster and faster. The space between her thighs and the jiggling of her flesh felt good. She sat up enough that her breasts could get air and that felt good too along with the sensation of being outside, naked. They kicked and splashed, the vibrations and the suds making them both laugh until Heather's foot hit the bottom side with such force she punctured the vinyl on an old rusty nail left behind from the remains of the deck. As the pool deflated it started to rain. They stumbled inside laughing so hard Heather began to pee. It poured down her legs and they watched in amazement, howling, as the yellow liquid puddled on to the linoleum.

Heather was hungover and none of her tops fit. She stumbled to the basement in search of the one top that was her true friend. It was in the hamper. Didn't smell too bad so she pulled it over her head. As her head popped out, she happened to catch a look at the back wall. Keith was stepping out of the shower as the shrieking started. Every part of his body tightened. He leaned against the wall, slid down and collapsed to the floor, looking like he'd been shot.

"I can't take it," Heather said miserably as they stood watching water trickle from between the cinderblocks.

"I can't either," said Keith.

"Well you have to. I'm too stressed. And fat. And broke."

Keith said nothing.

"Aren't you supposed to be a born actor? Just fake it."

Keith called Gerald who came by looking sheepish but not guilty. A small argument took place.

"Look," he said, "I can fix this again and again. Same thing will happen. What you need is a dry well. All the houses around here have them. Your property slopes and no matter what I do, water will find its way in. Water is incredible," he lectured. "You can't stop it, you can only redirect it. Especially since you don't have any weeping tile." They went out back. Gerald looked at the deflated pool. "Been swimming I see."

He went to his truck and brought back a big blue tarp. "We'll put this here in case it rains. But don't expect it to necessarily work good."

Gerald knew someone who might be able to help them build a dry well.

"But I'm not responsible, you understand?"

If nothing else, Tony was enthusiastic. "Gerry tells me you need me!" He stepped through the doorway flashing bright teeth and a video camera, which he used to show them wide-angle panoramas of a project he'd worked on in California — a monolithic stone embankment for a house built precariously on a cliff above the ocean. He was tanned and handsome and had an unusual formality about him. He looked like a guy who, no matter what life brings him, still manages to shave every day. His fingernails were clean and he oozed the confidence of someone who knows how to be around extremely wealthy people. Heather asked him what he'd been working on and he mentioned the street and number of a house the other end of town where he'd done a walkway and put in some garden beds. Oh yes — he'd done a few dry wells in Santa Barbara — few years back. "Santa Barbara, wow!" said Keith. They work beautifully. In a downpour all the water goes right to them, you just need to grade everything properly. Keith said he was a sleek and graceful white-tailed deer; Heather said she didn't care what he was as long as it worked.

Tony said he could do the work in a week. Heather said that's good, wondering how they were going to find eighteen hundred dollars. She arranged for a meeting with Sandra, the woman who said she'd done gymnastics to get them their mortgage. She now called herself their financial advisor and was eager to help. "I think we have a good rapport. I've checked your NOAs, talked to my boss, and because I want to work with you I've managed to bend the rules. I can offer you an equity line of credit for $5,000. It's at prime plus three and you can use it for anything you need. Just go online and transfer the funds as you need them."

It seemed easy. And painless. As they shuffled through the papers signing every line flagged with a yellow removable piece of tape that said SIGN HERE, Sandra tapped her nails on her desk.

"This one's for the lien we'll be putting on your house. Standard procedure."

"Of course," said Keith.

"Let's go for dinner," he suggested once they were back on the street, ears plugged from the elevator ride down forty-five floors. It was the first blazingly hot night of the year and even if a lien sounded like trouble, like an ongoing pressure that could cause them both to develop scoliosis, he didn't care. Despite his basic mistrust of human behaviours: eating, breathing, working, owning things, believing that love reigns supreme — that we should fill our lives with it the way we stuff our mouths with food — despite all that, his faith in this house stuff was being restored. They'd passed the two-month mark. The reign of terror was coming to an end. And he'd heard about a new little wine bar with a great patio that specialized in local foods and healthy alternatives — like bison. "My treat," he said.

They got home just before ten-thirty to a house turned psychotic. The sound was deafening — a persistent, piercing throbbing that screamed: *run away while you still can.*

"Hit the breaker," Dutch yelled, leaning over the front porch. "I think it's your smoke detectors." Heather was too furious to go inside so Keith ran downstairs and randomly started flicking switches on the panel until the alarm stopped. Which it did. Immediately. Like magic. The silence was full of numbing echoes that pierced through his heart as he ran back outside.

"They're sensitive to humidity," Dutch said, suggesting they keep a few windows open and a fan blowing.

"They're supposed to detect smoke, not humidity. This is fucked," complained Heather. "And we can't keep the windows open. We don't have an alarm system."

"We've done what we can," Keith observed sensibly.

"You don't get it," snapped Heather. "It means we need to put in air conditioning or we'll always have this problem." Fully charged, she paced in front of the house chewing her fingernails.

"Come on inside," Keith pleaded.

"I can't. I'm too stressed. See this," she said, pointing at herself. "This is what angry looks like." Her body was full of rage, the kind that explodes when hope can't attach itself to anything. She picked up a rock and released a huge scream as she flung it at the house. It smashed right through their bedroom window.

"Wow! Well, see this. This is what sane looks like," said Keith, patting his chest.

"Really? Don't make me laugh."

Dutch appeared behind Keith, holding a floor fan. Heather turned on her heels. Stormed down the street vaguely aware that she was headed for the convenience store and livid that now on top of everything, they had a broken window to fix. The house was supposed to be a respite from the pressures of the world and work. But this one was evil. This Tony guy better work out or she'd kill him.

"Always something, isn't it? When the root burst our sewer line, it was Mother's Day, no less. I hope this helps," Dutch said, handing Keith the fan and giving him a hug that Keith thought strange and comforting.

Two weeks later it was Tony's last day. It had taken him longer than expected and he wanted more money but Heather was firm. "No can do." And that was the truth. He told her about his ex and his two lousy kids back in California who'd taken him for most of his assets and his girlfriend here who kept asking him to buy her things. "I can't work for nothing," he said.

"You're not. You're working for what you asked for."

Eventually he conceded defeat with a comment about how she really knew how to grab a man by the balls and yank on his wallet. He stood back looking like he was admiring his work, but actually he was admiring Heather as she leaned over the dry well to look inside. Heather looked up at him and he nodded.

"How does it look? Is it what you wanted?"

The element of doubt was so off-putting it almost smelled. "Is this a dry well?" she asked.

"You bet," said Tony. "Just need to fill it with gravel and spread a little crushed limestone around to grade things and we're done ... You know, you're awesome," he said, shifting his weight from one leg to the other. Lowering his voice he added, "I'm always telling my girlfriend that we should do something, you know. Another woman."

"Well good luck with that," said Heather, before storming inside and slamming the door. Two hours later Tony knocked. *Done,* he stated, and Heather wrote him a cheque.

A week later the middle of the night brought a magnificent summer storm with big warm drops that splattered noisily. The sound would have been comforting in the way news of disasters can make you feel safe, except that despite applying several containers of tar filler to the roof shingles, Keith still hadn't been able to stop the leak. And the plastic that he'd taped over the broken window wasn't holding.

Heather looked at the plaster ceiling. During a torrential rain it was definitely going to burst and water would pour on their heads and drown them. She had an important presentation the next day — floor decals for gas stations and convenience stores. She lay in bed repeating the key points but she couldn't relax. She looked at Keith. Recalled the times he's rushed through the front door with a new sealant, heading to the roof, announcing it's going to work. Even though it never does. Gently she woke him. "I'm an asshole," she said, "I love you." And they made love, tenderly, like they were scared of hurting each other.

Now neither of them could sleep. Keith suggested they get up and check the dry well.

Outside the rain was turning torrential. Keith popped open an umbrella and they dodged the puddles and stood peering at the well, listening to the pounding of the rain. They were the sentinels waiting for the attack. After a

244 I'm a Registered Nurse Not a Whore

few minutes, the surface turned soupy. Then water bubbled up like it was looking around to see where it was, before splitting into two streams that slowly snaked toward the house.

Heather made a quick dash inside and stood on guard in the basement.

Keith grabbed a shovel that Tony had left behind and tried to redirect the water but he couldn't tell if it was working. Drenched, he kept moving the gravel around until Heather's shrill screams rang out. Keith dropped the shovel and looked up at the sky. Rain falling on his face stung his eyes and pooled in his ears. He held his hand to his head like a gun. *POOF.*

Tony agreed to come back the next evening. He swaggered in through the back looking sweaty and anxious. "There it is," he said, shooting an accusing look at Heather as he grabbed his shovel.

Tony insisted it wasn't his fault. Obviously something was wrong with the side of their house. He'd been hired to build a dry well and that's what he'd done. There was no explanation for why it wasn't working.

Heather struggled to keep her voice from turning shrill. "I don't care if you don't know why." She didn't succeed. "I paid you to build something and it's not working."

Keith ran inside the house to look up dry well on the Internet, thinking he'd ask a few technical questions to help determine where the fault lay.

Heather and Tony argued on. Heather insulted Tony's skills, said he was a complete incompetent fraud; Tony said Heather was a fat bitch who needed a good hard fuck. Heather grabbed his shovel and swung it over her shoulder like a baseball bat. Glaring at the dim-witted, smarmy idiot whose slick demeanour she'd mistaken for competence, she swung with all her might. In the second just before the edge would have entered the side of Tony's head, he ducked, and she released it. The shovel sailed through the air and over the fence. They stared at each other for a long time, the air heavy with the residue of calamity. Tony stepped back and spat, then turned and walked away. Heather looked down at the glutinous gob on her shoe and started to shake. Her strength, unflinching a minute earlier, was gone. She was broken.

"Fortunately it missed the inflatable wall," Keith said, after sneaking over the fence to retrieve the shovel.

"I can't do it anymore," Heather wailed as she kicked a baseboard in the living room.

"I'll call Gerry," Keith said.

"What's he going to do?" Tears leaked from her eyes.

Who knows? thought Keith. Come check the dry well? Call Tony and talk to him?

Gerry told Keith he was sorry but like he'd said, he couldn't guarantee anything. After a long discussion, Keith convinced Gerry that he clearly understood this was their problem. "But we need help."

"Okay," Gerry said. "I might know someone." He didn't really know the guy but he'd heard his work was okay and not too expensive. "I think he's from the islands. Gotta be used to heavy rains."

"Great!" Keith said excitedly.

Jackson called back that night. He was charming and attentive. Kept repeating, "We're in God's hands, what is, just is, don't worry."

Obviously he was religious. That boded well. He must want to do unto others as he would want done unto himself. Keith had a good feeling about the guy. It made him happy. He snacked on cereal and played games on his computer while Heather lay in bed watching TV, eating popcorn and thinking about how she almost killed a man. About how she could have killed a man. About how easy it is, too easy, to lose control. Never ever again would she even look at anyone hired to work on the house. She'd done enough; Keith needed to take over.

In the morning, the Shreddies were in the fridge and the milk in the cupboard and Heather couldn't handle it. She needed coffee before she could even think and under no circumstance could she have coffee without milk. "It's ruined, everything's shit," Heather screamed as she held the carton and let the milk gulp down the drain. Keith suggested maybe she needed help.

"Why? You think I got mental problems? Look," Heather pointed at her mouth. "That's what this house has done to me. I've lost my upper lip and gained twenty pounds." She hurled her coffee cup into the sink, smashing it into several sharp-edged pieces.

Jackson came quickly. Excitedly. Drove his truck right up on the sidewalk and came bounding up the walkway, his graceful movements full of energy. "You rang, Jackson's here." His voice was rich and deep.

He refused to walk through the house and told Keith he'd meet him around back. He trailed along the side of the house whistling, then waited for Keith to get to the back and open the shaky fence. "Show me what's causing you so much grief," he said.

Keith showed him the dry well. Said a few things about what it was supposed to do. Jackson put his hoe down and started digging with the shovel while singing and shouting out a litany of advice about how Jesus wants us to be loose, hang back. He worked like crazy, without reservation. Every part of his clothing and his hands was covered with flakey bits of concrete and mud. Keith could smell the skunky perspiration as he stood admiring Jackson's energy and strength. Abruptly, Jackson stopped. He grabbed Keith's arm. "Mister. Can I please have a glass of water?"

"Yeah, I'll be right back."

Keith came back with a glass of clinking ice water.

Jackson poured it down his throat. He handed back the glass. "You need to do that when I come by. You ask me, can I get you some water? That's hospitality, that's what we all need. Take time, slow down, that's what the Good Lord wants us to do."

Keith nodded, slipped back in the house, put the glass in the sink and stared out the window. Jackson was back at it, back in the hole shovelling and digging himself deeper and deeper, merrily and heartily, like a hard-working billy goat.

As Keith stepped outside Jackson looked up, his face glistening and beaming as he yelled out "Whoooo weeee."

"What is it?"

"This isn't a dry well," Jackson boomed. "You got a swimming pool." Standing several feet below the ground, he jumped up and down, rubbing his stomach. "A dry well, a french drain as I call it, doesn't have a floor. Ever! That just don't work. Some clown put a concrete bottom on this thing." Jackson started laughing. "Water'll just fill up and overflow, the deluge!" He starting running on the spot like a boxer doing an intense warm-up.

"We gotta get rid of this and make a big one." Jackson spread out his arms. "Six feet wide and six feet deep, with no bottom, so it drains, into the mother, into the earth. Whoooo weeee! How's that sound?" He pulled his shirt over his head and rested his elbows on the edge, his powerful shoulders wet with sweat.

Heather stepped out of the house.

Jackson started jumping up and down in the hole, gleefully. "Whoooo weeee! I like what I see," he hollered up to the sky. "Lord Jesus," he said, and whistled loud and long. "Yes, yes, I like it, I like it." Heather immediately went back in the house slamming the door behind her.

Keith worked out a deal. Jackson said he could get the work done over the next week or so. It would take a few days. Keith told him he was really tapped out, but he'd pay him $300 after the first day, another $1000 when he finished and the last $300 after the first few downpours. "Why are you so worried?" asked Jackson. Keith didn't say anything as he tried to figure out whether it was Heather or Tony or Jackson or the rain he was most worried about. Or the fact that he'd lost his job. Or rather, not been hired on after his probation period. Apparently he was not suited to data entry. "Like water off a duck's back," Jackson urged. "Let it go."

Later that night Heather asked what the plan was. "He's a billy goat and a holy fool but I think he knows what he's doing." Heather had no comment. Keith told her not to worry, he had the bases covered. He lay in bed listening to the slow clank of the ceiling fan and tried to see ahead to a time when all this would seem insignificant. As Jackson said, like water off a duck's back. He imagined himself a bird, slightly wounded but still able to fly, the dove being sent from the ark to see if the waters had abated. Keith prayed, promised to be good and kind, to be patient with Heather and do everything he could to help Jackson. Just make it work, then help me find a job. It had been thirty-nine years since he'd talked to God and thirty seconds into it he was begging for favours. Ashamed, he rolled over, smelled the sunny sweetness that was his voluptuous wife and reached for her. She was ready for him. He entered her from behind and fucked her like a golden lab, a white-tailed deer and a billy goat — all at the same time, while promising himself he'd tell her he was jobless in the morning.

But in the early daylight, lightning flashed and thunder rattled and a violent summer wind tore off a huge branch of their chestnut tree. It slammed into their roof, removing a section of the trough and damaging the soffit. This latest disaster rendered Heather temporarily mute. She had a pained look on her face, like a basset hound and she refused to go outside to see the damage.

Dutch offered to take the branch. "Gonna dry it out in my garage — old wood like this makes the best firewood." He gave Keith a big wraparound hug. "Our basement was filled with the most godawful brown sludge, full of a soupy mud and chunks of vegetables. Keep strong. It'll all work out," he said, holding Keith's face in his hands.

Jackson showed up a few days later. Heather was puzzled — had they agreed to a start date? Yes, Keith insisted, it had just slipped his mind. Did they have enough money? Yes, Keith insisted, knowing they didn't. He'd already dipped into the line of credit to cover this month's mortgage payment. He watched as Jackson swung a sledgehammer at Tony's work. He brought out a jug of ice water, a glass, a bag of oatmeal cookies, then hid in the house. In the afternoon he told himself it was just stuff, and stuff doesn't make you happy, and headed out to hock his Thorens turntable and some of his prized vinyl.

The next day was a scorcher. Keith spent most of the day in the library searching the net for jobs, getting home in time to make sure everything appeared to be going well — whatever that might look like. "What do you think?" Jackson asked, eager for praise.

"Until I see how it handles rain I haven't got an opinion."

"Faith, have some faith," he said, jumping up and down on top of the gravel. "Just got to pack it down and I'll finish it off tomorrow." Jackson asked for a hose and sprayed around the well for the longest time, shouting, "Look, look, it works!" He stripped naked and was hosing himself off as Heather stepped outside. Jackson looked at her and let out a holler. Heather went back inside, slamming the door.

"Jesus," Keith shouted. "Turn around at least."

"Verily, verily, verily," Jackson said, putting on his pants. "I'll make my way out back so as to disturb no one," he said.

Inside the house Heather was in a state. "It's too much," she shrieked. Keith stood watching her, pissed that his wife was more concerned about a naked man in the backyard than she was about the dry well. About whether or not it was working. About whether or not these stupid house troubles were coming to an end. Trinity next door was screaming.

"Fucking fucking fuck," screamed Heather at the wall.

"What the hell's wrong with you?"

Trinity screamed louder. It was bath time.

"Get outta my life," she wailed at the wall.

"Fucking shut up," ordered Keith.

Heather glared; Keith glared back.

"All I want is quiet," she shrieked, before picking up a knife from the kitchen counter and stabbing the common wall, not once but twice, then once more.

Keith recoiled, ran upstairs to the bedroom. The sound of his wife yelling, stalking the house, pounding the baseboards, reverberated off the walls. He wanted to evaporate. Stupid house problems. They're just stupid house problems. He imagined not living with Heather. It would be quiet. Peaceful. Was it just the house? Was it better before the house? It was, but what did that prove exactly? As his heart slowed down he decided to give it back to her, knowing nothing the house could present him with could ever crush his soul as much as the wretched disappointment he lives with, every day, because he'd never been able to make it as an actor. At the top of his lungs he did what he does best, and let it rip:

> *Even with a turkey that you know will fold,*
> *You may be stranded out in the cold,*
> *Still you wouldn't change it for a sack of gold –*
> *Let's go on with the shooooooooow.*

Keith left Heather standing in front of the open door to the pantry. He stepped outside. Felt like rain. Jackson's metal tool box was sitting in the mud. He moved it inside, then took his bike out for one last ride. Tomorrow he would sell it. He had no choice and he was pretty sure he could get five hundred. Maybe a bit more. As he rode along the winding trail he saw himself — a man out alone in a bar with his thoughts, and it was good, so he stopped at a friendly cavernous dive he and Heather used to go to. Before the house. The place was halfway between hopping and falling down. He grabbed a stool and a couple minutes later had a cold beer in front of him.

Heather had just finished eating a loaf of raisin bread when she noticed Jackson's tool box. She stared at it, then walked over and kicked it. It barely moved. She was angry at Keith. Where was he? The fact that she was worried about him when he so obviously wasn't worried about her convinced her she needed some wine.

As she finished her fifth glass of shiraz she plopped herself on the floor in front of the tool box. Slowly, like it was the mouth of a dead animal, she pried it open and snooped. The metal box contained an assortment of implements coated with grease and grit. She pushed and shoved her hand around until she saw a small silver pellet gun in the bottom, below a roll of duct tape. She couldn't resist. It was beautiful, shiny, surprisingly light. She pointed it at herself, then at the wall. A voice told her it couldn't possibly be loaded so she squeezed the trigger. A shot rang out. She couldn't believe it. Had she really fired? She held it up to her nose. It smelled hot and musky. She threw it into the box, stood up, and went to the wall. Such a very small hole. Had she killed someone? She could have killed someone. Certainly, it will look like she tried to kill someone. She peered through the hole. So tiny but she could see inside their house. It was brighter. Everything was quiet. But the ambulance will come soon, and the police, and there will be no way to hide. CSI will determine the angle, the distance, locate the source, and that's how they'll ascertain who the shooter is and uncover the motive. And the jury will never understand what happened — that all she wanted was for the house to suffer as much as she had.

"Another one?"

Keith looked at the bartender. "One more would be great." He looked around. The bar was host to a retro night called Thunderpussy and whenever someone went in or out of the back room the disco mix poured into the bar drowning out the pop chart-toppers. Keith watched the baseball game and wondered if Heather was missing him. He was a little worried about her but he sure wasn't missing her. At least not yet. During the seventh-inning stretch he looked around. Not much happening, just a few people at tables sitting quiet, looking like they're doing hard time. An older guy wearing only a Panama hat, big sunglasses, terry cloth shorts and cork-heeled sandals, entered from the back room. He had nipple enlargements that looked like incense cones and his ribs were visible, like an aging glam rocker. It can't be, thought Keith, but he knew it was. Dutch. No longer a Pomeranian, but more like one of those hairless little Chinese Crested dogs that look like ancient babies, susceptible to sunburn, good at performing tricks and vulnerable to attack. He recognized the shoulders, the way he moved his torso.

"Keith?"

"Dutch, hey! Everything going okay?"

Flapping his arms like they were the wings of a flightless ostrich, he peered into Keith's face. "Who aims for okay?"

"Exactly."

Dutch ordered a cran-soda. He was fidgety, every joint in his body seeming to vibrate. Dutch looked at himself in the mirror behind the bar, then blew Keith a kiss. "They're playing our music tonight. Want to join me?"

"Maybe another night."

"Fine. Give us a cuddle then."

Dutch leaned over as Keith reached up and they squeezed shoulders.

"This superfly must dance dance dance." Dutch twittered off with a fluttering wave of his fingers.

Keith watched him disappear into the back room. He wondered where Gloria was. Was she here? If she wasn't, did she know where Dutch was? Did she care? He ordered a shot of tequila. All couples make some kind of bargain with life he told himself as he poured it down the hatch. His marriage, since the house, had proven to be such a constant source of strife. But did he really want to split from Heather? Or did he just want to split from what their life had become? He didn't know. He slapped a twenty and a five on the bar top and left.

It was raining when he stepped outside. A warm wind pushed at him and the rain pelted his leather jacket and the top of his head. He stood, stunned, staring at nothing. "Fuck," he screamed as he kicked the remains of his lock, left as evidence, on the wet sidewalk.

Inside there was no sign of her but he could feel her presence. The sight of Sabrina hiding under a chair near the back door worried him.

The bedroom was dark and the bed was pulled out from the wall. Heather sat slumped in the middle of it like a rag doll surrounded by an assortment of confectionery delights. A tiny stream of water was pouring down from where the tree branch had crashed into the roof. Her housecoat, thrown on the floor, was drinking it up.

Keith sat on the bed. Water was ballooning inside the plaster and he could see the ceiling and the wall sweating through the thick layers of paint. They stayed that way, breathing in each other's presence, until Heather couldn't take it any longer. "Look behind the bed," she said, her voice hoarse. Keith got down on his knees, eyed a large mound of mouse turd.

"I'll clean it up," he offered.

In the kitchen he grabbed a newspaper, dustpan and a plastic bag. Upstairs he scraped the dung with the dustpan. It was glued together and he toiled until he got all of it onto the paper and into the bag.

"You self-deluded, lying, two-faced coyote," Heather said. "You don't even have a job."

Keith tied up the bag, twice.

"I talked to Bill tonight," she said. "After I ate a whole loaf of bread and before I shot the neighbours."

Keith put the dustpan down, tossed the bag on the floor and sat back on the edge of the bed. "Heather," he said softly. "I know you're upset …"

"Upset! That was so yesterday," she hissed. "I need Hickory Sticks."

Keith peered closely at her. In the dim glow her mouth and teeth were the witchy, ghostly purple colour of someone who has finished an entire bottle of wine and is working through another.

"Was I not clear?" Heather said fiercely. "I need Hickory Sticks."

Keith walked briskly to the store, his heart beating in his ears. He told himself that this is what you do when big things fall apart. You do little things. You mind the candy store. You sing in the rain.

Having something to do helped revive his spirit. He arrived back home telling himself he would not be defeated. He would find some kind of work. Some way to make some money. Even if his wife no longer believed in him. Fuck it. Or her. And if the house was too much, fuck the house. People buy houses because they don't know any better. They think a nice bathroom means they've reached some measure of success. It's all a big sadistic scheme to keep us slaving away at a job. If we're lucky enough to have one. As he ran up the stairs a trail of water rolled off his leather jacket. The bedroom door was locked and the doormat from the front door had been placed in front of the bedroom door — *Go Away* face up. "Ha!" Keith shouted. He kicked the door, then leaned into it. "I have Hickory Sticks."

Heather wanted Hickory Sticks but she didn't want to get off the bed again and walk all the way to the door. Her fat thighs were glued together. She used her tongue to rub the fur that was growing on her teeth. Her hard palate stung. Her life was in her stomach — her marriage, her house, her job, her wish to have a beautiful bathroom — and nothing went together. She popped the last Cracker Jack in her mouth to fill some small hole inside her but everything just sloshed around, drunken and disturbed, ready to explode out her ass or her mouth at any given moment.

"Heather." Keith kicked the door. "Let me in." He kicked the door again.

"Leave me alone," Heather said, as if Keith were a man she'd just met in a park.

Keith kicked the door some more. Pain shot through his foot but eventually his boot crushed through the cheap hollow-core construction. He kicked harder with his heel, big strong karate kicks, each time knocking out another piece.

Heather sat listening to her husband destroy things.

She opened a bag of mini fruit gums and tried a red one and a yellow one and a green one all at once. They were soft and fresh and pulled hard on her molars. "I don't know why I married you," she said, wrenching her teeth apart. "I don't even know why we're together."

Keith told himself to break a leg as he backed up, took the full charge position and went for it. He crashed through the door, slid across the floor, fell to one knee and held his arms out horizontally — the front one straight as a mic boom, the back one clutching Hickory Sticks.

A flawlessly executed entrance.

Graceful and weightless, he felt he remembered who he truly was. He looked at his wife. Loud and tri-umphantly, he sang out: "*It's bet-ter than be-ing a-looooooooooooone.*"

As Keith held the last note, Heather rose to the occa-sion and in what would become their single greatest memory of this night, hurled a fruit gum at him. Even with the room swaying, her aim transcended her natural abilities and the candy flew straight into his mouth, banging right into the fleshly lobe at the back of his throat. It blew him away.

She was incredible. He'd never been better. The house applauded.

THANKS AND ACKNOWLEDGEMENTS

For kindness, generosity, wisdom, enthusiasm and editorial insight: Julie Lemieux – luminously talented intelligent inspired dramaturge, Shaughnessy Bishop-Stall – the real deal fearless wizard, Lee Gowan – the brilliant and funny gem, Gillian Rodgerson and Mike O'Connor of Insomniac Press – I am so fortunate. Very special thanks and deep gratitude to Samantha Haywood, University of Toronto, School of Continuing Studies, Marina Nemat, Nory Siberry, Kim Echlin, Priscila Uppal, Phyllis Bruce, Karen Connelly, Marnie Woodrow, Kent Nussey, and Michael Winter. Big thanks to my sisters Marilyn and Meg, Danny Lemieux, Philip Lemieux, Margaret Webb, Nancy Lyons, Anna Khimasia, Sophie Collins, Matthew Zuccaro, the games girls: Em, Les, Kimwun, Dee and Isabelle; David Pereyra, Jessica Heafey, Candace Macpherson, Colleen Craig, Brin Bymin, Lorna Somers, Maureen Kennedy, the Zuccs, the Goodmans and WJP. And the late great Sandy Saunders for pure, never-ending love. Thanks also to Scott Bujeya and the OPID team, Dr Frank Lo and Jackie, Sarah Weatherwax, Lynda Murtha, Dianne Lococo, Audrey Hadfield, Pearl Richard, Irene Spadafora, Joan Haberman, Dale Flexman, Brenda McMillan, Marianne Miller, Andrea Accinelli, Bruce Geddes and Lisa Cruji. I thank my lucky stars for Bob Bright, Carla Bley, Cabbagetown, and the craft brewers of Ontario.